Reckless Abandon

J.C. HANNIGAN

booktrope

Booktrope Editions
Seattle, WA 2016

Cover Design by Yosbe Design
Edited by Lisa Davall

This is a work of fiction. Names, characters, places, brands, media, and incidents are either the product of the author's imagination or are used fictitiously. Any resemblance to similarly named places or to persons living or deceased is unintentional.

PRINT ISBN: 978-1-5137-0648-1
EPUB ISBN: 978-1-5137-0749-5
Library of Congress Control Number: 2015921048

Acknowledgments

There are so many people I would like to thank. Without their help, I wouldn't have been able to complete *The Damaged Series*. Thank you to Sarah Fader, Lauren Jones, Christina Harris, and Kristen Johnson for letting me talk about the heart of this story. Repeatedly. Thank you for your suggestions and encouragement. Those early on days of novel writing are crucial, and the input I got from each of you definitely helped craft what this book is today.

I would like to thank my beta readers for providing the feedback I needed so that I could polish and buff things up.

Another huge shout out goes out to my Booktrope team for making this book a reality – Chelsea Barnes, Nikki Colligan, Yosbe and Lisa Davall, as well as all those working hard in the background.

And to my husband Matt – you saw exactly what I needed you to see from this project. You knew Grayson better than I knew him, and you helped me find his redemption. You also helped man the home front while I spent hours in my writing cave bringing this to life.

Finally, thank you to ALL of my FANnigans! You each have a huge part in me completing this novel as well – if it weren't for you guys, I probably wouldn't have dared to release a second book, let alone a whole new series. Your encouragement and support is just the push I need to keep going! Special thanks go out to Cassandra Smith, Amanda Hall, Samantha Soccorso, Karie Deegan, and Donna Ash for relentlessly shouting my name from the rooftop.

This one is for he who inspired the essence of *The Damaged Series*.
I truly believe this story has magic because of you...

Prologue

Grayson

I'VE MADE A LOT of mistakes in my life, and I've hurt a lot of people I cared about. I was angry and weak and walked around with a chip on my shoulder. I missed what could have been the best time of my life, and worse—I pushed away the only girl I've ever loved... all because I hated myself.

Five years later, and I still hated myself—probably more. Only I didn't hate myself for no good reason. I hated myself because I sabotaged everything good and pure about my life.

Letting Everly Daniels walk out of my life had always been my biggest regret. For a guy that always acts first and thinks later, I really dropped the ball on that one.

It was a blessing and a curse, seeing her everywhere I went. I was happy for her success, but it was the sweetest kind of torture to know that I lost her and that I could never have her again. I had only myself to blame.

After I broke her heart, I dropped out of high school. I couldn't stand the idea of seeing the pain in her eyes—the pain that I put there—when she looked at me. I crushed her. At the time, I wanted to make her hate me as much as I hated myself because I didn't feel worthy of her. I *wasn't* worthy of her.

I got my GED and left for an oilfield work camp in an isolated Alberta town in a pitiful attempt to put her—and everything else—behind me. I worked my ass off, saving pretty much every penny. I didn't have anybody but myself to spend it on.

Within four years, I was restless and ready to blow all my money on something stupid. I felt myself sinking into a deep depression, seeking the comfort of whiskey and faceless women all too often.

When I started to hate myself more than I already did, I knew it was time to leave Alberta.

I had no sense of direction, though. The only thing I could do was return home to Orono, to my dad's place.

When he opened up his door and saw me standing on his porch in the middle of the night, I expected him to freak out about how I'd taken off without a word all those years before, or about how I hadn't come back to visit once since I had left. He didn't say anything. He just hugged me gruffly, handed over the keys to the apartment over the garage, and told me I had a job at his construction company if I wanted it. Then he forced me inside to say hello to Vanessa.

I started my life over again for the hundredth time, trying to shed the tattered skins of my former dark self. This was all in an attempt to finally become a man that could be worthy of a woman like Everly.

Chapter One

Everly

BETWEEN THE OVER-SIZED sunglasses obscuring the majority of my face and the smoky gray beanie that I'd tucked all my hair under, I was unrecognizable...or at least I *felt* unrecognizable. That was the point, of course. I didn't want to be noticed by anybody in Pearson International Airport. I wanted to get my luggage and get out. I wanted to be home.

My throat constricted with the thought of home. I hadn't been there in almost three years. I'd been so busy with the band and touring and performing, with interviews and red carpet events. Selfish reasons.

I should have gone home more, I thought, the tears brimming under my glasses. *Now it's too late.* I tried to push the thought away, but it was pointless. It was too late. I hadn't gone home enough, and now that I was returning, it was to bury somebody that I loved.

I kept my head down and my lips tightly closed as I walked. I was traveling for the first time in a long time without any security, without anybody at my side. Our manager with the label hadn't had time to clear anybody to go with me because they didn't even know I'd left.

I'd gotten the phone call the night before and had gone straight to the airport to board the next available plane, ditching my bandmates at a promotional event for our new album without any thought. It had been the longest flight I'd ever been on, and that was saying something. I'd been on every single kind of flight imaginable.

The lump in my throat got significantly larger when I glanced up and saw my parents waiting, clinging to each other as if they couldn't stand on their own feet without the support of each other's arms. I let out a strangled gasp, the air suddenly slicing into my lungs.

Dad caught sight of me first and smiled through his pain. The sadness lined his eyes and made him look as if he'd aged ten years in barely a month. I'd flown the entire family out to spend Thanksgiving with me in

Los Angeles a few weeks before, and he hadn't looked like this. Seeing them like shattered made it all too real.

I didn't want it to be real.

The tears escaped from my eyes, pouring down my cheeks without restraint as I flew into my parents' arms. They hugged me tightly, both of them unable to contain their own tears and sorrow. The three of us stood there, shaking uncontrollably as we sobbed into each other's arms.

"Where is she?" I demanded, my voice shaking with emotion as I pulled away. I felt frantic, panicked. My heart was beating incredibly fast; the pain was unlike anything I had ever felt before and I thought I knew heartache. "I need to see her."

Mom nodded, her face crumbling. "We'll head straight over," she promised, stroking my face as if she wanted to comfort me...or herself.

I nodded, taking a deep, shaky breath as they put their arms around me. The three of us stumbled out of the airport and piled into the car. Snow flurries danced in the pale gray sky, hinting at the holidays that were fast approaching.

I was silent on the drive to the hospital, completely lost in my own numb thoughts. I couldn't take anything in. I tried to focus on my breathing, counting each deep breath as it passed my lips.

Dad dropped us off in front of the hospital. My eyes blurred with tears that I fought desperately to control while Mom led the way to the seventh floor.

"Wait here," Mom said gently, rubbing my shoulders quickly before disappearing to check in at the nurses' station. I took a deep breath, trying to get my emotions under control. I couldn't go in there bawling my eyes out. I would only upset her.

Mom approached again, giving me a pained smile. She put her hands back on my shoulders, guiding me down the hallway.

We stood outside of the door, me shaking and trying to rein it in while Mom squeezed my shoulders again. I took a deep breath, wiping my cheeks dry.

Pushing open the door, we walked into the private hospital room. She looked so tiny lying in the bed. I let out a choked sob and willed myself to keep it together. I could fall apart later. I slowly approached the bed, Mom following directly behind me.

She was awake, her dark lashes fluttering against her cheeks as she blinked at me with recognition.

"Hi Cadence," I said, falling into the chair closest to the bed. She turned her head to follow my movements. She had several lacerations on her face as well as a fractured wrist from the accident, but she was okay. She was *alive*.

I couldn't hold back the tears that escaped when I leaned forward and gently pressed my lips to Cadence's undamaged cheek. I was never very good at holding in my emotions.

Cadence didn't say anything. She was groggy from the pain killers and the beating her tiny body had taken from the accident. Her eyelids softly fluttered closed. I remained in the chair, watching her face in peaceful slumber.

"How long until she can come home?" I asked, my voice sounding alien even to my own ears.

"She's scheduled to be discharged tomorrow afternoon; they want to keep her for one more night."

I nodded, accepting this answer as I studied the thick lashes resting against Cadence's cheek. I raised my hand to my mouth, hoping to hold back the ugly emotion that was going to spill out of me.

I sobbed into my hand, my shoulders shaking. Mom approached me quickly, wrapping her arms around my body. I hadn't had time to grieve. I hadn't had time to process anything. I hadn't even slept yet.

Mom helped me out of the chair, gently guiding me away from Cadence's sleeping body. She stopped once we'd reached the hallway. "Oh, honey," she said, her voice breaking as she rubbed my back.

"I can't believe she's gone," I sobbed, my entire body shaking. I'd just talked to Julia two days before. I didn't realize that it was the last time I would ever get to speak to my sister again. If I'd known that, I would have told her how much I loved her and how appreciative I was of her. Now I would never get that opportunity.

* * *

"I can't do this," I sobbed, my entire body shaking and trembling with fear. Julia stepped up to me, wrapping her arms around my waist. She held me tightly, quieting the tremors. I gasped, struggling to breathe against my panic.

"Yes you can," Julia assured me. "I'll help you."

The gentle pressure of a hand on my shoulder jarred me awake from the dream. I looked about, disoriented. The pale green walls of the hospital room reminded me where I was.

Mom glanced down at me, her eyes full of exhaustion. The accident had happened less than forty-eight hours ago, and I honestly didn't think she or Dad had slept at all either. I knew they hadn't left Cadence's side; that much was obvious from their rumpled clothing and the heavy bags under their eyes.

My chin quivered as I looked at her. The dream of Julia that I'd woken up from was actually not a dream at all; it was a memory, and it made the pain of losing her even more acute. I wanted to see my sister. I wanted to tell her that I appreciated her for all that she did for me... for all of the sacrifices she made so that I could chase my dreams.

"She knew," Dad said, his voice breaking as he took in the crumbled expression on my face. He rushed to my side, gently rubbing my back.

"I'm so selfish," I sobbed, my shoulders shaking as I looked at Cadence's sleeping form. I brushed her hair out of her face. I wanted to gather her in my arms, hold her close to my chest and cradle her. She looked so much like Julia had at that age. "If I'd never..."

"You did a lot for Julia, and for Cadence. She knows it. She never begrudged you anything. She was proud of you, proud of all your accomplishments," Mom told me. "We all are."

"My accomplishments took away from hers," I pointed out, tears pouring down my cheeks. I shook my head, beyond angry at myself.

"You can't think that way," Dad said, kneeling down in front of me. His eyes searched mine sadly. "Cadence was everything to her... and so were you."

I brushed away the tears, feebly attempting to stop their flow. It seemed endless, and I wondered if I would ever stop crying.

* * *

"The doctor will be here soon," Mom told me, her face pained.

"What?" I sat up straighter, brushing at my cheeks again with the back of my hand. "How long was I sleeping?"

"A few hours," Mom answered. There was movement by the door, and a man in a long white coat picked up Cadence's chart from her door before he walked in.

"Everything looks good. Her vitals have remained stable. She'll probably be drowsy for the next couple of days. The nurse is typing up her discharge paperwork now and I've already included a prescription for her to have when needed. This will help her with the pain. After the first week, Tylenol should be sufficient but please let me know if anything changes. I'll need to see her back here in about two to three weeks for a routine follow up and then again in six weeks to obtain an x-ray before removing the cast," the doctor said while reviewing the chart. He barely looked up while speaking; however, when he finally did, his face looked grave. "Please accept my condolences for your loss." His soft brown eyes were full of compassion as they met mine.

"Thank you." Mom's voice was weak, but she didn't cry. She didn't seem to have any moisture left. She was staring at Cadence with a broken expression.

"I've also written a referral for a child psychologist, to help Cadence process the accident and her loss," he added, handing me a copy of the referral and the prescription.

An hour later, I was pushing Cadence in a tiny child sized wheelchair, followed closely by Mom. Dad had left to bring the car around. Mom carried the balloon bouquet that Kyle, Marcus and Cam had sent for Cadence. I had left in a hurry, but made arrangements to fill Kyle in so that he could handle things with the band and the record label. I had pleaded with him to keep it from the tabloids; the last thing I wanted was the media to intrude on our time of grieving.

Dad was waiting in the drop off zone of the hospital and he darted out from the driver's seat to open the rear passenger door. I carefully lifted Cadence up from the wheelchair, her body limp in my arms as I lifted her inside the car. They'd given her a light sedative to make the hour long trip home.

I placed her in her booster seat, buckling her in securely. My eyes filled again at the sight of the new booster seat. I closed the door, walking around with stiff legs to climb in on the other side. I sat in the middle of the car, as close to Cadence as I could get.

Cadence slept the entire drive home. I held her tiny hand in mine, staring out the window as my thoughts raced and I struggled to keep my breathing steady.

I couldn't help but think about all the summers that I'd have Cadence and Julia at my place in LA with me—when I wasn't busy touring or recording, that is. Cadence always enjoyed coming to LA and swimming in the big in-ground pool. Two days ago, Julia had called to finalize their plans to come out for a Christmas visit. Mom and Dad were going to come along too.

Now I was home, and Julia was gone.

The drive home took less than an hour. We'd made it before the rush hour traffic clogged up the highway.

My parents still lived in the house that I grew up in, in Newcastle. Things were almost completely unchanged, except for the new sofa set they'd gotten and the flat screen TV. My beloved dog, Stella, had passed away a few years back when I was on tour. My parents hadn't gotten another dog, and it was surreal to come home and not have her waiting for me at the door, her tail thumping against the banister in welcome.

But it was nothing compared to the massive puncture in my heart from losing Julia.

My heart seized in my chest at the reminder. I would never see Julia lounging on the couch with her feet up again. I'd no longer fight her for the last baked cookie, or cry on her shoulder when everything got to be too much.

I forced the tragic thought from my mind. Cadence was awake and alert... and silent. The relief I felt for Cadence being safe was inexplicable.

Positioning her carefully on the sofa, I propped her up with a bunch of pillows and blankets, and her favorite purple stuffed bear...the bear that Grayson had won for me at the fair. Even after everything I went through with Grayson, I still hadn't been able to part with it, and I'd given the bear to Cadence on the day that she was born. I had found solace in the fact that she now carried it close to her heart.

She clenched the bear to her chest, her eyes focused on my face. I stared at her in turn, forcing all other thoughts out of my head. I didn't want to break down crying in front of her.

"Hey, my rhythm," I whispered, stroking her face. Usually, Cadence's lips would split into a wide grin and she'd throw her arms around my neck. Cadence said nothing; she barely even blinked. "I'm going to go get something to eat. Do you want something to eat?"

She shook her head, burying her face in the worn material of the purple bear. "I want Mommy," she whispered, big fat tears rolling down her plump cheeks. I brushed back a strand of her dark hair, my heart breaking all over again. I didn't know what to say. I looked up at my parents, who were lingering in the foyer, holding each other and watching us with destroyed expressions on their faces.

"Oh, Cadence," I said, my voice breaking as I gathered Cadence's tiny body into my arms. I held her close to me, wanting to draw out all the pain and confusion she must be feeling.

* * *

I lay in the bed of my old room, gently rubbing Cadence's back as she drifted off to sleep. Cadence had barely said a word all day, and had barely eaten either. I was at a complete loss, not knowing how to help her.

I watched as her breathing slowed with sleep. I remained there for several more minutes, making sure that she was truly out. I glanced around my old bedroom, the shapes and shadows as familiar to me as they had been when I was still living here.

I hadn't been back in years, but everything was mostly the same. My lilac bedspread and the furniture I grew up with were still there. The photos of me and my friends from our high school days were still taped to my mirror.

The only changes that were made had been minor. There were more stuffed animals that were slowly accumulated over the years for Cadence, as well as a crayon drawing that had been scrawled on my old white desk.

My sister and Cadence hadn't lived with my parents; Julia rented a house in town. Cadence went for sleepovers at Gramma's and Papa's every other weekend since she was a baby to give Julia a break. Naturally, she had needed an army of stuffed animals to sleep with.

Mom told me that Cadence used to sleep in Julia's old room until she started insisting on sleeping in mine. I didn't know why she'd chosen my room, but I couldn't help but wonder if it was so she could feel closer to me. The ever present guilt welled up, roaring over me in waves.

I pressed my lips gently to her forehead, feeling exhausted and broken and completely lost. I longed for somebody to tell me what I was supposed to do now.

My relationship with Julia hadn't always been perfect, but we'd grown close in the past five years. Julia was there for me, always rallying for me and coming to my rescue when I needed it...like the night of semi-formal, when I'd called her in a panic. She'd been there the day that I signed on with the record label. Julia believed with utmost confidence that we were going to make it big. That *I* was going to make it big. Her belief in me was unwavering and solid.

I wiped a tear from my eye, my heart yearning for just one more conversation with my sister. She'd know what to do. She always knew what to do.

Slowly and carefully, I pulled my body out from the bed, tucking the purple bear closer to Cadence. She grabbed it, hugging it tightly underneath her chin, and rolled over. Soft snores filled the room as I tip-toed out. I closed the door softly behind me and stood in the hallway.

Julia's bedroom was just across the hall, where it had always been. I swallowed hard, blinking away the tears. It was too soon for me to go in there and see her in my memories, in the things that she'd left behind when she moved herself and Cadence to their own house.

A gentle but firm knocking on the front door broke my attention from staring helplessly at Julia's old, closed bedroom door.

My parents were finally sleeping for what I could only guess was the first time in over two days, and I didn't want to wake them so I descended the stairs quickly and silently. I opened the door, peering outside to see who it was.

I was engulfed in a sea of auburn hair and arms. "Oh, Everly," Aubrey said, her voice full of emotion. "Kyle called me. He asked me to come check on you, said you weren't answering your phone."

"Of course I wasn't answering my phone," I said, pulling away rather abruptly. I stood aside, motioning for Aubrey to come in while I warily checked the outside bushes for paparazzi. Now that I was a well-known celebrity, it wasn't uncommon for reporters to lurk outside, trying to snap a quick photo of me for some stupid tabloid magazine.

I eventually stopped coming home because every time I did, the news broke out and then my parents' front yard was swarmed by fans... and none of them were local. They came from *miles*. The townspeople had watched me grow up, and while they were just as proud of a small town girl making it big in the music industry, they respected my family enough to not intrude on the time I was there with them. The other fans though... they didn't seem to care if they snapped photos of me and my family, and almost all of them would end up on some trashy magazine cover.

The last thing I wanted was for my family to be harassed by the paparazzi. It was easier to just invite them to LA, where all security would expertly ensure that nobody trespassed for a picture.

The bushes were clear, but I still closed the door quickly behind her. My heart felt incredibly heavy in my chest.

Aubrey looked at me with concern, like I would break and shatter if the wind blew the wrong way. "I'm so sorry," she said, stepping toward me. I allowed my old friend to draw me back into her arms and comfort me.

Aubrey and I still spoke regularly. She came to any show that we played locally and she'd also visit me in LA. She remained close to our hometown, pursuing her teaching career. She was no longer dating Marcus—she couldn't handle him being on the road all the time—but they were still friendly...*really* friendly.

"I can't believe she's gone," I said, shaking my head with disbelief. The tears threatened to start up again. I blinked them away furiously. I had plenty of time to cry later.

"What are you going to do?" she whispered, her head automatically turning toward the stairs.

"I don't know," I whispered back, my face still buried in her shoulder.

Chapter Two

Grayson

"YOUR USUAL, GRAYSON?" Katrina's sleek voice purred as she leaned over the bar and eyed me suggestively, her cleavage spilling out from her tight tank top. I pulled out a barstool and sat down, scowling at her while I gave a curt nod.

She grabbed a tumbler and poured me a whiskey on the rocks, sliding it over to me and using her bar towel to quickly wipe up the trail of condensation. I lifted the glass to my lips, the ice clinking against it while I took a deep sip. The whiskey warmed my throat. I set the glass back down on the bar, aware that Katrina was still staring at me.

"Don't you have someone else to serve?" I muttered, still scowling.

"Dude, this is Tap's on a Monday night. You and Tom are my only customers." Katrina rolled her eyes, gesturing to the almost empty bar. It was true; the night life in this town was prehistoric.

I raised my glass to old Tom Grady, the only other person at the bar, and took a deep gulp. Tom was damn near ninety years old, and he was there every night, staring into his glass of brandy with a defeated look on his weathered face. I knew this because *I* was there almost every night.

It had been two years since I returned home. In that time, I'd learned the ins and outs of my father's business and officially took it over after he suffered from a heart attack. He was still kicking around; he just decided to step down from his position and spend more time with Vanessa and the girls, leaving me to manage the company and the crews.

I bought land and built a house on the outskirts of Newcastle. I had no reason to leave the area. Once I was settled in, all of our clientele came to seek me out. Dixon Construction Ltd was a big name, and I was busy trying to meet the demands of our massively growing clientele with my three separate crews. Work was crazy enough that I was in the midst of putting together a fourth crew.

Work kept me busy during the day, but when the night came, my demons came out to play. I usually tried to drown them before they could wear me down, using either whiskey or women.

Judging by the patrons at and the person behind the bar, my coping method of choice was going to be whiskey tonight.

Tom Grady lifted his empty glass at Katrina without raising his tired eyes, signaling that he needed another drink. I had no idea what Tom's full story was, but from the town gossip I'd managed to overhear, it was similar to mine.

He had lost the love of his life, only Tom hadn't lost her to his own stupidity. He hadn't forcefully pushed her from his life. Tom had been married for sixty-five years to her, and when she'd passed away two years previously, he lost half his heart and soul. He started spending more and more time at Tap's because he had nothing else, just like me.

I stared into the dark honey color of my whiskey with a grim face. I had nobody to go home to either, and I didn't want just anybody. I wanted the one girl that haunted my dreams and my every conscious moment. I wanted the girl that made me give a shit, the girl that made me want to be better. I wanted the girl whose voice I heard all the time.

I frowned, my ears perking up to the sound of her actual voice as it poured out from the speakers. My heart started to race as her soulful lyrics brought her flawless face to mind. I closed my eyes, the familiar hurt and pain of losing her consuming me. I didn't usually listen to her music. I couldn't. Her voice unsettled me and reminded me of all that I lost. It didn't help that almost all the lyrics she harmonized were about love and loss and relationships falling apart.

Katrina was humming along to it distractedly, wiping down glasses and setting them on the underside of the bar. I glared deeper at her, tossing back the rest of my drink and slamming the empty glass down with enough force to make her jump.

She clued in, quickly changing the radio station to a different song and guiltily pouring another two fingers of whiskey in my glass while avoiding my eyes. She kept biting the inside of her cheek, like she had something to say but was afraid to broach the subject.

Katrina had changed since high school. She was no longer the catty girl who tried to sabotage my relationships, mainly because I hadn't had a relationship since Everly, but also because my five-year disappearing act had rattled her. While I would have never called us close, Katrina did. I was the person that remained longest in her life. I was her familiarity. In high school, she wanted me. We'd hooked up a few times but she read more into it than me.

When I started dating Everly, when I was *really trying* to be a decent person, Katrina got jealous. She came over uninvited the night of semi-formal, the night I laid a fraction of my rage into Kyle Russell's face. She'd stood at my door all but sobbing, telling me that some asshole at that party forced himself on her.

I was trying to be a good friend, trying to comfort her. Then she got all grabby with me, and I didn't react at first because my brain seized and I froze. I made the biggest mistake of my life— I kissed her back.

I wasn't used to saying no to the girls that threw themselves at me. If they wanted it, I was happy enough to oblige. I was seventeen. What seventeen-year-old doesn't pop a boner if a pretty girl is stroking up against their jeans? But as my lips pressed against Katrina's, all I could think about was Everly, how I needed to make things right with her.

I shoved Katrina off of me and told her as much. She started to cry again, saying that I could do better. Katrina seemed convinced there was something going on between Everly and Kyle.

Hearing that pissed me off. I didn't think Everly would ever betray me; she'd chosen me time and time again. It pissed me off because of Kyle's words, and the fact that he was right.

She deserved better than what I had to offer.

When someone knocked on my door, I figured it was just my dad or Vanessa. I threw it open, shocked to see Everly standing on my porch. Her cheeks were rosy from the cold, and her eyes shone bright with emotion and confusion.

The events that followed set the foundation for me breaking her heart. She demanded to know why Katrina had been sitting on my bed looking freshly fucked. Katrina's gloating didn't help. Before Everly or I could speak, she called out from my bed, "Who's that, babe?"

The expression on Everly's face had turned my blood to ice. I told Katrina to get the fuck out, and she did...but not before she whispered as she passed, "Remember what I told you."

I tried to explain to Everly what happened, but I couldn't lie. Hearing that I had kissed Katrina back, just for an instant before my mind stopped seizing, completely broke her heart. That was when I decided I was done hurting her. I was done letting her down and disappointing her. She didn't ever say I did, but the look in her eyes was enough. I knew I'd only continue to fuck it up, and I panicked.

Everly was going places, and I wasn't. I tried to make her hate me. I tried to make her walk away without looking back so she could live the life that she deserved and find the person that she was supposed to be with— the person that could truly make her happy. She deserved happiness and I knew I couldn't give it to her.

That night, I paced the floor of my bedroom. I knew that if I stayed in town, I would undoubtedly try and make her mine again, because I wanted her more than anything. But I didn't want to hold her back. I wasn't giving her what she needed, what she deserved. I took a week agonizing over what to do. Then I heard that the band got signed with the record label, and I knew I needed to escape.

I couldn't drag her down anymore. I had to let her go so she could move on, even if I couldn't. When I got the job on the oilfield work camp in Alberta, I moved without looking back...at least physically.

Mentally and spiritually, I never left. It took three years—and the help of one co-worker turned friend, Brock—for me to realize that I was never going to outrun the memory of Everly, and it didn't matter where I was. She would follow me.

"Do you want another refill?" Katrina gently prodded me back to the present. I shoved the glass away, standing up. I'd lost my taste for whiskey. The only taste I had now was for Everly.

"No," I said stiffly, tossing down a couple of bills and heading for the door.

"Grayson," Katrina's voice made me take pause by the door.

"What?" I said without turning around.

"She's back."

The blood roared to my ears as I slowly turned my body to face Katrina, my eyes hard. "What did you say?"

"She's back," Katrina repeated. She tossed the bar towel over her shoulder, pressing her palms against the bar, her eyes calmly fixed on my face. My breath hitched. I hadn't heard wrong.

"She hasn't been back in years," I argued, my teeth clenching as I looked away. I suppose another part of the reason why I returned and why I stuck around was because I kept *hoping* she'd return. I told myself that I wouldn't seek her out, but if she came to me, I wouldn't let her go again.

Only she hadn't come to me. She hadn't been home for the past several years. She flew her family out to see her at her place in California. Even if she did come home to Newcastle, it didn't mean anything. Her parents and sister still lived here; she wasn't back for me. As far as I knew, she'd moved on. Tabloids rumored that she was now engaged... to Kyle. She'd been spotted with a ring on her left ring finger while grabbing coffee at a Starbucks. Not that I paid attention to the trash reporting coming from Hollywood, but it was hard to turn away from her when her face was on my television screen.

"She's back now," Katrina insisted, shaking her head at me. She bit her lip, considering her words. "You should go to her."

"It's been five years, Katrina," I said tiredly, rubbing my index finger and thumb against my temple. I was getting a headache from all the yelling that was happening in my head. *Go to her. Go now. Make her understand.*

"Yes, it's been five years." Katrina's voice was shockingly gentle. "And you're still as in love with her as you were the day you shoved her out of your life. And she needs you now." Katrina pointed her finger at me as if she was scolding a child.

I glowered at her, but she didn't wilt away as usual. "She doesn't need me. If she needed me, I'd know it," I told her, sure of it.

"I've already apologized for my part in... what happened. But *you* were the one that let her walk away. You were the one that just disappeared. You are the one that's holding yourself back from moving on. I just want to see you happy, Gray," Katrina added, looking at me sadly. "And she does really need you."

"How do you know?" My voice rose with anger. Tom finally glanced up from his glass, sparing me a bored look before his gaze dropped back down.

Katrina's chest heaved as she inhaled deeply. "I saw a photo of her at the airport with her parents."

"So what?" I tried to feign indifference. I tried to hide the fact that my heartbeat was pounding frantically in my chest at the mere prospect of her being back in town.

"So...she looked upset. You should go to her. It's your chance to make things right...or your chance to truly let her go." Katrina arched an eyebrow at me, willing me to decide.

I said nothing. I just turned around and stomped out of the bar to my truck. I drove home, unable to pull my thoughts away from Everly. Was she really in town? What had brought her back? Was she with Kyle? Did thoughts of me torment her like thoughts of her tormented me?

The first thing I did when I got home was pour myself another glass of whiskey and sink heavily onto the leather couch in my living room. It was the same couch that I used to have in my loft at my dad's house. The same couch that I'd spread Everly out on more than once. I closed my eyes against the torrent of memories, blindly grabbing the remote from the coffee table.

I needed a new fucking couch, but if I was being perfectly honest, there was a reason why I didn't go out and buy a new one. I could afford it; it wasn't a matter of money. I was afraid to replace the couch and lose the memories. As much as it pained me to think of her—and hell, as much as it held me back from moving forward—I couldn't imagine a world without her face, even if it was just in my memories.

And so, I held on to every last piece of her that I had. The truck. The bed. The fucking couch. It was pathetic, but that didn't stop me from doing it anyway.

The possibility that she was home sent me into a weird spiral. What I was doing to myself could basically be described as torture. I flicked through the DVR, finding the interview *Rolling Stone* had done with Everly a year ago. I was feeling sorry for myself. What better way to feel sorry for yourself than continuously replay all your fuck ups over and over again in your head while watching an interview of your ex-girlfriend, the one that got away...the one that you *pushed* away?

She looked the same as she did in high school... only not. Gone was the shy and reserved girl I knew, the girl who was too timid, the girl who didn't believe that she should stand out. The girl sitting down for the interview was sensual and confident, posed and collected. She also had massive tits and hips that I wanted to sink my teeth into. She'd filled out in those departments since high school, although she was still as lithe as she'd always been.

She shimmered like the star she was. She was the embodiment of what I had always known was beneath her shy exterior.

I didn't listen to the questions the interviewer asked; I just watched Everly's expressions as she laughed and smiled. I allowed myself an evening of being mesmerized by the sparkle in her eyes when she spoke about her music, her passion. Her eyes used to sparkle like that for me.

I took another heady sip, my fractured heart aching to be put back together using the only remedy I had ever known—*her*.

Chapter Three

Everly

I PINNED UP MY ASH blonde hair, twisting the length of it into a French twist. I wore dainty pearl drop earrings in my earlobes. I stood back, staring at myself in the bathroom mirror and running my hands over the black lace of my dress. I didn't look like a woman who had spent the last four days crying every opportunity that I was alone. I looked like I was about to go out to another swanky album release event, not to my only sister's funeral.

My limbs felt weak, but I pressed on anyway, moving them when all I wanted to do was crawl under the blankets and wake up in my room in LA, to all of this being a terrible, horrible dream. It wasn't a dream, and I wasn't going to wake up from it.

I took a deep breath, attempting to prepare myself for the day, but I knew it was impossible. Burying a family member was never an easy thing, but it was exceptionally shitty when you were a goddamn A-lister that couldn't escape the media.

I couldn't believe that I'd only been back in town for three days, and within one day the tabloids had exploded with my face. Someone had snapped a photo of me at the airport, and the tabloids boasted that I'd returned home to mend my broken heart after catching Kyle with someone else.

Total bullshit, but I suppose it was better than the tabloids spilling the details of my family's private tragedy. Still, I was angry that I couldn't even get away to mourn.

We had purposely kept Julia's name out of the newspaper obituary and the article detailing the accident. We'd started a rumor that the funeral would take place in Toronto, hoping to throw the paparazzi off the scent so the funeral wouldn't be overrun with reporters. Instead, the funeral would be held in our tiny hometown.

I paused by my old bedroom door, spotting Cadence staring out the window. She was dressed in a black velvet dress, and her dark hair hung down her back in a tight French braid. She was clenching the purple bear, cradling it against the white cast on her arm.

"Are you ready Cadence?" I asked her, my voice hoarse from all the crying I'd done the night before.

Cadence didn't say anything; she just slowly slid off the bed and walked to me, her head down. I crouched down, picking her up in my arms. I held her close to me as we walked down the stairs.

Mom and Dad were waiting by the front door. They'd been giving me more and more time alone with Cadence. I was the only one that she'd let hold her when she woke up screaming and crying from the nightmares.

Cadence started to tremble as we approached the car.

"It'll be okay. I'm right here with you," I muttered to her gently, securing her in her booster seat.

The drive to the funeral home was short and silent. Conversation wasn't easily flowing for any of us. The parking lot was packed already. Julia had been a popular girl her whole life; it didn't surprise me that a lot of people had turned up to say goodbye to her.

I walked into the funeral home, Cadence's uninjured hand clinging to mine tightly like she never wanted to let go. I avoided going into the room where Julia's casket rested. We'd requested a closed casket ceremony, but I knew it was open so people could say their final goodbyes.

I closed my eyes against the intrusive thought of seeing my sister lying in her open casket. It wouldn't be *her*. She was gone. Just her body remained, and the difference would undoubtedly be noticeable. I didn't want to see her body, I wanted to see *her*...to talk to her.

Mom put her arm around my shoulders, pulling me tightly to her side as we joined my grandparents near the doorway to the room where Julia's casket rested. We greeted the visitors one by one as they came to give their condolences.

My bandmates and a few of my old friends joined the receiving line. Kyle Russell threw his arms around me, pulling me close. I shut my eyes against the familiar scent of him, tiny tears filling my eyes.

"Don't worry about a thing," he whispered, kissing me on the forehead. "I'll take care of it all." I nodded my thanks, unable to form words.

Marcus Muller hugged me next. "We love you, Ever," he said, his voice gruff with emotion. Aubrey stood beside him and she wordlessly took me in her arms again, whispering that she loved me too. Cam Roberts was next, and he gave me a pained smile as he hugged me. Cam was usually a talker, a joker, but when tragedy hit, he couldn't seem to form a sentence.

Cam moved on, and Alicia Garcia stepped up. I hadn't exactly been the best friend in the world within the last five years— at least, not to Aubrey or Alicia. I still spoke to them, but I didn't make as much time as I should have. Aubrey had come out to shows and to visit us in LA because she was still in love with Marcus, although their relationship was complicated, so I'd seen her more often the last few years. Despite that, we still stayed in touch and I knew that Alicia was busy with her own life, working as an art therapist and seeing a nice girl named Mandy.

Alicia had come by with Aubrey a few times after learning about the accident, helping any way that she could. She released me, unable to speak, her brown eyes full of sadness for me. There wasn't anything that she could say anyway. The fact that she was there was enough.

"I'll see you in a bit," Alicia finally said, her voice strained.

After Alicia came Maddie Markham, my personal assistant. Her long dark hair was pulled up into a trendy bun, and her sharp bangs cut across her forehead. She pushed her glasses up on her nose before pulling me in for a massive hug.

Maddie was an incredible force when it came to chaos. She not only managed my schedule, but also handled pretty much all of the other details of my life. She found the best outfits for red carpet events, managed the guys and helped run interference with our jackass agent.

"I'm sorry I didn't call you," I told her.

"Don't," Maddie warned sternly. She pulled away enough to stare at me. "I have to leave right after the funeral to catch my plane, but I wanted to tell you that everything is taken care of. Take as much time as you need. Call me and keep me updated but *don't worry about anything* except what's happening with your family, okay?" Sincerity filled Maddie's soft hazel eyes. I nodded gratefully and bit my lip. She hugged me again before moving on.

A couple more of Julia's friends and co-workers stepped up to give their condolences and the line kept moving. Panic was beginning to swell in my chest. The air felt stifling, and I needed to break away from this room full of people before it consumed me and I broke down. Before I could snag Cadence and escape, a voice that I hadn't heard in many years stilled me.

"Everly." I turned, noticing the golden mane first before Lindsay's arms wrapped around me. She pulled me to her. "I'm so sorry for your loss."

"Thanks," I murmured in response, my body rigid. I hadn't spoken to Lindsay Little since high school—since the whole Alicia thing. She hadn't changed much, I realized when she pulled away. She was fashionably put together and as thin as ever, but she carried herself with a defeated set to her shoulders. I finally met her gaze to see that her eyes were full of sorrow and regret.

Lindsay looked as if she had more to say; her mouth opened and closed before she gave me a small smile. "I'll see you later," she said instead, looking at the line behind her. Her gaze flitted down to Cadence.

My heart pounded in my chest as she looked at Cadence for a moment, giving her a tiny smile. I could tell that Lindsay wanted to say something comforting to Cadence, but that she didn't know what to say. Instead, she looked back up at me. "Let me know if you need anything... anything at all. I'd be happy to help anyway I can."

"Thank you," I said, watching as she disappeared into the crowd.

I picked Cadence up in my arms, just needing to hold her. I still felt like a funeral was too much for a four-year-old—hell, it was too much for *me*, but at the same time, how could she miss it?

"Are you thirsty?" I asked her. She nodded solemnly against my chest. There was a water cooler in one of the sitting rooms. I'd seen it when we first walked in. I put Cadence down in front of the cooler and grabbed a paper cup from the dispenser. "Do you want to press the button?"

She nodded timidly, pressing the button quickly while I held the plastic cup under the nozzle. "You have to press and hold," I instructed gently. Cadence tried again, this time she kept her finger on the button. "Okay, that's enough," I warned as the cup started to overflow. Cadence removed her finger soundlessly. I took her hand and we walked to one of the empty sofas.

I spoke softly to her and stroked the soft hair on her head while she sipped at her water. I glanced up, watching as Aubrey and Alicia walked into the sitting room. They had both been so much help in the last four days, keeping Cadence busy while my parents and I tried to sort out the funeral and burial arrangements, plus being there for me. We'd spent the night before sitting in the living room after Cadence had gone to bed, drinking wine and relaying stories of Julia from back in the day.

Although talking about Julia had been incredibly painful, I needed to do it.

"Lindsay's here," I remarked, tilting my head. Aubrey nodded, giving me a small smile.

"I know, we just spoke to her." Alicia didn't look upset or tense to receive a blast from the past. She was obviously over the burn.

I wished I could say the same about myself. I swallowed hard, my eyes roaming to Cadence's face before I spoke. "Do you guys talk to her often?" I asked.

"We see her around town now and again. She works at the restaurant," Aubrey said. Aubrey's parents owned a successful restaurant downtown. It was one of the best local places to go. Not only was the food incredible, but the service was too. The employees and the customers all had that small town friendliness that you definitely didn't see in LA.

The funeral director, Bonnie Strong, poked her head into the room. Bonnie's eyes were red-rimmed too. She'd gone to school with my mom and they had remained close friends into their adulthood. Bonnie babysat us when we were little. She didn't have kids of her own, and used to joke that we were the closest she would ever get to experiencing parenting. I was surprised to see that she was directing the funeral, but also happy. I couldn't imagine a stranger handling this. "Are you ready?" she asked, looking at me as if she knew the answer.

No, I wasn't. I would never be ready.

My parents had asked me if I would do the honors of singing "Hallelujah" at the beginning of the ceremony before they gave their speech. I hadn't wanted to say no to them, but singing was the furthest thing from my mind. Julia had always loved to hear me sing, so I agreed to do it anyway. It was the perfect tribute for my sister, and I hoped it would bring my parents some kind of peace.

I stood up and took Cadence's hand, walking her toward Aubrey and Alicia. "Can you stay with Aubrey and Alicia?" Cadence nodded solemnly, taking Aubrey's offered hand.

Bonnie led me to the podium that my parents and grandparents were standing beside and adjusted the microphone for me. I took a deep breath, my eyes seeking out and finding those familiar ice blue eyes from my past. The room was full of people I recognized. Growing up in a small town meant you grew up with everyone; you knew them and you didn't forget their faces.

I couldn't lie to myself. I knew that I was looking for one face in particular. Even as my heart stopped in my chest, I drew strength from those eyes. I took another deep breath before I started to sing.

I made it through most of the song before the tears welled up in my eyes. The final chorus was what tore me up.

"I did my best, it wasn't much
I couldn't feel, so I tried to touch
I've told the truth, I didn't come to fool you
And even though
It all went wrong
I'll stand before the lord of song
With nothing on my tongue but hallelujah!"

Finally, the last *Hallelujah* fell from my lips along with a couple of tears. My voice had wavered one too many times with emotion, but nobody seemed bothered by it. The silence of the room was broken every so often by the sniffling or quiet sobbing of our friends and family. I looked away from the grief reflecting within those intense blue eyes, my chest rising and falling as I struggled to breathe against the emotions crushing me.

* * *

After the funeral service, we returned to my parents' house for the wake. The house was packed full of people. So many clammy hands reaching out to clasp mine, so many lips whispering condolences and apologizes, talking about Julia like she was a saint.

It's an angering thing, having people tell you just how remarkable your sister was. I already *knew* that. Julia had loved fiercely, fought fiercer, and made sacrifices that most people her age wouldn't have considered making.

She had given up her college party lifestyle to raise a baby.

I grabbed a flute of champagne off the counter and tossed it back, not prepared to think about any of *that*. I had no idea why my grandparents had decided that champagne was an appropriate post-funeral drink, but I wasn't going to argue with them. I'd already pissed them off enough. The scowls they sent in my direction were not lost on my numb eyes. Besides, the champagne was helping to take the edge off the pain. I tossed back another one, and went to grab a third when the sound of quiet footfall alerted me to the arrival of Aubrey and Cadence.

"She doesn't want to be here," Aubrey told me, arching a brow at me and tightening her lips with sadness. *That makes two of us,* I thought.

"Okay, let's go then," I told Cadence, setting the full champagne flute down on the counter beside the two empty ones and extending my hand to her. She gave me a small smile and took it. "We'll just be upstairs, if Mom or Dad ask."

Aubrey nodded, giving me a sad smile as I led Cadence up the stairs.

It was quieter in the bedroom. I lay down on top of the lilac comforter, motioning for Cadence to join me. She crawled up beside me and nuzzled into my arm. "I miss Mommy. Could you tell me another story about her?" she asked, looking up at me with her wide eyes.

My heart felt lodged in my throat as I looked into Cadence's ice blue eyes. I swallowed hard as the memories resurfaced, smiling at her. Being around Cadence was the best and the worst thing. She resembled two people that I had loved and lost.

"Sure, my rhythm," I told her, stroking her dark hair. "When we were kids..." My voice got stuck on the lump in my throat. I cleared my throat, racking my brain to think of one story to share with her. There were so many to choose from, anecdotes of our childhood together. I started to tell her about the time Papa built the tree-house for us, and how we'd spend almost all of our time in it, coloring and playing together. I told her about how I'd fallen out of it and broken my arm, and how Julia had run inside crying worse than I had at the time. She had always hated seeing me in pain, even if we had drifted off when we were teenagers.

By the time I finished with my story, Cadence was fast asleep. I slipped out from under her, tucking an extra blanket over her sleeping body and adjusting the purple bear in her arms.

I crept out of the bedroom, remembering where the creaky parts of the floor were, and closed the door slowly and gently behind me. I turned around, mentally preparing myself to go downstairs.

Voices drifted up the stairwell. Mostly everyone that remained at the Daniels' house was family or close friends. I could hear my parents in the kitchen, talking softly as the fragrance of fresh coffee wafted out.

I spotted Kyle, Marcus and Cam lingering in the living room, waiting for me with Aubrey and Alicia. I walked up as Kyle stepped forward, his brow knitted together with concern. He wordlessly put his arms around me, pulling me to him.

I wrapped my arms around his neck, resting my head against his shoulder and drawing in his clean scent of comfort.

The tabloids liked to print breaking news stories about me and Kyle. They liked to flip images of me so that the ring I wore on my right ring finger appeared to be on my left hand and insist that Kyle and I were engaged.

It wasn't true, though—the engagement thing. Kyle and I were just friends, bandmates. He'd been a very big part of my life for five years now. He knew my secrets, and he covered my back to help me hide them, but we were not together.

Kyle loved me, and I loved him...but it wasn't like that. Kyle's romantic feelings for me had dissipated over the years of touring and seeing me at my absolute worst. He was now discreetly dating a girl that we had met three years ago at a concert in Ottawa. She was a private person that preferred to stay out of the tabloids. She was pretty and kind and she made Kyle happy.

The ring on my right finger was definitely not an engagement ring. It was a ring that Julia had given me four years ago; a beautiful, dainty platinum ring that had diamonds on the band and a beautiful red ruby in the middle.

"Where are we at with the tour?" I asked him, needing the distraction. I hadn't really thought about work over the last few days. I'd been busy with the funeral and Cadence. It was something that I needed to discuss though.

We were just about to go on tour for our new album, *Free From Blame*. The tour was supposed to start in January, only I knew I wouldn't be ready to perform any time soon—not until everything here was sorted. In fact, I couldn't bear the thought of leaving my parents and Cadence at all right now.

Tours were intense, and I'd been excited about this one before everything happened. I felt like this album was our best yet, and I knew the tour was going to be incredible. I was looking forward to it ending, too. After this tour, I intended to take a break. That had been in the cards even before everything happened. Touring was hard, putting in sixty hours a week at a studio was *hard*. As much as I loved doing it, I was burning out... and fast.

I dreaded thinking about the upcoming tour now. Six months of traveling, doing multiple venues each week was *hard* when you hadn't lost someone extremely important to you. I didn't know how I was going to get through this. *I didn't want to*, but I was afraid to let the guys down.

The guys knew how conflicted I was about it, but they were torn between worrying about their professional careers and my sanity.

"Everly!" Grandma Daniels said angrily. I glanced over, wincing as I realized that my grandparents were standing by the mantel. Grandma Daniels looked downright livid. She stomped over to me, Grandpa trailing behind her warily. "How dare you discuss your Hollywood antics at a time like this!"

The little color I had left in my face faded as everyone turned to stare at me. Aubrey weaved around the guys to stand beside me, placing her hands gently on my arm. "Let's just go, Everly," she hinted, trying to rouse me to walk away. We started to move, but I froze as my grandmother's voice rang out like a whip across the silent room.

"That's just like you, ready to take off again and your sister isn't even cremated yet!" Grandma Daniels venomously said. Her words were like punches right through my heart. I opened my mouth, about to tell her that I was trying to rearrange my schedule so that I could figure things out, when her next wave of words came spewing out like acid. "You don't even care that you left your sister to handle your responsibilities while you strutted around in Hollywood! You are selfish!"

The air left my lungs and my shoulders crumbled at the impact of her words.

"Mother." Dad's voice made the attention of the room snap from Grandma and me to him. He looked destroyed. "That's enough."

"No, Robert. It's not enough," Grandma argued. Grandpa put his hand on her shoulder, trying to calm her down. She wrenched free, her eyes flashing back to me. "Everyone else may have accepted and forgiven your selfishness, Everly, but I don't and I won't."

The living room was heavy with the uncomfortable silence that followed Grandma's sharp words. All eyes were on me as I drew in a shaky breath. Every inch of my body was trembling.

I couldn't respond; there was nothing to say. She was right.

Grandma Daniels gave me one final, disgusted look before she took off, barreling out the door with Grandpa almost chasing her.

I let out a strangled sound halfway between a gasp and a cry and pulled away from Aubrey. I needed to escape. I needed to get away. Where I planned on going, I had no idea. I didn't even have time to think about it before I came to an abrupt stop as my eyes fell on the familiar ice blue eyes of Grayson Dixon.

My tear-filled eyes widened in shock. I had dreamed about seeing Grayson Dixon again every night since he'd left. His blue eyes still haunted my dreams and a lot of my waking moments. All I could do was blink at him as he stood in the foyer looking into the living room at me. He had an unreadable expression on his tragically handsome face. Nobody in the room moved or said a thing while Grayson and I stood directly across from one another, our eyes locked. He didn't even seem to notice or care that we weren't alone.

Grayson had changed a lot over the past five years. He must have been over six feet tall. His dark blue button up dress shirt did little to conceal his muscular chest and waist. He no longer wore the facial piercings he had in high school.

He was a man now. An undeniably attractive man. I couldn't even help the swell of longing that exploded in my lower belly as my eyes roamed across his chest and shoulders. His dark hair was still on the unruly side, as if he'd spent the better half of the day running his hands through it. Knowing him, he likely had.

It was those eyes that got me. They were still swirling pools of intensity and passion, the same intense shade of blue, fixated on me as if I was all he could see; as if I was all he *wanted* to see.

I gulped. Coming face to face with him again was surreal. He looked so much like...

I forced the thought to stop in its tracks. I couldn't think about that right now.

"Everly." Grayson's voice was deep and gruff with a thousand words left unsaid. The look in his eyes was all-consuming. I took an involuntary step toward him, forcing myself to stop. My body and my heart were at war with my mind. My body wanted to go to him, while the thoughts in my head advised against those impulses. All eyes were on us. It was so quiet that I could hear my panicked breathing. "I'm so sorry."

More tears welled up in my eyes at his words, at the mere sight of him. Suddenly, he was closing the distance between us, taking me into his arms. They still felt like home, like where I wanted to be. His scent awoke all of the emotions I desperately tried to conceal for years.

I'd never gotten over Grayson...over what had happened between us. The tangible evidence of our passionate relationship would never let me forget it. I wore him on my skin, in my heart, and in my soul.

I had, however, gotten skilled at repressing my emotions. I was accomplished in pasting on a perfect smile for the camera. I had to in my field. I had to learn how to play the game to succeed. If I let the media tug on my seams, I would unravel and spoil it all for everyone. I couldn't *just* think about me, and I hadn't in a long time. But I was already fractured, and I was one more gentle probe away from shattering completely.

Grayson's hands seemed to roam over my hips without restraint, truly uncaring to the fact that we were not alone. It was almost as if nothing had changed between us. The electricity still zapped and sizzled; time still fell away. My heart still jump-started in my chest and my eyes still fluttered at the gentle grazing of his fingers across the small of my back.

I stepped back quickly, out of his arms. Each touch that Grayson probably meant as comforting set my skin on fire, just as it had all those years ago. It was unsettling, and I knew I couldn't have that. I couldn't let myself get sucked into the vortex that was Grayson and my feelings for him.

He'd hurt me once before, gutted me completely, and the last thing I needed right now was for Grayson to come into my life and complicate it further.

"What are you doing here?" I demanded.

Chapter Four

Grayson

EVERLY STOOD BEFORE ME with a hard set to her delicate jaw as she stared, waiting for me to answer. I couldn't seem to untangle my tongue. There was so much that I needed to tell her, but now wasn't the time. She'd just lost her sister.

"I just wanted to make sure you were okay," I explained, trying to keep my own emotion from clouding my voice. I'd expected to walk into a depressing atmosphere, but I hadn't expected to walk in to *this* atmosphere. The room was full of people, but nobody was moving and every eye darted back and forth from Everly to me, like some kind of pinball game. The air felt heavy, suffocating.

Kyle Russell was standing behind her, his brow furrowed as he glared at me with contempt. I didn't even react; I couldn't. I was still stunned that I'd actually shown up, that she was standing in front of me. My hands twitched with the desire to pull her to me and never let her go.

It felt so fucking surreal, like a dream sequence. Everything was bright, as if movie lights were pointed directly on us. Everyone seemed to be holding their breath, waiting and watching. I swallowed hard, my eyes finding Everly's face again. Everyone else fell away as I looked into those pale green eyes.

"To ask if I was okay?" she repeated, her eyebrows arching up. Her beauty took my breath away. She'd twisted her caramel hair up in a strange bun, exposing her slender neck. Her skin glowed, the black lace of her dress illuminating her perfection. She used to be the girl next door, all soft and malleable. Now, she was still and cool, emotionally untouched, posed and harder to read. Only her eyes gave way to the hardened pain she felt. "I just lost my sister, and my...my Cadance..." Her stoic mask finally fell apart as her voice broke. The depth of pain in her eyes made my own spirit crack a little.

I didn't wait for an invitation; I took her in my arms again. I held her close to me while she fell apart, her tears soaking the dark blue dress shirt I'd thrown on for the funeral. It was so crowded, that the funeral home had set up an additional room, connecting cameras to TVs so those of us sitting inside the additional room could watch the ceremony.

I had debated for days on whether to go to the funeral. I hadn't known Julia, and had only met her a few times in passing. I ended up going because not going felt wrong. I wanted to be there for Everly. Her pain was always my pain, even if I had a shitty way of showing it in the past.

I was late getting to the wake because I'd been agonizing over if I should go. The wake was more intimate than the funeral, and I didn't want to impose, but I couldn't wait to see her. She'd left so quickly after the funeral, carrying a little girl—her niece—in her arms. It had taken me half the afternoon to man up and just go.

Everly seemed to realize that she was falling to pieces in my arms in front of her family and friends. She pulled away again, tucking her arms around herself tightly, still staring at me like she'd seen the sun for the first time in years. Like I blinded her.

"Can we talk?" The three words fell off my tongue with difficulty. Everly's pain was gutting me. I gestured with a slight nod of my head to our audience. She nodded, leading the way to the kitchen. She stopped near the sliding door, looking out into the backyard. It was snowing, but it wasn't sticking. I watched her face in the reflection of the glass.

"You should go," she whispered, her voice broken, her back still to me. I watched her reflection in the glass as she closed her eyes. Two large tears escaped from under her thick lashes, trailing down her face.

"Is that what you want?" It almost hurt to speak, or rather...to hear her answer.

Everly didn't reply right away. She slowly turned to look at me. "Why do you suddenly care what I want?"

"I've always cared," I argued, keeping my eyes locked on hers. I swallowed against the agony I saw there.

"You left, Grayson." Her voice shook. It seemed like those words had been stuck on her tongue for years, turmoil rattling around inside her head. "Before I even had a chance to tell you…"

"Tell me what?" I demanded, the look in her eyes making all the saliva dry up in my mouth. I stepped toward her.

She inhaled sharply, her eyes fluttering at my nearness. I brought my hands up to frame her face, gently brushing the tears away from her cheeks.

"It doesn't matter," she said. "Why are you back? Why now?"

"I've been back for two years," I told her, my hands still framing her face. The pad of my thumb brushed over her lips, and she let out a soft sigh. She wasn't objecting to my closeness, to my hands on her skin, hungering to touch her.

My lips pressed against hers, gently at first, testing the waters. Her lips parted, and I took that as an invitation to deepen the kiss. She moaned softly, the sound vibrating against my lips.

Suddenly, she was pushing me away, her eyes flashing with anger, hurt and regret."You can't just come back and kiss me like that!"

"Like what?" I challenged. I raised my eyebrows, alluding truth. "Like I've missed you? Like I've longed for your touch ever since I stupidly made you walk away? Like I love you?"

Everly was shaking her head, tears pouring down her cheeks.

"I never stopped, Everly," I told her, running my hands through my hair and tugging at the ends. I was sure I looked frantic. I *felt* frantic. I reeled it in, dropping my hands to my sides and approaching her slowly. "I was an idiot; I made a mistake. I've never stopped loving you."

I realized it was shitty of me to say that right now. Everly had just lost her sister; she was going through hell and there I was showing up to announce my feelings for her. I was all too aware of the fact that I had never told her I loved her before. It had always been my biggest regret— letting her walk away without her knowing the depths of my feelings.

"I know you're going through a lot, and I understand that. I'm not asking you for anything. I just needed to tell you how I felt. I've been carrying it around for years. I never thought you'd come back, but if you did, I just needed to tell you." I brushed the tears away from her cheeks again. My heart felt like it had been blown to pieces, and I knew it was my own fucking fault. All of it was. "My feelings for you haven't changed. And I'm here. I want to be here for you. I won't run this time."

The sound of someone clearing their throat dragged our attention from one another. Everly and I looked toward the sound. Aubrey was standing there apologetically.

"What's wrong?" Everly demanded, stepping away from me. I let my hands fall to my sides, shoving them in my pockets.

"She's screaming for you," Aubrey apologized. "Your Mom asked me to get you."

Everly was running before the words were even completely out of Aubrey's mouth.

Aubrey was still standing in the doorway of the kitchen, studying me. Aubrey and I had never been tight, but she'd never looked at me with animosity before.

"Who's screaming?" I asked.

"Cadence," she answered shortly. "Everly's...Julia's..." she trailed off awkwardly, looking away.

Oh, right. The little girl I'd seen Everly carry to the car. There was an awkward pause while I thought about my next course of action—stay or give her some space to digest the verbal explosion I'd showered over her.

"Maybe you should go. I'm sure that she appreciates seeing you again," Aubrey's face pinched slightly at this, "but she's dealing with a lot right now."

I nodded, my jaw tense. "Tell her to call me," I said, feeling like the world's biggest imbecile for handing my card to Aubrey. She took it.

"I'm sure she'll be calling you," she said ominously, unable to meet my eyes.

Walking away from Everly physically hurt, but Aubrey was right. Everly was dealing with a lot, and the last thing she needed was the added drama of dealing with me. So I left, the quiet conversation from the living room following me out the door.

I pulled up to the curb in front of Tap's. I wasn't one to day-drink normally, but special occasions and what not. I sank down into a bar stool, nodding at Tom Grady. Tom inclined his head slightly, but otherwise remained still.

Katrina was behind the bar. She set down a glass of whiskey in front of me and I drained it. She arched her eyebrow at me questionably, grabbing the empty glass to refill it. "I take it she didn't run back into your arms right away?" Katrina chuckled at the expression on my face. I stared at her, conveying I wasn't in the mood for her antics. "Sorry. But what did you expect? You haven't said boo to her in the past five years."

"I know that." I frowned. I wasn't expecting Everly to run back into my open arms. I wasn't even expecting her to give me another chance. I hadn't gone there with the intention of kissing her; it just happened. It was just how our bodies reacted to one another. I was helpless against my primal urges for her, and I was a fucking asshole for it.

I took another swig of whiskey, the cold liquid soothing my raw throat as I thought about how it had felt to hold Everly in my arms again, about how her eyelids had fluttered against my touch, her face relaxing and her lips parting. How she'd tasted against my tongue...the same taste that was always her, with a hint of champagne and tears.

I remembered how Everly's body felt. I remembered the expression she used to get when around me, the breathless way her lids would softly close and her lips would slowly part.

The same thing happened today; I touched her and she reacted like she always had. The *thing* between us was as strong as ever, only now it was tangled with hurt and regret and years of longing.

I set the glass down, my brows furrowing as I kicked myself for being such a guy. I could have handled our reunion with more tact.

Exhaling, my lips tightening over my teeth as I stared into the amber liquid. I swirled it around carefully before taking another sip. I continued to swirl it, staring into its depths. "So...Julia had a daughter?"

"Yup," Katrina replied, not looking at me. She seemed to be counting in her head while she checked her liquor stock.

"I didn't know that." I swallowed back more whiskey.

Katrina looked up at me curiously. "Why does that matter? Is Everly going to take custody or something?" she asked.

The thought had never even occurred to me. If she took custody, did that mean she would stay in town to raise the girl? Or would she just take the girl with her to LA? Everly was successful enough that she could easily afford a full-time nanny while she toured. I swallowed, my Adam's apple bobbing against my dry throat.

"I don't know," I said honestly, dropping my gaze.

"What's on your mind?" Katrina sighed, leaning forward to capture my gaze. "You know how much I *love* when drunken patrons unload their problems on me. Have at 'er." Katrina waved her hand as if encouraging me to unload those problems. She grinned wickedly.

"First of all, I'm not drunk...yet," I corrected, polishing off the rest of my drink. It burned my throat on the way down, but it was the good kind of burn. I trailed off, looking away from Katrina's intense gaze. I sighed deeply, feeling resigned. Seeing Everly had opened up the floodgates of my repressed emotions.

I'd been trying to act like the sting of losing her didn't still hurt every day, but there was no lying anymore. My own walls were stripped bare, and it became abundantly clear to me that I could never come back from Everly. She was it for me.

I was relieved to know that I still affected her, I wasn't sure what it would ultimately lead to, but at least I hadn't burned her feelings for me to the ground completely. There was something left. The big question now was, could it be salvaged?

Swallowing again, I raised my eyes to look up at Katrina. She was watching me, patiently waiting for me to resurface.

"It's nothing," I said gruffly, narrowing my eyes. I couldn't put my thoughts into words yet. I didn't even truly comprehend them.

I tossed back the remainder of my whiskey, gesturing for Katrina to pour me another.

* * *

The next morning, I awoke feeling as if someone was taking a jack hammer to my skull. I wiped the sleep from my eyes, rolling over. The movement made me wince and I opened my eyes gingerly.

Katrina was lying beside me, watching me with one eyebrow arched and a smirk on her lips.

"Jesus!" I bolted out of bed, startled. Katrina effectively got rid of my morning wood faster than a cold shower.

"No, *Katrina*," she corrected sarcastically, sitting up. "You're welcome, by the way."

"For what?" I asked warily, scratching the stubble on my jaw while I tried to recall from hazy alcohol soaked memories exactly *what* had happened after I left the bar. I was dressed from the waist down, and Katrina was fully clothed as well. Still, that didn't mean much when it came to my track record.

"For dragging your drunk ass home last night. You're a heavy asshole." Katrina shook her head, grinning. "I almost broke my spine."

I frowned, some of last night coming back to me. I didn't know how many glasses of whiskey I'd tossed back; I'd lost count after five.

"You drank the entire bottle, and then demanded shots," Katrina clarified, pursing her lips. "It was the most fun you've been in a while. You even had Tom Grady taking shots with you!"

"Hmmpf," I said, my frown increasing. I hadn't meant to get that wasted. I just needed to get wasted enough that I wouldn't do something stupid.

Like drive back to Everly's house and push her up against the wall and kiss her until she let me back in...back to where I belonged.

I suppose getting completely trashed with Tom Grady was the lesser of two evils. I glanced at Katrina again. "Did we...?" I trailed off, raising a brow in question. It was definitely an awkward question—to ask the girl in your bed if you'd drunkenly screwed her the night before. I honestly didn't remember. I could have met the Pope and wouldn't have known it.

"Trust me, Dixon, if we did, you'd remember." Katrina rolled her eyes, getting up out of the bed. "I crashed here because I didn't feel like driving home at five in the morning."

"There were other beds," I muttered, scowling.

"Oh get over it, Grayson." Katrina sighed, aggravated. "I'm going to need a ride home. But first...go shower. I can smell your nasty whiskey pores from over here."

"Fine." I shut the bathroom door on her.

"We should go out for breakfast," Katrina suggested as I walked back into the bedroom ten minutes later, using a towel to dry my hair. I scowled at her. "Friends can go out for breakfast, Grayson. I'm starving, and you owe me."

"Why do I owe you?" I demanded, barely sparing her a glance as I dropped the towel and stepped into my boxers. Katrina looked away with a smirk. It was nothing she hadn't seen before, though several years had passed. She was mostly over her feelings for me, but it was hard for a girl not to be affected by me—and I didn't mean that in an egotistical way. I worked out, I took care of my body, and I was blessed in more ways than just having great muscle memory.

"Because I blew off my boyfriend to take care of you and make sure that you didn't go over to Everly's."

I buckled my jeans, scowling deeper. I didn't *think* I'd broached the topic of my desire to go back. But then again, I couldn't very well say that with the utmost certainty, considering I didn't even remember leaving the bar.

"You were babbling on and on incoherently last night about making it right, and it was weird. I was worried," Katrina continued, her brown eyes seeking mine out. She'd long since ditched the weird cat shaped contacts. It was easier to read her emotions now. She was concerned about me.

She was the closest thing I had to a friend, and I wouldn't even call her that. I could never tell her about the crazy shit that went on in my head, but she was determined to keep me in her life, no matter how much shit I threw her way.

Katrina was like a termite. She was impossible to scare away, and she was almost indestructible. I had been home for two years now, and she'd come knocking the moment she heard I was back in town. She hadn't let me continue with my self-imposed isolation.

"Fine, breakfast. But no talking." I pulled my shirt over my head and left the bedroom, knowing that Katrina would follow.

We piled into my work truck and drove to a local restaurant to grab the breakfast that Katrina insisted I owed her. Day Breakfast was packed with the Saturday hangover crowd. I said nothing as I sat across from Katrina and waited for the waitress to bring me my coffee.

I had a billion things going on in my head. Everly was at the very front of my mind, but the list of work demands I had coming up was there as well.

"Are you going to try again?" Katrina asked, leaning back against the booth while she studied me. She was dressed in the same black tank top she'd worn to work the night before, her ample cleavage all but staring me in the face. The saddest part was that it didn't do a damn thing for me.

"I said no talking," I reminded her gruffly. I didn't want to talk about what I was or wasn't going to do when it came to Everly. I didn't know what the plan was. I knew what I wanted. I wanted her to come back to me, to be mine again. But I had fucked up royally, and I didn't know how to go about getting her back. Besides, the last thing she wanted right now was me to complicate things. I'd witnessed the destroyed look on her face in the moments before she realized I was standing there.

But at the same time...*I* wanted to be there for her. I wanted to help her heal. I wanted to be her safe place and her hideaway from grief. Lord knew I should have done it years ago, actually been there for her when she needed it.

"Sorry," Katrina said, raising her hands in mock surrender. "Jesus. Didn't think you were serious about that."

"I was. Very," I retorted. I leaned back in the booth, my gaze drifting out the large window that faced the street.

There wasn't much to see. Most of Newcastle was either still asleep or already inside Day Breakfast. The waitress appeared by my arm, setting down a black coffee in front of my hands for me, and a tea for Katrina.

"Are you guys ready to order?" she asked, bored. I peered up at her, recognizing her face but barely. I figured it was another one of those small town things. Her eyes widened while she looked at me. The recognition faded to intrigue, and she tilted her head as she stared into my eyes with a calculating look that almost made me feel uncomfortable.

"I'll take the Hearty Breakfast. Eggs sunny side up and extra bacon," I ordered, handing the menu back, my brows knitting together while I tried to place her.

"Same, only make my eggs over easy and give me extra sausage. You should get one for yourself too, how about a big thick one?" Katrina smirked, winking at the waitress. The waitress took the menus from our table, rolling her eyes at Katrina as she left.

"Who was that?"

"Lindsay Little," Katrina replied, still smirking as she watched Lindsay disappear to slide our order to the kitchen window.

"Hmm." I frowned. I'd barely recognized her at first, but after Katrina told me who she was...I recalled her from my high school memories. She had been one of Everly's friends before a bunch of drama went down. I couldn't even remember what the hell had happened. Everly took up so much space in my head that the mundane memories had fallen away.

I took a sip of coffee, distractedly looking out the window across from me. It faced the street. I watched as cars drove by and the occasional person walked past.

I reluctantly looked up at Katrina, hating the way she was quietly assessing me.

"You know," she said slowly as she grabbed a sugar packet from the bowl. She ripped it open, pouring it into her tea before she continued. "You've always been a fighter, Grayson. You've always been the guy that rushes to defend. Hell, you react with your fists before your brain even registers what the fuck is going on. You always have. But the *one time* that you should have fought, you didn't."

I snorted, shaking my head. Katrina struggled with minding her own damn business. The annoying thing was that she was right.

"I swear to God if you don't fight this time, Grayson, I'll rearrange your face with a pipe. A guy with *your* good looks shouldn't be so stupid."

Chapter Five

Everly

I SAT AT THE KITCHEN island in a barstool, my hot mug of coffee sitting on the counter before me. My hands cupped around the ceramic mug, drawing the warmth of it into my fingers. I purposely kept my eyes focused on the mug, avoiding the plain white business card on the counter beside my right hand. Grayson had given it to Aubrey for me. It had his contact information; he wanted me to call him.

I sighed, the sound of it loud in my ears. The house was dark and eerily quiet, a vast change from the chaos of family and bodies it had seen over the last few days. I was the only one awake.

As I stared at the steam rising, my thoughts became a swirling, confusing mess of 'what ifs' and 'if onlys'.

I'd started out my final year of high school with the intention of finding out who I was. I hadn't really understood anything about life back then. I thought I knew it all.

Everybody thought I was so sweet and docile, but it turned out that I was just a selfish, weak person that was ruled by emotions and impulses.

When I found out that I was pregnant, I had a breakdown. Privately. I felt like I couldn't tell anyone. I was embarrassed and ashamed of myself. Grayson was gone, and I'd been stupid enough to somehow get pregnant. I couldn't remember a time when we hadn't used protection though, but the articles that I read said it could still happen. And it *had* happened; I was pregnant at seventeen. Pregnant and alone.

Plus, I'd just signed a contract with the band. We were working on our first album in the studio, putting in seven hours a day. We were set to go on tour in early November. I couldn't have a baby and tour with a band, but the idea of having an abortion made me ill. I couldn't do that either. The baby was the last piece of *him* that I had and despite my fears, I loved it.

I kept it secret for four months. I lost weight because I had difficulty eating and keeping anything down. My parents assumed that I was stressing about the release of my first album.

Julia clued in first. She stood outside of the bathroom door one day while a particularly bad case of morning sickness kept my face firmly positioned over the toilet.

"How far along are you?" she demanded, cornering me in the hallway as I attempted to make my way back to my room.

"What?"

"Don't play dumb, Everly. I'm not an idiot. You're pregnant. How far along are you?" Julia's deep green eyes were focused on my face. I started to cry. She wrapped her arms around me and waited for my tears to ebb so I could speak. I was so relieved to finally tell someone the truth, to finally get it off of my chest.

Julia immediately stepped up and helped me get through the next five months. She was there for me, offering her unwavering support. She went with me to doctor appointments, tried to help me track down Grayson, and held my hand when I finally told my parents.

Telling my parents had been a terrifying experience. They didn't know what to say at first—they knew the situation with Grayson. We'd broken up and he'd left the province without any way of reaching him. I'd already tried to get his step-mom to tell me how I could reach him, but all she'd said to me was that he had left without leaving a forwarding address or number.

It was clear that Grayson didn't want to be found, and I had no choice but to accept that fact and try to move on.

I hid the entire pregnancy from almost everybody. I acted as if I had thyroid issues, and that excuse explained the little weight that I'd gained. I wore clothes that hid my bump, posing in ways that obscured it from view. We were still new, so I didn't have to worry about the paparazzi snapping bump pictures of me. I was still careful though. I still kept it secret. Only my family, Aubrey, Alicia, my agent, my personal assistant and the guys in the band knew. Half of them would never betray me, and the other half had signed confidentiality contracts.

I didn't know what I was going to do when the baby was born. I knew that the baby couldn't come on tour with me, and I knew that I couldn't bail out on the band. We were opening for *Sevens*, a popular band from Vancouver, and the shows had already sold out.

It was a challenging time. Instead of enjoying putting together our first album and doing radio shows, the guys and I were all twisted with anxiety. Tensions ran high because nobody knew what I would actually do once the baby was born. Every time my parents tried to talk about it to me, I shut down. I just couldn't process it. Thinking about it made me think about Grayson, and how he should be here for this...but he wasn't.

Julia had been the one to come up with the plan. She offered to take care of the baby while I toured. "She's young enough that she won't even remember," Julia assured me.

When Julia presented her plan to our parents, the house exploded into chaos.

"Think of how much money Everly is going to make doing this," Julia had argued, a few tears of her own escaping. "How many people get a shot like this? I can't let her pass it up—"

"You shouldn't be offering this." Mom shook her head, biting her lip. They exchanged a meaningful look with one another. She could see where Julia was coming from; where I was coming from. It was no secret that I wasn't ready for this kind of responsibility. I could tell that my mom wanted me to stay, to step up, but she worried about how I would be able to get on my feet if I didn't take this opportunity.

Julia was right about the money. From the raving reviews our debut album received, we had the potential to make it big...and I hadn't exactly graduated high school. I was doing correspondence, but between recording and the pregnancy, I hadn't had much time or will to focus. Regardless, my family was going to have to help me and they knew it. The problem was deciding which was the lesser evil.

Less than two days later, my water broke. Cadence was born on the twenty-ninth of July. Her name meant rhythm. She was my rhythm.

I didn't think I could do it. I looked down at the tiny being bundled up in a pink blanket, her wide deep blue eyes focused on my face, and I broke. I shattered into a million pieces.

There was a little over four months before the tour started. To say that I wasn't prepared for it was an understatement. I wasn't prepared to leave my home, my family...and Cadence.

However, Julia insisted I go. She sat with me in my hospital bed, her arms around my shoulders while I cuddled Cadence and cried, snot and tears flowing down my cheeks without constraint. I felt like my heart was breaking all over again, only worse. It was twisting and squeezing in my chest. It felt like it was ripping apart, shredding into irreparable fragments.

"I can't abandon her," I had wailed, my shoulders shaking. Cadence's little body moved with my trembles, but the motion didn't bother her. In fact, it seemed to put her to sleep.

"You aren't abandoning her," Julia insisted, her own tears freely streaming down her cheeks. "She's still very much a part of your life. You're still her mommy. You're just going off to work for a bit. Mommies have to work, Everly."

Julia was almost finished with her dental hygienist program. She'd been doing incredibly well, and had decided to fast track it. She was set to graduate in two months. I would be paying for everything that Cadence needed. Mom and Dad would help Julia with Cadence, and I would return home whenever I had a break in shows. Still, I couldn't understand why my sister was offering this. I didn't understand why she was willing to give up her freedom for me.

"Why do you want to do this?" I asked, my chest heaving with the panic and desperation I felt. Every time I had asked before, Julia would shrug off my question and tell me that I deserved a chance at my dreams and being a mom. This time, she sighed heavily, pulling me closer. I felt my hair grow damp from her tears.

"I was pregnant, Everly. Just before you. When I told Liam, he made me feel like an abortion was the only option for us. He said he couldn't handle being a dad so young. He said he would be with me the entire time. So...I got one. He held my hand, and the next day, he broke up with me."

I didn't think it was possible for my heart to break any more, but it did. I was so locked in my own despair, I hadn't even seen what pain Julia was carrying. She hid it so well. "Julia, I'm so sorry. I wish I'd known. I wish I'd been there for you."

"I wouldn't let anybody be there for me. Dad still doesn't know, and he never will...and I only told Mom after the fact when I had an infection," Julia confessed, peering down at Cadence's tiny sleeping body in my arms. Her jaw trembled. "I regretted that decision so much, Everly. I can never explain to you the hollow feeling that I'll carry around forever. I should be holding my own baby..." Julia gasped, choking on her tears. "I didn't want you to experience that sense of loss. This way, you can still do what you set out to do and you won't lose her, because we'll be here. She'll be yours."

So, when Cadence was just under four months old, I left with the band for the tour, placing Cadence in the arms of my sister and parents. I knew she was safe and loved, and that was all that mattered. I didn't want to chance anything happening while I was gone. I was paranoid that if I admitted the truth, then the media would stalk my family. And I was honestly afraid to have Grayson find out about it by looking at a magazine that covered the "breaking" news.

Julia saw where I was coming from and completely understood, and Cadence helped fill a void in her heart too. Watching them solidified my decision, even if it didn't make it any easier.

"What are you thinking about?" Mom asked, her sudden appearance in the kitchen taking me by surprise.

"Everything." I sighed, my head dropping into my hands. My hair was tangled and I was still wearing my pajamas. I was a mess, but I was all cried out.

Mom put her arms around me. "I'm sorry about what Grandma said," she said, stroking the hair from my eyes.

"She was right." I laughed, the sound bitter as it echoed throughout the kitchen. "Can't blame her for being right."

"She wasn't right," Mom argued, arching a brow. "You did what you thought was right for Cadence. You made sure that she never went without anything."

I didn't argue with her, even though I didn't agree. What was the good in making sure she never went without anything if I was never there? Cadence spent four years with Julia and she called her Mommy.

I swallowed hard as the memory surfaced.

The town car pulled into the driveway of my family's house. The driver parked and got out, going to the trunk to grab my suitcase for me.

"Thanks, I've got it," I told him, taking it out from his arms. I set off up the walkway, my heart pounding in my chest.

I hadn't been home for eight months. Cadence was a year old. I'd missed her first birthday, although we were celebrating it this weekend. Julia told me that she was starting to walk and talk. I was nervous and excited to see her again.

Pushing open the door, I was greeted with the gentle thumping of Stella's tail against the banister. She was moving slower these days. Stella was suffering from arthritis.

I scratched her ears while I walked toward the living room. Julia was sitting on the carpet, her arms outstretched as Cadence crawled over to her, babbling while bits of drool dropped down her chin and onto the hardwood floor in front of her. Slowly and cautiously, she stood up.

"Mommy, oouk!" Cadence was saying as she took her first tentative steps, straight into Julia's arms, and nuzzled her head into Julia's neck.

Hearing her say that while looking at Julia with eyes wide and full of wonder knocked the wind out of me. I smiled through the pain of my heart squeezing in my chest as I realized that it didn't matter what Cadence called Julia or me. Julia was her mother. Julia was there for the everyday things. Julia rocked her to sleep at night and was there to kiss her in the morning.

Just before our second tour took off, the band was interviewed by Owen O'Malley from the *O'Malley At Night* show. It was after I'd heard Cadence call Julia Mama. The interview started off harmless enough; Owen O'Malley asked us how it felt to be where we were.

Then, just as I started to relax, I was asked about Cadence. A photo had surfaced of me tearfully kissing her small bundled body goodbye before I left for the first tour, as well as a photo of Cadence and me when she was just over a year old. It was grainy, as if someone had snapped it on their phone. When the photos came up on the screen, I froze.

"Who's the kid?" Owen asked, his white teeth flashing against his tanned skin.

"My niece," I quickly answered, pasting on a smile.

"She looks a lot like you!" Owen pressed, smiling mischievously.

"My sister and I could almost pass for twins." I'd laughed, trying to keep it natural and easy. It was true; we could.

"Well, she's cute as a button and has one incredibly talented aunt! You guys are doing incredible. It's only been a year, and your last two records have topped the charts for months! That's huge!" Owen grinned.

I shook my head, bringing myself back to the present. I blinked up at Mom. She was staring at me expectantly. "Sorry, what did you say?"

"I said, what did he want?" Mom repeated as she crossed over to the counter and poured herself a cup of coffee.

"I don't know." I frowned, my stomach flipping in memory of the feel of his hands and lips on me again. My body hadn't even argued his presence. My body had melted in to him like he'd never hurt me before. But he *had* hurt me. He had hurt me *badly* in all the ways that he predicted he would.

I knew that I had only myself to blame, that my reaction to the breakup wasn't Grayson's fault. It wasn't Grayson's fault that I loved him as much as I did. It wasn't Grayson's fault that his love for me hadn't been enough, or as strong as mine was for him. I couldn't blame him for leaving if I hadn't been what he wanted.

But still, you'd think after everything he had put me through before, my body wouldn't melt like butter in his hands; my heart wouldn't collapse at his words, desperately wanting to believe them.

"What did he say?" Mom was trying to get me to talk to her, to fill her in on what I was thinking. I knew she wanted me to tell her what the plan was. We had avoided talking about it over the last few days, desperate to grieve and get through the funeral. Now the funeral was over, and the uncertainty of the future loomed over us all.

Grayson's voice invaded my head. My cheeks were warm where his fingers had carefully brushed my tears away. *"I know you're going through a lot, and I understand that. I'm not asking you for anything. I just needed to tell you how I felt...I've been carrying it around for years. I never thought you'd come back, but if you did...I just needed to tell you. My feelings for you haven't changed. And I'm here. I want to be here for you."*

"It doesn't matter." I sighed heavily. It didn't matter. It didn't matter whether I believed him. It didn't matter because it wouldn't change anything.

I had loved—and lost—Grayson before. I'd experienced the best highs of my life... and the worst lows. It had been a whirlwind love affair that nearly destroyed me. I wouldn't survive a repeat.

"I know you're about to start the tour..." Mom continued as if I hadn't just shut her down. "Cadence is attending school here. Your father and I don't think that it's a good idea for her to move to LA right now. She's just been in an accident and she lost her—Julia." Mom paused, clearing her throat before she met my eyes.

I inhaled slowly, knowing that I couldn't avoid the subject anymore. "I don't want to do the tour." I brushed away a lone tear. "I can't bear leaving, but the venues are already set, the shows are already sold out."

"So what are you going to do?" Mom asked. I had no idea how to answer her question. I knew that if I bowed out of the tour, I would let the guys down...and they didn't deserve that after all they'd done for me. I wasn't concerned about the fines for canceling; I knew I'd lose money if I did it but I didn't care about the money. I had plenty of it—more than enough to cover the fines and still live comfortably. I just didn't want to let *them* down; they'd be out money too. The whole thing made my brain strain and my stomach tighten with anxiety.

I sighed, massaging my aching temples with my fingers. "I can't think about this right now, Mom. I can't think." I hid my face behind my hands as more tears escaped, spilling onto my fingers. My shoulders shook. Every time I tried to think about what I was going to do, I became so overwhelmed with it all and longed to ask Julia what I should do. It was the worst reminder that she was gone.

Mom pursed her lips, nodding. She understood what I felt.

"Is the truth ever going to come out, Everly?" Mom's question caught me off guard. I took a deep breath, my shoulders shaking slightly. I couldn't meet her eyes.

"My agent thinks it'll be bad for my image for the media to get a hold of the truth. He wants me to act like I took custody of my niece, not re-took custody of my daughter," I said this with a voice void of emotion.

"What do you think about that?"

"I don't know, Mom." My brain felt as if it were pushing against my skull, trying to break free and explode everywhere. "I don't care about that anymore. Cadence has always known the truth, and that's always been enough for me."

The cover story I'd given Owen O'Malley was just a way to save my ass and to protect Cadence. And it stuck. As far as my fans knew, I was the aunt and Julia was the mom. Cadence knew the truth—or at least a variation of it. She knew that she came from my tummy and I was her mama; however, she had always referred to Julia as her mommy. We'd never corrected her because essentially, she was right.

It was like a weird version of the game of house we used to play as kids. I spoiled Cadence like a part-time parent would. I invited my sister and Cadence up to LA whenever our schedules correlated. I bought her the best birthday and Christmas presents and I showered her with affection every chance that I got. I truly loved that child more than anything because everything I did was for her. Almost all of my money went directly into a high-yield savings account for Cadence's future.

But Julia was Mommy. Julia was the one who kissed skinned knees and brushed away cranky tears. Julia was the one who was *there* for all of it; the good, the bad, and the mundane. And she deserved that title.

Mom exhaled heavily. She couldn't think of a solution for our predicament either. None of us could have possibly ever imagined something so tragic happening, leaving us helpless and defeated as to what should be done next.

"Are you going to tell him?" she asked, her voice soft and gentle.

I stared at the remaining contents of my cold coffee. "It wouldn't change anything." My jaw trembled.

"I think he deserves to know the truth," Mom said sagely.

"How do I tell him the truth?"

"By using your voice." Mom shrugged, smiling sadly.

* * *

I left Cadence with my parents while I drove to the house that Julia had rented. I'd tried to buy them a house, but Julia refused to accept that kind of help. I was headed there to start packing up. There was no reason to keep the apartment; Cadence was going to stay at my parents' for a bit, and so was I. The landlord had been excessively calling my dad, demanding to know what was going to happen to his unit.

Some people had no tact. I decided to handle it before my father had an aneurysm.

I was hit with another memory as I pulled my parents' car into a free parking spot.

"You're already giving me enough money for Cadence. She doesn't need half of what you give!" Julia argued. We were talking on the phone, miles away from each other.

"The rest is for you, for whatever you need. A sitter so you can go on a date, maybe," I hinted.

Julia laughed, the sound rich over the phone. "I don't need a man. I have BOB."

"Bob?" I repeated, frowning. I hadn't heard of a Bob before. Maybe they'd just met.

"Battery Operated Boyfriend." I could hear her smirking over the phone. I snorted with laughter. "Besides," Julia's voice quieted my laughter as I waited for her to continue, "I don't like bringing too many guys around. It's confusing for Cadence."

"Oh, right." I hadn't thought of that. It just proved in my head that Julia was better suited for the job than I was...

A gentle tapping against the window startled me from the memories. I wiped at my cheeks, startled to see that I'd been crying again, and rolled down the window.

"Are you Tom?" I asked, eyeing the elderly gentleman. Tom Grady was the name of Julia's landlord. He was a short old man, his back curving forward. Gray hairs sprouted from his ears and he wore a brown tweed newspaper boy hat that matched his trousers and jacket.

The man nodded solemnly. He waited until I'd rolled the window back up and stepped outside to speak. "I'm sorry about your loss," he said, his voice gruff and hoarse, as if he wasn't in practice of using it often.

"Yeah, thanks," I said, resisting the urge to roll my eyes. If he was so sorry, he really had a funny way of showing it. "I'm sorry for pressuring you about the unit. But I do need to know what's going on, and I'm sick of taking care of that damn cat."

"What damn cat?" I asked, raising my eyebrows.

"They've got a cat," Tom croaked, using his key to unlock the unit door. "It's an asshole. Keeps scratching me when I try to feed it."

"Sorry," I said, peering around him and looking in to the apartment. Julia kept the apartment fairly clean. There was clutter here and there, toys and discarded sweaters, the usual mess that came when you had a kid. I watched as a tabby darted from under the couch to the hallway off to the left of the living room, disappearing from sight.

Tom left me to it, handing over the spare key and asking me to give him an update on when everything would be cleared out. I stood alone in the middle of the tiny living room, wondering where to begin.

Chapter Six

Grayson

AFTER BREAKFAST, I pulled up to Katrina's house. She hopped out of the truck and stood in the driveway, holding the door open.

"What?" I demanded. I knew I hadn't exactly been the greatest company at breakfast; I'd been quiet, staring off into space and thinking about Everly. When I wasn't lost inside my own head, I was acting like a miserable, antsy prick. I couldn't help it. Knowing that I was so close to her and yet so far drove me absolutely insane.

"I'd better not see you at the bar tonight," Katrina said, her voice dangerous.

"Don't worry, I think I've had enough of your company," I retorted, smirking at the offended look on her face.

She shook her head, smiling as she slammed the door. "Asshole," I saw her mutter as I pulled away.

I had a long list of fuck all to do, and I sort of wanted to get to it. I turned on to the main road and drove for a few minutes before my eyes were drawn to the painted on jeans and long slender legs that I forever pictured in my dreams, wrapped around me while I sank deep inside her.

Everly was carrying boxes out to the silver Subaru parked in the driveway of a house. One of Tom Grady's rentals, from the look of it. I'd done a renovation on the back deck the year before.

She leaned forward, placing the box she'd been carrying into the trunk. I swallowed hard and pulled my truck up to the curb. She didn't look my way until she heard my door slam shut, the sound bursting the quiet early November morning.

Everly brushed her hair out of her eyes, squinting against the sun. Her eyes widened with surprise as she took in the sight of me walking over to her. She was dressed in tight jeans and a soft gray thermal shirt that clung to her breasts and her taunt stomach. I admired the curves of her body, not bothering to hide the desire I knew was apparent in my eyes. I wore it all over my face; there was no point in trying to deny it, and I didn't want to.

The hairs on my arms stood up on end as she returned the coveted look, her eyes pausing on the buckle of my jeans before rising quickly to my face, a faint blush appearing on her cheeks. She shivered, either from the cold or from seeing me standing in front of her. Looking into my eyes didn't seem to help her uneasiness. She turned away, staring at my truck.

"New truck?" she asked. I glanced back at it, the heavy 4x4 quad cab I'd bought to haul my equipment around. It said *Dixon Construction* on the side.

"Yeah," I answered almost uneasily as I turned my head back to her. I didn't tell her that I still had the old forest green truck, that I'd held on to it all these years...and probably would hold on to it forever. Hell, the halo from Everly's angel costume still hung off the rearview mirror, so I would always be reminded of her when I looked back. As if I could forget.

I swallowed hard. That was the night I realized that my feelings for Everly were more than just lust, although that was definitely there...tenfold. I cleared my throat, trying to draw my thoughts away from the memory of her beneath me, waiting and ready.

"It's nice," she said. There was an awkward pause that came from a million words left unsaid. I stepped towards her and she stepped back; like a prelude to a dark dance.

"What are you doing here?" I asked, glancing up to the house.

"My sister rented this place. I'm cleaning it out."

"By yourself?" I asked, my brow furrowing.

She shrugged, avoiding my gaze. "It has to get done," she said simply.

"You shouldn't have to do this alone," I told her. "I can help."

"That's not necessary, Grayson," she said stiffly, turning around and walking back inside. She left the door open, and I followed warily after her, waiting to see if she'd protest my presence. When she didn't, I let out the breath I had unknowingly held at the sight of her walking away from me.

She stood in the middle of the half-packed living room, her back to me as her shoulders shook. She was cradling her face in her hands. The sight of her pain made me ache worse than anything I'd experienced over the last five years...and those years had been *hell*.

"Everly..." I breathed her name, closing the space that separated me from her. My arms wrapped around her from behind. I brought my hands up to cup hers, holding her tight. She fell apart there, safely tucked into my arms. I lowered us to the ground, amid the furniture and boxes.

I didn't know how long we stayed there like that, with me holding Everly while she released her grief and confusion. There was more behind her tears than the loss of her sister. That was there, and that was raw and sharp... but there was more beneath that. I could taste her lingering heartbreak just as easily as I could taste mine.

Finally, Everly shifted out from under my arms. She timidly used her palms to dry her cheeks, avoiding my penetrating gaze. We were still on the floor, my legs on either side of her and her legs folded beneath her.

She took a shaky breath. "Thanks," she said, her voice barely above a whisper. I leaned forward, gently brushing her hair back from her face. Although her eyes were red-rimmed from crying and her cheeks were blotchy, she was still the most incredible kind of beautiful. Not only did I ache with desire for her; it was the need of healing her broken heart that resurfaced in my mind. I wanted to bring the smile and the light back into her eyes, the smile that my dumbass seventeen-year-old-self had extinguished.

"I meant every word that I said to you yesterday," I told her. Every fiber in my body wanted and needed her to believe me.

"Why?" she asked, looking up at me with the most heart-wrenching expression on her face. I swallowed hard, her eyes following the movement.

"I was fucked up, Everly." I didn't want to get into this, not like this... not right now—not in the middle of her dead sister's living room. But she asked, and I couldn't lie to her. "My mom's death screwed me up worse than I already was. I didn't...handle it well. I didn't handle *anything* well. I saw the disappointment in your eyes every time I let you down, and I couldn't handle that."

"So it was my fault." Her lips were a thin line as she looked away.

I caught her chin in my hand, turning her face back to mine. "No," I said firmly. "It was my fault. I was stupid. Instead of letting you in, I shut you out. I told myself it was better for you, that you'd be happier if I wasn't disappointing you. I thought you deserved better than what I had to give... you were going places, Everly. I couldn't stand in your way."

"You wouldn't have," she argued, her eyes flashing.

"I would have," I countered, raising my brow. "Would you have left for the tour if I had...stayed?"

Everly's face paled and she didn't reply.

"I wasn't ready then, but I'm ready now," I added, my voice vulnerable as my eyes searched hers out, willing her to understand. I just prayed it wasn't too late.

"What makes you ready now?" Everly demanded, refusing to accept what I was telling her. I sighed, almost wanting to chuckle at her defiance. She was desperately fighting against me, against giving in to me. I couldn't blame her.

I paused, taking time to think about my answer while my eyes hungrily lapped up Everly's face. I cupped her face with my hand, needing to touch her. "I've denied myself happiness long enough, and you're it for me. You're my happiness."

She closed her eyes and leaned into my hand. Thick tears escaped from under her long lashes and ran down her cheek to fall into my palm.

"You broke me, Grayson," she said, admitting the truth I'd always known. Her eyes remained closed against the painful memory.

"I broke myself too," I assured her, the emotion making my voice break. "I don't expect you to forgive me. I still hoped..."

"There's nothing to forgive, Grayson." She sighed, cutting me off. Everly opened her eyes, watching me warily as she stood up. She folded her arms across her chest. "I'm over it."

I stood too, a reluctant smile teasing the corner of my lips. I knew when Everly was lying, and she was lying now. "Are you with him?"

"With who?" Everly frowned, her expression changing to one of confusion. "Kyle?" I nodded, my heart in my throat. I tried to prepare myself for the answer. "No, and we've never been together..." She hesitated and looked away from my face again. "It's only been you."

* * *

I remained with Everly for the rest of the day, helping her slowly pack away the living room and kitchen, watching her while she watched me out of the corner of her eye. The sexual strain between us was heavy; even the air pulsed with it. I was overly aware of every soft breath as she exhaled.

"I'll do the bedrooms later," Everly said, darting in front of me to prevent me from going down the hallway. "I should get home now. Thanks for your help."

She was dismissing me, or trying to. Her eyelids fluttered against her cheeks in response to the heated look I gave her. She was standing too close to me. Her fragrance invaded my senses. Everly smelled like she always had...like creamy lemon and jasmine. It was just as enchanting to me as it had always been. My stomach rolled with a desperate desire. The arousal was just as apparent in her pale green eyes. I swallowed hard, knowing I was seconds away from losing control.

Everly licked her lips quickly, drawing the bottom one in with her teeth. The action maddened me, and took away the last of my self-control. She exhaled as I brought my lips to hers. I kissed her, hoping to convey the depth of my feelings, the depth of my regret and apology. It was the surest way to express it all; the language of our bodies, hearts and souls.

She lost herself again, forgetting to put her guard up as she matched my desperate kiss with a searing one of her own. Her hands came up to my chest, gripping my shirt in her hands. I reacted by pushing her against the wall with my hips, the evidence of my arousal pressing into her lower stomach. Five years of denying myself of her touch, five years of basically starving for it. Nothing could fill the void that leaving her had left in me. No amount of one-night stands, no amount of whiskey could erase the taste of her from my lips.

Everly fit against me in a way that nobody ever had or ever would again. Her head fell back against the wall, and I dropped my lips to her neck, sucking and biting gently. With our bodies dancing in the familiar tango of passion and need, she spoke clearly, arching her hips toward me in welcome. I felt the years melt away between us; I tasted the underlying ache of abandonment and heartbreak. I wanted to mend it with my body, show her just how much I needed her.

She moaned, opening her eyes again for the first time since our lips met.

Everly shoved on me abruptly, pushing me away from her. Her breasts rose and fell with each frantic breath she took. I could see her nipples through the thin material of her shirt. She wasn't wearing a bra, and my hard dick twitched at the realization.

"We can't," she said breathlessly, tucking a strand of hair behind her ear. She avoided meeting my eyes. I knew why—she'd always been powerless against the spell of them.

Everly was harder to read, but not impossible. She'd learned how to mask her emotions better, and it was more of a challenge to tell what she was feeling simply by looking at her face...but I could still read her body with ease. She was tossing up her guard, frantically trying to keep me on the other side of her walls, but she wanted me. That meant there was hope. I was used to walls—I was the *king* of walls. I could smash through hers if it meant making her mine again. I was certain of it.

"Can I see you tomorrow?" I ignored her protest, knowing she didn't mean it. An impish smile teased my lips upward. She glanced behind her, toward the bedrooms down the hall and bit her lip. The action did nothing to calm my primal urges. My hardened cock strained painfully against my jeans. I rubbed up against her, my hand catching a strand of her hair. It felt like silk between my fingers.

"I don't know." She sighed. "I have a lot I need to do before..." She frowned.

"Are you leaving again?" I asked, the dread settling heavily in my stomach.

"I'm supposed to go on tour in two months. Our shows are all sold out and the fans...and the label...won't be pleased if we cancel it. It'll go against our contract." She sounded uncertain, though.

I nodded, understanding that. "What about the girl?"

Everly jumped like I'd electrocuted her, her eyes snapping back up to mine. "What about her?"

"What happens to her now that Julia..." I tried to word my question sensitively enough that I wouldn't set Everly off. "Will she be going with you?"

"I don't know," Everly said carefully, her eyes guarded. "My parents are here. Her school is here. Her friends are here. I don't want to bring her away from the comfort of home and tossed into...that lifestyle. Especially not after she lost..." Everly trailed off, unable to say her sister's name.

"Makes sense," I said, my eyes dropping to her lips again. I couldn't help myself. I drew in a shaky breath, beyond affected by her. It was vexing; I didn't react this way to people—to anything, really. Except for her. I'd always reacted that way to her.

Everly had been the only person who ever made me feel. Everything was brighter, illuminated by her beauty and the only real thing that I'd ever felt—my love for her, my desire for her. "So we have time then."

"For what?"

"To make up for five years of missing you," I told her, my voice husky with emotion.

Chapter Seven

Everly

MY BODY TREMBLED and my heart fluttered in my chest at his words, at the way he was looking at me, setting my skin on fire. I closed my eyes, counting to ten in my head and trying to calm my racing heart.

"Grayson," I whispered, my eyes still closed, my heart twisting and squeezing painfully.

"Do you want me, Everly?" he asked, pressing his hard length against my body. My stomach clenched with desire and anticipation. I swallowed hard, my silence the only answer I could give.

It wasn't a matter of wanting or not wanting Grayson. It was the fact that he'd shattered me completely, and my life was beyond changed by what we had. There was also the painful thought that he would never forgive *me* once he found out what I'd done. I knew how much he hated and resented his mother for abandoning him in heartbreak. I could only imagine what he would say about *me*.

The tears built behind my closed lids, and I desperately tried not to show them. I didn't need him pressing on the open wounds, trying to help but really just making it worse because the past could never be forgotten. I could never forget the hell I went through after he left, or undo my decision to leave for the tour anyway...leaving my daughter. *Our* daughter, the one he didn't even know he had.

"Tell me there's not a chance in hell you want to give this a try, and I'll walk away, Everly. I swear I will. If you're happy with your life...if you've moved on, I won't bother you. I just need to know before I give you up completely." Grayson looked frenzied, the desperation in his ice blue eyes piercing into me.

My heart tore further at the thought of Grayson walking away again. I let out a strangled cry that I quickly silenced by biting down on my tongue.

"This isn't just about us," I tried to argue, my voice shaking.

"What are you talking about?" Grayson demanded. "Of course it's about us. It's always been about us. About you and me."

"You've always seen me as this angel that deserves so much more than what you can give," I told him, shaking my head while the fresh tears finally escaped. I was so goddamn tired of *crying* all the time. "What if that isn't true, Grayson? What if I'm not the perfect person you thought I was?"

"I don't care." Grayson's voice was sincere, and his eyes were determined. He attempted to brush away my tears with his thumbs. "You couldn't be more perfect to me. Every flaw you may have is still perfect."

"No," I said earnestly, shaking my head again. I turned away from him, my chest heaving. I ran my hands through my hair, brushing it out of my eyes. *Tell him. Tell him now,* the voice in my head demanded. I turned back to face him again. "Grayson...I tried to find you."

He winced in response to my words, like he had suspected it to be true but hoped it wasn't. "I'm sorry. I'll spend forever proving it to you."

"You're not listening," I said, my expression grim. "This isn't me making you feel guilty for leaving, Grayson. You did what you had to do, and yeah...that sucked. And yeah, I don't know how I would come back from it...how we would if we were to try. But I'm trying to tell you something here."

"What are you trying to tell me?" Grayson asked warily. He was finally picking up on my keyed up mood. I didn't say anything. I turned around and headed down the hallway, towards the closed door with the *Cadence* nameplate on it. I opened the door, entering her bedroom. I hadn't started packing anything yet; I'd been focused on getting the main rooms packed away and trying to chase down that damn cat.

Cadence's bedroom at Julia's house had an abundance of stuffed animals and dolls. She had a pink bedspread with matching pink curtains. Her furniture was light, similar to mine at home. She had an easel in the corner, with an abandoned crayon masterpiece.

Grayson followed me into Cadence's bedroom cautiously, keeping his eyes on me. I stopped in front of the white dresser, picking up the framed photo that sat on top.

The photo was of Cadence and me. Julia had snapped it when they'd visited me for Thanksgiving. We had been lounging by the pool, and Cadence's hair was damp from the water. Her eyes sparkled with happiness as I'd held her in my arms. I wordlessly handed the photo to Grayson.

He took it, his eyes lingering on my face for a moment before he looked down at the photo. I heard the sharp intake of breath as he studied the photo. I knew what he was seeing. The ice blue eyes, the same shape and color as his own. Cadence had inherited his eyes, his hair, my father's olive complexion and my lips.

Grayson looked up at me, a conflicted expression on his face.

"Do you get it now?" I asked, my eyes hardening. I wanted to protect my heart from the fallout, but I knew I couldn't. His mouth opened and closed while he looked from me to the picture. One hand shot up, tugging at the roots of his thick hair, a habit Grayson always had when he was overcome with complicated emotions.

I could see the questions on his face.

"I couldn't find you, I tried to...but nobody knew where you were. I sent you messages on MSN and your cell phone. You never saw them?"

Grayson shook his head mutely, words still escaping him for several long minutes. He was wounded. "I've been back for two years. I live in the same goddamn town as...as they did. Why didn't you tell me?"

"Because I was never back, Grayson!" I shouted. "I couldn't come back here. I didn't think you were here, and even if you were, what could I say to you?"

"How about 'hey, you have a fucking kid'?" Grayson supplied, his eyes narrowing.

I folded my arms across my chest. His words physically hurt. "I tried to find you, Grayson. You wanted off the grid, you got off the grid," I told him, my own eyes narrowing at him in return. We stood across from each other, posed for a fight; old wounds resurfacing, new wounds being inflicted.

"Why did you..." Grayson's jaw clenched as he repressed the remaining words.

"Leave her? Because I had to, Grayson. I found out about...the pregnancy after I'd signed the contract. The guys and I were already in the studio recording, the tour was already booked. It was either bail out on the band, or go through with it."

"So the band was more important than our kid?" Grayson shot out hotly, his words slapping me across the face.

"You have no right," I said, my voice dangerously low. "I had to choose the best future for her. I had no other prospects. How was I supposed to afford her formula? Her clothes? You were gone, I couldn't find you and I had no intention of dumping more responsibility and commitment on your shoulders when you couldn't even handle a high school relationship. My sister...she refused to let me bail out on the band."

"So the entire town thinks that Cadence is Julia's?" He had a right to ask, I knew it. But his questions, as he attempted to dissect everything he'd missed, made me bristle.

I smiled sadly. "I really don't know what the entire town thinks, and frankly, I don't care. I just didn't want to chance someone trying to get a picture of Cadence for some sleazy tabloid. I couldn't have her getting hurt. Grayson, I never abandoned her. She was never off my mind. I just wanted to secure a bright future for her...since I didn't know..." I choked on my own words.

Grayson eyed me warily for a moment. Then he sighed, approaching me with the frame still clenched in his hand. He used his free hand to tip my chin up.

"I told you I wasn't the angel you thought I was," I told him defiantly.

He watched me, his eyes flickering with icy flames. The smirk that came to his lips at my jab took me by surprise. "Darling, you've never been an angel...except for that one night," he said suggestively.

I laughed without humor, rolling my eyes. The heavy weight that I'd been carrying on my shoulders for years lessened considerably after telling Grayson the truth, but the uncertainty for the future still kicked around.

The mood shifted as he looked down at the photo again. He dropped his hand from my face, touching the glass of the frame. His brow was furrowed and his lips were drawn down in a slight frown. He stared at the photo while he sank down to sit on Cadence's neatly made bed.

"How old is she?" he asked, his eyes still fixed to the photo.

"She's four. She was born July twenty-ninth." I could see Grayson doing the math in his head. "I got pregnant sometime in November."

He swallowed hard, closing his eyes and drawing in a deep breath. He opened them again, looking down at the photo with an unreadable expression on his face.

"Motherhood isn't a role you can just drop and pick up as you choose." Grayson's words were hard, but his tone was gentle, given the circumstances.

"It wasn't like that." I shook my head, trying to ignore the hurt that stabbed at my beaten heart. "Cadence knows that she came from me, she knows I am her mother, but she called Julia *Mommy* because that's what Julia was to her—more than I was." The words stung coming out. The truth really did hurt.

"What does this mean...for her?" he asked, looking back up at me.

"I'll do whatever I need to do to keep her safe. I'll be wherever I need to be for that. I'm in the process of getting out of the tour...of breaking the news to the label company, the guys and the fans," I answered. I'd already called and spoken with my lawyers. I'd already gotten the ball rolling on that because I knew that my agent would give me a terrible time about it. The prospect of bowing out now still terrified me, but less so than leaving Cadence.

I'd almost lost my daughter the night that my sister died. Had Cadence's car seat been behind the driver's seat, I would have lost her when Julia's car was t-boned at an intersection. I hadn't lost her, and I was so thankful for that. I didn't intend to let her out of my reach again.

"Where does that leave me?" The vulnerability in Grayson's voice nearly broke me again.

"Where do you want to be?" I asked, my heart pounding frantically in my chest as I awaited his answer.

Grayson looked slowly at the photo again. "If I haven't made that abundantly clear by now, I guess I still suck at expressing my emotions," he said dryly, his eyes catching mine. "I meant everything I said before."

"Even knowing this?"

Grayson stood up at my question, his eyes intense enough to burn through the weak shield I was trying to throw around myself. "Everly, we both fucked up...a lot. And it was my fuck ups that started it all," Grayson said darkly as he made an attempt to hand the photo back to me.

"It's yours...if you want it," I told him, my voice shaking.

"Can I meet her?" Grayson questioned, his eyes searching mine.

I inhaled sharply, forcing a smile to my shaking lips. "Yes...as soon as I decide how I'm going to tell her who you are."

* * *

I'd finally managed to catch the damn cat, with help from Grayson. Tom was right—it was a goddamn asshole. The cat hadn't taken to being shoved in the cat carrier very well, and Grayson's arms were covered in angry scratches. The cat had managed to knick him on the cheek, too. The expression on Grayson's face as he set the cat carrier carefully on the front seat of my parents' car made me want to laugh, but I bit it back.

"Thanks," I said, touching the cut on his cheek gingerly.

"Don't worry about it," Grayson told me, his gaze ignited me. I shivered in the thin coat I was wearing. The temperature had dropped, and our breath came out in little puffs in front of us. He looked deeply into my eyes, the storm moving across his. "I want to see you again."

He saw me hesitating, and his hands came up to cup my face. I watched as his gaze leisurely drifted across my face, lingering on my lips. "You kind of dropped a major bomb on me. Don't shut me out now," he pleaded.

I was hopeless against the spell of his eyes, full of yearning and need. He was right; I couldn't shut him out anymore. He knew the truth, and I owed him a chance...for Cadence's sake. Even if it broke my heart. But there was a change in him, a change that I wasn't blind to. I could sense it and I could see the sincerity behind each of his words.

Grayson had only ever promised to try before, and he had tried. He'd never promised me forever. He had already laid it all out on the line for me—more than once. I was more scared than I'd ever been before, but I was hopeless against him. He was the missing piece of my soul.

I just had no idea how I was going to explain it to Cadence — or the rest of my family.

My parents didn't know Grayson very well, but they knew that he had broken my heart and disappeared. They hadn't been stoked that he had showed up at our house after the funeral, but what could they say? It was my decision, my life. It didn't seem to matter what course of action I took; Cadence's life was going to change drastically regardless.

"I could meet you back here and help you finish packing up," Grayson suggested, his hands still hot on my skin.

I bit my lip. "Okay," I said softly. A smile broke out across his lips, lightening his eyes and transforming his face. Grayson had an incredible smile. Between his smile and his eyes, I was completely powerless.

"Tomorrow morning then," he whispered, brushing my hair out of my face and kissing me chastely. "Meet me here at ten. We'll finish the rest of it. And we'll talk; we'll try and figure out...this." The burning look he gave me made my blood pressure go up.

He waited in the cab of his truck as I drove away and I watched as it slowly faded from the rearview mirror. The uncertainty, fear and regret that had reflected in his eyes when he had pleaded with me to see him again made my heart ache.

I pulled up to my parents' familiar driveway, frowning when I noticed Kyle's rented convertible in place of my dad's truck. It looked completely ridiculous in the snowy driveway, but that was Kyle.

Grabbing the carrier, I walked into the house, finding Kyle and Cadence coloring on the living room hardwood floor. Cadence was lying on her stomach. She looked up at me with her wide blue eyes when I walked in the room.

Kyle had a good bond with Cadence and always had. He had visited her the day that she was born, being the first man aside from my father to hold her, followed closely by Marcus and Cam. When Julia brought Cadence to LA, Kyle would always visit as often as he could and spend hours playing with her and just hanging out. He had a soft spot for her. All the guys did, but Kyle seemed to take more of an interest. Marcus and Cam were a little unsettled by having a child in their midst.

"Uncle Kyle drew a turtle," she told me matter-of-factly. Kyle grinned, hopping up effortlessly to cross the room and pull me in for a hug as Cadence lifted the picture to show me.

"Is that so?" I asked, arching an eyebrow as Kyle released me. He grinned, proud of his work. "Look who I found!" I said, crouching down and setting the cat carrier on the floor in front of Cadence.

"Jinx!" Cadence squealed, a bright smile lighting up her entire face.

"Now Jinx might be a little scared, okay Cadence? This is a new place for him and he'll be uncertain for a bit. He might hide, but he'll come out when he's ready, okay?" I warned her. She nodded, watching as I opened the metal door of the cat carrier slowly.

I expected the cat to dart out of the metal cage like a bat out of hell. It had certainly put up the fight when I tried to catch it. Instead, it went straight for Cadence and started to purr the second she wrapped her arms around its body.

"Well, that's shocking," I said to Kyle, shaking my head with a grin. "He wasn't that friendly when I tried to catch him."

"Is that where you've been?" Kyle asked, tilting his head and frowning slightly. He still wore his light hair on the longer side. It brushed against his collar and drove our female fans wild. They'd been helpless against his charming dimpled smile and boy-next-door looks.

I gestured to Cadence with my eyes. He nodded, catching my unspoken request. I walked over to her, crouching down so I could see her face better. "Cadence, Uncle Kyle and I are just going to go in the kitchen for a minute. Could you draw me a picture of Jinx?" She nodded, burying her face in Jinx's soft fur. I smiled at her again before I stood up and followed Kyle into the kitchen.

"Where are my parents?" I asked.

"They went to the grocery store. I said I would hang out with Cadence until you got back. I wanted to talk to you anyway."

"About what?" I frowned, my gaze flitting to Kyle's face. The easy smile he'd worn upon seeing me had vanished. He studied me curiously, lines of concern crinkling his light eyes.

"Are you okay, Everly?" he asked. He kept his distance, his arms crossed as he leaned against the counter, but his eyes never wavered from my face. "Maddie says you haven't been returning her phone calls or messages..."

"I'm as okay as I could be, given the circumstances," I answered as honestly as I could while ignoring the part about Maddie. I hadn't answered her calls or texted her back because I knew she was going to be pissed. Kyle nodded, accepting my answer.

"What did he say?" Kyle didn't need to spell it out for me to understand who he was talking about. The hard set of his usual gentle eyes was indication enough.

"I'd rather not get into it right now," I warned him, crossing my own arms.

Kyle sighed, rubbing his temple with his fingers slowly. He could sense my reluctance to talk about it and wisely switched topics. "Brent is giving us another month until we need to leave for the tour, so instead of January, we'll be leaving in February. We've had to cancel two shows that were already sold out, and a bunch of appearances. The public isn't happy about it. Brent wants us in California in two and a half weeks for an interview...all of us. Hell, mainly you. He thinks the fans will understand things a little better if they hear from you. He's been trying to reach you too."

"I know." I frowned. I'd been ignoring everyone's calls, especially people from the recording label—especially Brent. "I'll do the interview. I need to meet with the label anyway. Kyle, I can't do the tour," I added, swallowing hard. I couldn't look at him; I was too afraid. "I've already spoken to my lawyer and my financial advisor. I'm going to cover the fines myself. I just can't do it."

"Everly..." Kyle's voice was just as torn as his expression when I finally looked at him.

"Kyle, I almost lost her." I couldn't prevent the tears from spilling freely down my cheeks. Kyle stepped up to me automatically, drawing me toward him. "January—hell, even February isn't enough time for me. You know that."

He exhaled, his shoulders deflating slightly. "I know that. I get it, Everly, I do. It just..."

"Sucks? Yeah, I know. The last thing I want to do is let you guys down," I said, leaning against him. My knees felt weak. It was such a relief to finally tell Kyle where I was with things. "You knew I was done after this tour anyway...you all knew."

"I know." Kyle sighed. He rested his chin on top of my head. "And you aren't letting us down."

"Are you mad?"

"No, I'm not mad, Everly." Kyle pulled away so his eyes could lock on mine. "I just don't know what we're going to do without you. I kept hoping you weren't *really* done. You've been saying it for years, but this time, it felt different. Now...it's definite. I knew it the moment you got the call and I don't blame you."

"The rest of the guys will." I took a shaky breath.

"They love you too, Ever. You know that. They get what this means for us all...we'll figure it out. Let me talk to the guys."

Chapter Eight

Grayson

TO SAY THAT MY ENTIRE world wasn't completely rattled straight off its axis was a complete understatement. It wasn't every day that the one that got away returned bearing the shocking news that your idiot teenage self managed to unknowingly become a father.

I sat in the cab of my truck after Everly drove away, staring at the picture that she'd given me. It was of the two of them... her and Cadence. Our daughter. I was having a really fucking hard time wrapping my head around this.

I had always been careful with Everly—with everyone I'd been with. I wasn't careless when it came to protection. Still, condoms ripped, and all it took was one tiny unnoticeable tear or hole. There was no denying it; I didn't need a damn paternity test to know that she had my eyes and my hair, Everly's lips and the olive complexion of Everly's father and late sister. She was beautiful like her mother. It was surreal to see my features in hers.

Setting the photo down on the bench seat, I let my head fall into my hands. I was too stunned to be mad at Everly, that she'd kept this from me for so long. I felt shell shocked. I'd missed out on so much, and I had only myself to blame. If I hadn't run, if I hadn't left town, if I'd just stayed and tried to sort through my fucked up mind and feelings, I would have been there that day she went to my house. She would have told me, and I would have...

I frowned, trying to think of what seventeen-year-old me would have done.

Back then, I didn't have the emotional maturity to handle an intimate relationship. How could I have handled fatherhood? *I couldn't have.* I was certain of it.

But could I now?

Most men have nine months to adjust to the idea of fatherhood. Then they get an additional two years of figuring out their shit while the kid is still unaware.

Four-years-old was old enough to question why your father hadn't been there for you. It was old enough to *see* things, to understand them and certainly old enough to feel rejected and unimportant.

I didn't want her to feel rejected or unimportant; I didn't want my presence to cause her any confusion, but I couldn't just sit idly by after receiving that news.

I tapped my fingers against the steering wheel, scowling at the empty street.

Katrina had said not to return to the bar, but I was restless. If I didn't go to Tap's, I would have shown up at Everly's parents' house...and that wouldn't have been good. Not only was I not in the right frame of mind for that, but Everly likely would have been pissed at me. Besides, we'd made plans for tomorrow. I didn't want to push her too hard or too fast. I didn't want to drive her away from me again.

I needed to process things, to distract myself so I didn't do something stupid.

I pulled up in front of Tap's, thankful that the bar wasn't crowded. Only Tom and another patron that I didn't recognize sat along the length of the bar.

I sank down into the stool, snapping at Katrina before she could say anything. "Just get me a drink, would you?"

Katrina sighed and begrudgingly grabbed a clean glass and the bottle of whiskey. She eyed me critically as she slid it across the black walnut bar, wiping the condensation trail after I'd lifted the glass to my lips. "Grayson, you're spending too much time here again," she remarked, arching an eyebrow. "I'm beginning to think you're sweet on me."

I snorted, glowering at her. She laughed easily, the sound piquing the attention of the other two bar patrons. Tom lowered his eyes almost immediately, but the other guy's stare lingered. I took a slow sip of my drink, assessing him.

He appeared to be in his mid-thirties. He was dressed in gray dress pants, a button up shirt and a deep blue dress jacket. He had dark, pretentiously styled hair. I instantly mistrusted him, and not just because he looked completely out of place. Guys in this small town dressed in casual work clothes and checkered shirts. I didn't recognize him, and I didn't like how he looked as if he recognized me.

"Easy, killer. I'm kidding. I know who owns your heart." Katrina's voice brought my attention back to her and away from the stranger. "What are you doing here, Grayson?"

My visits to the bar were never a social call; they were my attempts to quiet the regret. Feed into one addiction to numb the cravings for another and what not.

I swirled the liquid around in my glass, staring at it. I felt a million questions ricocheting around in my head. "Can you tell me something, Katrina?"

"Probably," she responded sarcastically, the smirk falling from her lips when I looked up at her. She saw the torment and conflict in my eyes. "Yes," she amended.

"What happened after I left?"

Katrina watched me earnestly, her brown eyes sympathetic. "Well, you know they signed on and started recording." I nodded once and she continued. "So...once they started that, they all sort of stopped coming to school, and I didn't see them around often. If you're asking what happened with her, I don't know any more than you do. For a celebrity, she's pretty damn private— same with her family."

"Did you see Julia ever?" I asked in a low voice. Katrina had to lean forward against the bar to hear me. I glanced toward the stranger; he was occupied with his drink.

"Not really," she said after a moment.

"Have you ever met...her kid?" I asked, trying to keep my voice low and my question causal.

"I saw her around town a few times," Katrina answered, giving me an odd look as she automatically refilled my empty glass. "But no, I've never met the kid." She shrugged, placing the whiskey back on the counter behind her. She crossed her arms and leaned against the counter, a shrewd look on her face.

I grunted, staring back into my drink. For the first time ever, I wanted to confide in someone. I needed to process what I had learned. I wanted that somebody to be Everly, but she wasn't here.

But talking to Katrina would be a mistake. Everly had her reasons for wanting to keep things secret, and I had to go along with it. What other goddamned choice did I have?

Movement from across the bar caught my attention; the man was now joined by the waitress from Day Breakfast, Lindsay. Lindsay glanced over at me, her critical eyes assessing me carefully before she sat down on the stool beside him. She inclined her head to whisper something to him, her eyes never leaving my face.

I didn't know what her game was, but it didn't matter. The appeal of sitting at the bar had long since evaporated. It was one thing hanging out with Katrina and even Tom Grady, but the stranger and Lindsay were a different story. I tossed back the remainder of my drink before I stomped out of the bar without another word to Katrina.

* * *

The next morning, I pulled up to the curb in front of the rental unit. Everly was already inside. By the time I arrived bearing two coffees, she'd already managed to pack up all of Cadence's room. The mattress was stripped bare; the stuffed animals, toys, and clothes were all tucked away in boxes that she had piled on top of the dresser. The easel was folded and resting against the wall.

Everly was dressed in tight black jeans and a plain white v-neck t-shirt. Her long hair was pulled up in a messy ponytail, and she wasn't wearing any makeup. Everly was the kind of girl who didn't need makeup to look sexy. Her pale green eyes and thick lashes, her creamy pale skin and her sinfully sexy body didn't need the help.

My lower abdomen clenched with desire at the sight of her, her hips slowly swaying as she approached me. My fingers twitched with the urge to touch her, to squeeze the sides of her hips and pull her toward me.

"You brought coffee? Thank you!" she said, clearing my mind of the lustful thoughts and smiling as she took the paper cup from my outstretched hand. Our fingers brushed, and she startled at the electricity that passed between our fingertips.

"Yeah. I didn't know how you took it, so..." I handed her the bag of sugar, milk and creamers. I hadn't realized until I was sitting in my truck, in the drive thru, that I had absolutely no idea how Everly even liked her coffee.

That detail made the regret wash back over me, reminding me that I had left her and ran when I could have stayed. I could have let her in and learned every little thing about her; the details that couldn't be discovered by physically exploring and knowing one another's bodies. Like how she liked her coffee or even her eggs.

I could have spent the last five years raising a beautiful little girl with her.

I swallowed hard, forcing a tight lipped smile. Everly frowned, noting my darkened expression.

"What are you thinking about?" she asked, her voice vulnerable and curious. I could tell she was torn between coming to me and keeping her distance. It was the constant battle that Everly waged on herself since the moment she locked eyes with me again. Instead, she set her coffee down on the counter and selected a couple of creamers and sugar packets, busying herself with that particular task.

"Cadence," I answered, my voice gruff and my brows furrowed. "I just can't wrap my head around it."

Everly drew in a deep breath and looked at me, steadying herself for what she perceived would surely be an attack. She was the only person who knew about the struggles I'd had with my mother, and she hadn't even known the half of it.

My parents divorced when I was in grade seven, and my mom never recovered from that heartbreak. She let her despair consume her until there was nothing left but a bleakness that terrified the ever living shit out of me.

It was why I had been so terrified to fall for Everly, to let her get close to me. Because I knew what heartbreak could do, and I didn't want to feel that—or cause it. Everly knew I resented my parents for their parts in screwing me up. I had resented my father for breaking up our family, and my mother for not being strong enough to move past it for me. I'd lost her that year—the year that I finally let myself fall for Everly. The year that I left her, thinking it'd be better for her if I did.

Of course, my misguided attempt at avoiding heartache had me—and her—experiencing it at full force.

I couldn't be mad at Everly because this situation was entirely different from that one. In this situation, I was the one that walked away first. I was the one that made it impossible to be reached. I shut down my email account, my cell phone, and disappeared completely.

Everly did what she had to do with what I'd left her with, which was nothing. I'd left her with nothing but heartache and a baby that I hadn't even known about. But Everly had done a damn good job with the crumbs I'd left her, as far as I could tell. She had found someone who could take care of our daughter while she worked her ass off to make sure Cadence had everything she could ever need without any help from my sorry ass at all.

I took in another deep lungful of air before I stepped toward her, saying nothing at first. She set the coffee down on the kitchen table, her hands shaking. She kept her chin lifted and her spine straight, preparing for me to lash out at her.

I kept closing the distance between us until I cornered her against the tiny wall that separated the kitchen from the living room. Her back was against the wall, her palms splayed out on either side of her hips, as if she was trying to ground herself.

"What would you have done, Grayson?" Everly's voice was gentle, but she had a heartbreakingly wounded expression in her eyes as she looked at me, waiting for the angry words to come. It broke me that I'd conditioned her to feel that way; like I'd either flee or react with anger.

I wasn't going to lash out, but I wasn't going to speak until I touched her. My hand reached out, slow and hesitant. I rested it on the side of her delicate neck, feeling her pulse beating frantically beneath my palm. I brought my other hand up to cup the side of her face, my thumbs gently stroking her soft skin.

I had always struggled with expressing my emotions, feelings and thoughts. I was the kind of guy that bottled it up until I exploded. Words didn't come easily to me—at least not in conversation. But touching Everly always unlocked something in me, that ability that I didn't seem to have when she wasn't around to pull me out.

Focusing on the feel of her hummingbird heartbeat beneath my palm, I closed my eyes and breathed in the scent of her. I opened my eyes slowly, looking into the pale green pools that were staring intently at me with wide-eyed uncertainty.

"I kept running it all over in my head, wondering what I would have done if I'd known that you were pregnant," I finally said, my voice heavy with emotion as I gazed into her eyes with remorse. "I couldn't have done it, Everly. Not then..." my voice broke with shame and I lowered my head.

I felt Everly's fingers gently stroke the stubble on my chin, and I realized with embarrassment that my eyes had started to water. I raised my head again, blinking away the moisture as our gazes locked.

"I wasn't ready either," Everly pointed out.

"What now?" I whispered.

"I don't know," she whispered back, letting her hand fall. She was just as vulnerable and lost as I was. "All I know is that I have to be ready."

"Tell me what you need me to do, Everly. I swear I'll do whatever it takes." The words were hard to get out. I was basically asking her to forgive me, to move past what I'd done to her— to us.

She swallowed and I felt the movement beneath my palm. "I don't have any answers, Grayson," she said, her voice shaking. She was avoiding my eyes again.

"Could you forgive me? For...shutting you out and leaving you?" I pressed, arching my hips against hers with a need that was more than just physical, although that was there. This need was an ache that went straight into my bones. The need to connect with her again as I once had.

Everly was the only person I'd ever let into my stony fortress; she was the only one who understood me and accepted me. She'd known my flaws, and she had loved me regardless. I knew I could love her regardless of her flaws, too. I already did.

"Could you forgive me for giving up on trying to find you? For allowing my sister to raise our daughter?" Everly's voice was pained and her eyes were full of sorrow. Everly didn't forgive herself.

I couldn't form the words to express that I had already forgiven her, that I was desperately aching for her, that I'd walk through flames for the chance to have her again. I didn't have the words for that. Instead, my lips collided with hers fervently. I pressed my pelvis to her, grinding my hard length against her, fueled by her tiny gasps and moans.

Her head fell back against the wall as my lips grazed her neck, feathering kisses beneath her jawline. She clung to my body, rolling her hips into me as I returned to her lips. The friction of both our jeans rubbing against my engorged cock felt sensual. The way she was tugging on my lip with her teeth made my eyes roll into the back of my head.

"I need to have you," I told her, half crazed with desire and longing.

Everly opened her eyes, seeming to come to. Her chest rose and fell frantically. Her eyes widened as she took in the kitchen, the pleasured blush fading from her cheeks.

"Not here," she said, shoving at my chest with her trembling hand. I stepped back from her, giving us both space to catch our breath. "I have to pack up Julia's bedroom."

I inwardly smacked myself. I'd completely forgotten that we were standing in the kitchen of her late sister's house, packing up the rest of her worldly possessions. "Jesus, Everly...I'm sorry."

"It's okay." A small smile graced her lips as she raised her eyes to meet mine again. "You always could make the world fall away with your touch."

"Guess that means I've still got it." I smirked.

Chapter Nine

Everly

EVERYTHING IN MY SISTER'S house was packed away into boxes, lined neatly against walls. The clothes, the pictures, the knick knacks. The dishes, cookware and cutlery. Several boxes were piled by the door; they were Cadence's things or the items that I wanted, and the ones that I thought my parents and Cadence would want. Photos, her little keepsakes. Her favorite perfume and her pearl drop earrings I'd bought her for Mother's Day, from Cadence.

One of the items that hit me hard to see was the tiny box in Julia's closet that had special Christmas tree ornaments in it. I gently touched the *baby's first Christmas* ornament with a watery smile. It was nearly December; we would soon be celebrating our first Christmas without Julia. I added that box to the keep pile, my heart heavy.

My last task of the day was to clean out the entire refrigerator. I threw out what couldn't be donated to the town Food Bank and scrubbed the inside of her refrigerator furiously, using the physical labor to keep myself from thinking about the fact that I was packing away my dead sister's home.

Grayson helped...a lot. He did heavy lifting. He scrubbed the oven while I scrubbed the fridge. He was quiet, letting me grieve in the silent way that I needed. He didn't ask me why I didn't just hire someone to do it. I could have afforded it, but this was something that I felt *I* needed to do. Something that would give *me* closure.

I hadn't planned on having Grayson's help, but I was thankful for it. It likely would have taken me triple the time alone. I knew that Aubrey and Alicia would have helped had they known what I was up to, but I hadn't told anybody. Not even my parents. I hadn't wanted to upset them or make them feel obligated to help.

Now the only thing to do was wait for the local thrift store to pick up the remaining boxes and furniture. They wouldn't be coming until the next day, though, so at seven at night we finally called it a day.

"You haven't eaten," Grayson pointed out, as we carried the final boxes to the car. Some of Cadence's stuffed animals were poking out of the box Grayson was carrying. He gently set the box down in the back seat, beside Cadence's booster seat. I watched as his fingers briefly touched the stuffed animal's head before he closed the door and turned to face me.

It was true; I hadn't eaten. I'd been so preoccupied with getting everything done that I hadn't even thought about food. My stomach was growling now, awakened by Grayson's casual observation.

"Neither have you," I retorted, arching a brow.

He grinned. "I know. Let's go grab food," he suggested.

I hesitated. "I don't think that's a good idea."

"Why not?" Grayson was still smiling at me, as if he could sense I had very little fight left.

"I'll be recognized, I—" I started to explain, but Grayson's hands were suddenly cupping my face. The look in his eyes instantly silenced me before his lips crashed against mine.

He shifted me so that it was my back against the car instead of his. He pressed his pelvis to mine, pinning me against the car. It sent me back to high school, back to the night of Zoe March's Halloween party. It forced me to replay when he kissed me like that and I went with him, knowing it would lead me to heartache, but also knowing that I wanted it no matter the outcome.

Grayson kissed me until I melted completely into him, until he could have had me then and there on the roof of my parents' car in the freezing November night with the snow softly falling all around us.

As if he'd felt my surrender, Grayson stopped kissing me and looked into my eyes. He smiled wantonly. "So we'll order pizza and we'll go back to my place for a bit." He arched his eyebrow suggestively. My stomach rolled with desire and my heart fluttered frantically in my chest. "I'll drive," he added.

"Don't you always?" I remarked dryly.

He grinned, gesturing to his truck. "Your chariot awaits," he said with flourish.

* * *

Grayson eased his truck into a long driveway that led up to a beautifully designed modern house. It was two stories and all sharp, clean angles and shiny windows. Light poured out from inside, illuminating the beautiful front yard.

"Oh my God, Grayson. This is beautiful!" I told him, opening the truck door and jumping down. My feet struggled to find tread on the icy driveway.

I nearly slipped, but just as I was falling, Grayson caught me, his hand shooting out to grip my arm and steady me. "Guess I should put some salt down."

"I guess so," I responded, disoriented.

Grayson made sure that I was steady on my feet before releasing my arm, a smirk on his delectable lips. "Let's go inside," he said as he turned to lead me up the slippery walkway. He hesitated for a moment before his hand found mine. My heart thudded loudly in my chest. My hand felt so good in his, and from the intense way Grayson was covertly looking at me, I knew where this night would go. I swallowed, suddenly nervous.

I hadn't been celibate for the last five years, but my experiences were far and few between...and definitely nothing to write home about. I hadn't had good sex *since* Grayson. I didn't know if that was because of my intense feelings for him, or if he was just an incredible lover, or if the two different guys I'd met in LA were just more concerned with themselves getting off than with me getting any enjoyment.

Grayson though...Grayson was a very attentive lover and always had been. It was his mission to make me enjoy myself as much as possible before he allowed himself any kind of release. He'd always been focused on *me*.

"I'll be right back," Grayson promised, flicking on the lights. "I'm just going to put some salt down over that ice patch. Make yourself at home."

My heart stuttered in my chest at his words. I couldn't look at him. I was afraid to see his expression, afraid that he'd regret his choice of words when he saw how profoundly they had affected me. Instead, I focused on examining the beautiful rooms of the main floor.

Grayson's living room was located to the right of the main foyer. The south and north facing walls were completely made up of windows. I couldn't see outside since the light from inside caused a mirror image reflection. It made me a little uncomfortable to know that I couldn't see out but people could see in, so I crossed my arms and ducked into the kitchen.

His kitchen was modern, sleek and masculine with black walnut cabinetry and dark marble countertops. All of his appliances were stainless steel, and the backsplash was a light and dark gray tilted pattern. Everything gleamed; there wasn't a speck of anything out of place.

Grayson cleared his throat, surprising me; I hadn't heard him come back in. He was standing near the island, his eyes assessing me with pleasure. "You look good in my kitchen."

"Well, don't count on me cooking. I never learned how," I retorted, turning my back on him to inspect his refrigerator like the nosy house guest that I was. It was stocked full of yogurt, produce and beer. I closed it wordlessly.

"Excuse me? You don't know how to cook?" Grayson said with astonishment. "Even *I* know how to cook, Everly, and I'm fucking hopeless."

"You're not hopeless." I narrowed my eyes at him. "Besides, I never had to. My mom cooked for me until I left on tour, and...well. Who needs to cook when you've got an album that went platinum and a couple of Grammys?" I added, shrugging with discomfort. I was ashamed of the fact that I didn't know how to cook, and I hadn't really thought about it until this moment.

Grayson walked over to me, stopping just before me. His fingers came up to brush against my jaw. "Hey now," Grayson said soothingly. "I wouldn't have learned either if it wasn't a necessity. But that won't stop me from trying to teach you how to cook. *Everyone* should know how to at least make spaghetti."

"You can make spaghetti?" I asked, peering up at him skeptically.

Grayson grinned, stepping away from me so that he could inspect his refrigerator. "Do you care if our spaghetti is missing a crucial ingredient or two?"

"What?"

"Noodles? Meatballs? And...erm," Grayson opened and closed a few cupboards, "spaghetti sauce?"

"So...we're going to drink boiled water?" I smirked. So much for his plan of teaching me how to cook.

Grayson pulled his phone out of his back pocket, flipping through the contacts quickly. He raised the phone to his ear and waited for someone to pick up. "Hi there, I'd like to order a pizza. Large, deluxe. Two pops. One Dr. Pepper, one Pepsi. Yeah, toss in a couple of dipping sauces. Creamy garlic works?" I nodded in response to his question. "Yeah that's fine. Okay, thank you."

He flipped his phone shut and set it back on the counter, his eyes never leaving my face. He licked his lips. "Forty minutes or it's free," he remarked, arching an eyebrow while he leaned back against the counter. The way he was looking at me made my breath hitch and desire roll in my lower belly.

"We should talk first," I said, folding my arms across my chest and looking away from him. He approached me slowly, as if he was stalking me.

"What did you want to talk about?" Grayson asked, nuzzling his lips against my neck. My thoughts melted away from my mind, and suddenly I had a very difficult time recalling what I wanted to talk about.

"Cadence," I finally said, nearly gasping as he gently sucked and nipped at my neck. He paused, pulling his face away from mine so he could look into my eyes.

"Oh, I intend to talk about her, just as soon as I'm done making your legs quake," Grayson murmured, his hand traveling up my ribcage and lifting my shirt. He squeezed my breast, rolling my nipple with his thumb and index finger through my lace bra. "I've waited too long for this moment, Everly. If I don't have you...I'll explode."

My eyes fluttered closed and my head fell back. I wasn't sure if my response was to how incredible his fingers felt on my nipples, or his desperate words. I moved my hips against his, feeling the hard length of him through both our jeans.

"Grayson...the windows," I said breathlessly. Grayson sighed, regretfully pulling himself away from me. He disappeared for a moment, and when he returned all of the windows were slowly disappearing behind a motorized shutter system.

"There, now nobody can see us." Grayson sauntered towards me again, a hungry look in his eyes. Driven with five years worth of need, I closed the distance between us and jumped into his arms, hugging his hips with my legs. He caught me like he'd known all along I was going to jump. His hands gripped my ass and he gently squeezed as he pressed his hard length against me.

We looked at each other while my hands weaved through his thick hair. The smoky desire behind Grayson's heavy-lidded eyes made my lower abdomen clench with anticipation. I tugged gently, pulling his face up so I could kiss him.

I channeled everything into that kiss; I truly let go, let myself submit to him and my feelings for him. Thinking could happen later; right now I wanted to curl up in the bliss and stay there for a little while.

Grayson carried me to the counter, never breaking the kiss. He set me down on top of it and stood between my legs, his hands running all over my thighs while he kissed me with his own burning need.

He pulled my shirt off over my head, pausing to admire my black lace bra. His hands brushed across the tops of my breasts, and I shuddered with the pleasure of having his hands on me once again.

"God, Everly, you're stunning," Grayson told me, his eyes drinking me in with awe. I slid off the counter, pressing my body to his. The action made the desire even more evident in Grayson's eyes. His lips came to mine again as his hand gently unbuttoned my jeans. I worked on his shirt, pulling it up over his head and tossing it aside.

My breasts rose and fell rapidly with the hurried pounding of my heart. I could feel Grayson's heart beneath the palm of my hand, and it was beating just as chaotically as mine, matching the tempo beat per beat. His breath hitched as my hand traveled down the cut muscles of his torso and unbuttoned his jeans. I pushed down his jeans and boxers just enough for him to spring free.

I tugged on his bottom lip gently with my teeth while my hand pumped him once. Grayson moaned, almost shuddering. I squeezed him again, enjoying the look of tortured bliss on his face.

In a sudden movement that astonished him, I dropped down to my knees and took him in my mouth. In the short time we'd been together in high school, I had never given him a blow job before. I was shy and inexperienced, and he hadn't really given me the opportunity to focus my attention on him like that. He'd been busy focusing *his* attention on me.

"Everly...what?" Grayson couldn't even form words as I sucked on the tip and pumped him at the same time. His eyes rolled into the back of his head and he bit his lip, making the most delectable sounds I'd ever heard.

"You. Need. To. Stop." Grayson's voice was strained, and he picked me up, his hands instantly gripping my ass and pulling me against him.

He struggled with my jeans, growing frustrated. "Jesus, I fucking knew they were painted on," he muttered, grinning mischievously. I laughed, backing away so I could shimmy out of them. He watched me as if I was performing the most exotic dance that he'd ever witnessed. I stood before him in my matching bra and panties, in the middle of his brightly lit kitchen.

I was no longer insecure about my body. Pregnancy had gifted me with curves that I still hadn't lost, but my stomach was tight from regular yoga sessions and semi-regular private training sessions. The pressures of Hollywood had shaped me to take very good care of my body, and I couldn't be more thankful for that as I watched Grayson's eyes drink me in.

I seductively reached my arm behind my back to unclasp my bra, my very core throbbing from the way he was looking at me. I dropped my shoulders and it fell to the floor. Grayson's eyes widened with anticipation and appreciation while I slowly shimmied out of my lacy underwear.

Grayson's jeans and boxers dropped to the ground in one fluid motion, and he stepped toward me. Our lips crashed against one another, and he effortlessly lifted me up as if I weighed less than a sack of potatoes. He squeezed my ass, his hard length rubbing delectably at my entrance.

Even though he hadn't really done anything to me yet, I was ready for him. I was too impatient to wait. While he held me against him, I wrapped my legs tighter to his hips and lifted myself up, guiding him with my hand.

He steadied me, his breathing heavy and his eyes tortured. "I have condoms upstairs," he said, trying to slow the roll.

"I'm on the pill, and I'm clean. I was last tested three months ago," I said, the words tumbling from my mouth as my lips brushed against his neck. I didn't want him to stop what he was doing, it felt right. I wanted to feel him without anything between us at all.

Grayson inhaled sharply and I froze, never having considered Grayson's past. I was positive that he hadn't practiced abstinence while we were apart.

"I'm clean too," he assured me, still sounding hesitant. I moved against him, causing his length to rub against my center. He moaned, his eyes fluttering before he focused again on me. "Are you sure?"

"I'm sure," I whispered as Grayson sunk into me slowly. He closed his eyes, exhaling as I squeezed my inside muscles against his large length. I almost came then, with him simply inside of me. I'd been craving him for years, and my body remembered the pleasure he always delivered as if no time had passed at all.

"God, Everly," he moaned, still gripping my ass and lifting me so that I could meet him thrust for thrust. He filled me completely and hit every spot I needed him to hit. Grayson inexplicably knew my body; he knew how to make it respond to him in ways I never thought I'd get to experience again.

This though…this was different. I couldn't find the words to explain *how* or *why*, but it was. He wasn't holding back *anything* now. He'd opened himself completely up to me, making the whole experience more raw and potent. I could *feel* his love with each stroke of his cock within me; I could feel it in every fiber of my body.

I felt myself coming undone around him, my legs quaking just like he'd intended, and I had to bite back a scream. Grayson moaned as he spilled his release into me, dropping his forehead against my shoulder.

"Fucking hell, Everly," Grayson muttered, still buried within me. He drew his head back, meeting my gaze with a euphoric expression on his face. His ice blue eyes were swirling with bliss and pleasure, with awe and love.

Before either of us could speak, the doorbell rang.

"That'd be the pizza." Grayson grinned mischievously.

* * *

Grayson turned on the gas fireplace in the center of the living room and placed the box of pizza and some plates on his coffee table. He gestured for me to sit, and I walked over from the kitchen.

I hadn't bothered to get completely dressed yet; I'd tossed my underwear and my t-shirt back on. Grayson was still just rocking his jeans, and I figured from the way he was looking at me that he wasn't done with me yet.

And I didn't want him to be.

I sat down on the worn couch—the same couch that had been in his loft in high school. I folded my legs underneath me, facing Grayson. He handed me a plate with two pieces of pizza on it, and I raised one to my mouth to bite it.

We couldn't help but watch each other out of the corners of our eyes, like the love struck teenagers we should have been.

That thought made my smile falter.

"What's wrong?" Grayson asked, catching it.

I shrugged, finishing chewing before I answered. "I was thinking about high school."

Grayson's eyes darkened slightly. He sighed, setting his plate down on top of the closed pizza box. He ran a hand through his thick hair and looked at me with regret. "I'm sorry about that—"

"I know, Grayson," I cut him off. I didn't want to hear him apologize again. "I guess what I'm trying to understand...is what has changed? Why now?" I tried without success to disguise the vulnerability in my voice. I swallowed hard, my throat suddenly dry. I realized that I'd asked that question countless times before, but I still felt like I didn't understand it, although I *knew* things were different with him.

Grayson took a few minutes to answer. He stared at the gas fireplace, watching the fake flame lick against the fake logs. "What's changed is that now I know what it's like to lose you, to *not* have you. And as scared as I am over how intensely I feel about you, I'm more scared of watching you walk away again. I'm a better person because of you, Everly. I was too dumb back then to realize it, but I get it now." When Grayson looked at me, his eyes were yearning for me to believe him.

I nodded, looking away while I digested his answer. My heart fluttered in my chest.

"I'm warning you now," Grayson added, his intense gaze locking with mine again. My breath hitched. "I haven't changed that much. I still have a temper, I still suck at dealing with complicated emotions and situations. But now I'm not afraid to fall. I'm not afraid to let myself love you the way you deserve."

"Why?"

"Because you're it for me, Everly," Grayson answered, his eyes raw and sincere.

Chapter Ten

Greyson

I WATCHED AS EVERLY inhaled sharply. She paused, as if consuming my words. The emotion in her eyes twisted my heart in the worst possible way. I could *see* the heartbreak, the longing, and the hope and confusion just as clearly as I would had she told me what she was feeling. I couldn't fault her for having doubts.

Running a hand through my hair, tugging on the follicles, I wished that I could rewind time and undo the number I had done on her. I honestly hadn't realized just how badly I'd broken her. I hadn't thought that I was capable of breaking her as much as I did, because I hadn't let myself believe that she was that in love with me. I had watched her the same way everyone else had over the past five years—I had seen her go from small town shy girl to shining star; confidence set in her shoulders and the easy smile on her lips. I fooled myself into believing that she *was* better off.

It wasn't until I was standing before her, seeing her in her rawest moments, that I realized exactly how badly and deeply I'd hurt Everly. It was enough to almost make me hate myself again, like I did back then. But I knew that had I not left, I would have broken her even more.

I wasn't worthy then, but I could be worthy now. That thought gave me the strength I needed to push past my own guilt. I cleared my throat, the heavy silence becoming too much for me.

Everly set her plate down beside mine on the coffee table, her eyes dropping down to her hands. Her chest rose and fell with each breath she took. She looked up, a thousand questions reflecting in the depths of those pale green eyes.

But I had a few questions for her as well; the elephant in the room, so to speak. "So, Cadence," I said, arching a brow. "I need to meet her, Everly."

"I know," she whispered, her eyes pained. I took her hand in mine, running the callused pads of my fingers across her smooth skin. Goose bumps raised on her arms, another indicator that Everly was inexplicably affected by my actions, regardless of the subject matter. I cleared my throat again, needing to keep my mind on track. It was hard to do with her sitting so close to me in so few clothes. I raised my eyes to hers again, my pulse jumping at the look in her eyes.

I had been running these thoughts over and over again in my mind since I found out about Cadence. I wasn't one hundred percent sure what I would have done if Everly *had* found me when she was pregnant. I was certain I would have screwed it up, and I knew that I might still screw things up now, but I couldn't ignore the fact that I had a child; I didn't want to. I hadn't even met the child, and I knew I loved her and would do anything to protect her. How could I not love my own flesh and blood? *Everly's* flesh and blood?

"We can figure out how we're going to tell her everything together, but I don't think it'd damage her if you introduced me to her. I was thinking..." I suddenly felt completely stupid. I turned my head, staring at the fake flames in the electric fireplace.

"What?" Everly's shy voice had my eyes returning to her face. She looked just as vulnerable and unsure as I felt.

"Well...I was going to decorate for Christmas," I admitted. The thought had crossed my mind once. It was nearly the middle of November, and Christmas was fast approaching.

Normally, I didn't bother with decorating. I'd never bought a tree, or hung lights around the house. The most festive I'd ever really been involved showing up to my dad's house that he shared with Vanessa for Christmas dinner. I only showed so I could give my half-sisters their gifts.

But this year...this year was different. I was no longer unaware of the fact that I'd fathered a child. Since Everly had told me the truth, I couldn't help but think about how painful the holidays were going to be for Cadence and the rest of Everly's family. I wanted to do something nice for her, something fun. I wanted to brighten her day. I wanted to know her. Was she shy, like her mother? Or was she a brooder, like me?

"Decorate?" Everly's expression was one of confusion. I raised my hand to stroke along her delicate jaw, trying my hardest to pinch back a smile.

"Yeah, like, Christmas lights and putting up a tree and all that shit." I couldn't prevent my face from splitting into a big, dorky grin. I knew how ridiculous I looked, how ridiculous I sounded. "I know, it's not usually my forte, but we need something to do together and we can't really go out, can we?" I challenged. She vehemently shook her head, as if that idea terrified her. Then she smiled.

"Alright, we'll come over. How's Saturday?"

My answer was simply my lips crashing against hers. Saturday was perfect.

* * *

I started Saturday morning by heading directly to Walmart to buy decorations, since I had none. I walked aimlessly through the aisles, pausing every so often to pick up cheerful boxes of outdoor lights and displays.

I must have been staring at a box of blue dangling icicle outdoor lights for thirty minutes, wondering what the hell I'd gotten myself into before someone gently tapped me on the shoulder. I turned around, scowling at the intrusion. My scowl faded a little as Aubrey paused hesitantly.

"Are you okay? You've been staring at that box for a while now." She tried to hide her bemused smile.

"Yeah, I'm fine," I said, tossing the box into the empty cart. I threw in another one just to make sure I'd have enough.

"Shopping for Christmas decorations?" Aubrey questioned, smiling politely. Her sea green eyes seemed to sparkle and dance. I could tell from the way she was looking at me that she knew that Everly and I had reconciled. I wondered how much Everly had told her. The kitchen scene was definitely replaying in my mind on a loop, and I didn't mind it in the slightest, although it made concentrating a little difficult.

"Yeah, Everly and...Cadence are coming over tonight to help me decorate," I answered, giving her a little information to see how she'd react. Aubrey's face split into a wide, energetic grin. The animosity I'd seen in her eyes the day of the funeral had disappeared.

"That's awesome!" she said. There was an awkward pause, where the both of us were at a loss for how to proceed with the conversation. She knew that I knew, and I knew that she knew. We settled for moving on, pushing our carts down the aisle. "What's next on your list?"

"No idea," I responded, my scowl returning. I'd been entertaining the idea of Googling "Christmas decoration must-haves" in the moments before Aubrey had tapped me on my shoulder. Not that I'd admit that to her.

"Well, do you have a wreath for your door?" she inquired. I shook my head. "Ornaments? *A tree?*" I continued to shake my head, slightly entertained by the shocked expression on Aubrey's face. "Seriously? You have *no* Christmas decorations?"

"Didn't see the point." I shrugged, feeling a little awkward. "It was only me."

Aubrey considered my answer, working her bottom lip while she thought. "Alright, I'll help you. But only because you desperately need it—and because I can tell you're nervous about tonight."

"I'm not nervous," I argued, frowning after her while she rounded the corner with purpose. I took off after her, pushing my cart warily.

Aubrey was on a mission, grabbing things off the shelves without a moment's consideration. She tossed some outdoor garland and another two boxes of regular outdoor lights and a large wreath into my cart. She paused in the ornament section, her eyes assessing the few different multicolored bulb packages.

"What's your theme?" she asked, not turning around to look at me.

"Excuse me?"

"Your decorating style...in your house...is it traditional? Contemporary? Modern?" Aubrey finally turned to look at me, noticing my look of confusion. She rolled her eyes with exasperation. "You know, your paint theme."

"Oh, I don't know."

She sighed deeply, selecting a couple of assorted ornament boxes. "We'll grab silver ornaments and gold ribbon," she declared, setting the ornaments in my cart and grabbing a large roll of gold glittery ribbon.

"What's the ribbon for?"

"Seriously? It's to trim the tree," Aubrey answered. She sighed when she realized that I still hadn't the slightest idea what she was talking about. I had celebrated Christmas growing up, but I'd never paid attention to those things. "You wrap it around your tree. Google it. In the meantime, just listen to me."

I nodded obediently and followed her down another aisle. She stopped in front of the pre-lit trees. "Now, you're going to want something that goes up easy and comes down easier," she instructed, glancing up at the display. "Which tree do you want?"

"A cheap one," I retorted, crossing my arms. This whole thing would be a lot easier if I could have just brought Everly and Cadence with me and told them to have at it. But Everly couldn't just show up at a store to shop for Christmas decorations—at least not without creating a bit of a scene. Aubrey picked up on my growing aggravation. She selected an eight foot tall pre-lit tree, pulling the box out and sliding it underneath my cart. "Now, grab a tree topper and you're probably good to go," she said. "Try not to freak out too much about it...Cadence is really easy to please. Especially if you have the *Shrek* movies."

"Shrek?" I shook my head, completely lost. "What the hell is a Shrek?" Aubrey smiled patiently. "Electronics department. In the family movie section. I would help you find that, but I've really got to get going."

"I'm sure I can take it from here," I remarked. She shrugged, her hands gripping her half-filled cart as she started to push it. "And Aubrey?" she turned, looking back at me. "Thank you...for helping with this," I told her, gesturing to my now full cart.

"No problem. Just remember, if you hurt my friend again, I'll castrate you. Have an awesome day!" Aubrey winked, disappearing around the corner. I chuckled, shaking my head after her.

Out of all of Everly's friends, Aubrey was the only one I'd actually liked.

I finished up my shopping, taking a little longer than necessary to find the aforementioned *Shrek* movie that Cadence supposedly loved after getting sidetracked by the title *family movie section*. Family. The word disoriented me and made my heart pound frantically in my chest.

I also spent a lot of time wandering the toy aisle, wondering if I should get Cadence something. The realization that I didn't know what kind of things she liked to do kind of burned in an unpleasant way, so I quickly headed toward checkout.

The cashier started ringing in my items right as I spotted the stranger I'd seen sitting in Tap's the other night. He was a couple carts behind me, in the same line. His cart was filled with random stuff, and he was reading a magazine. My eyes easily picked out Everly's face from the cover of the magazine, along with the headline of *Heartbreak at the Airport: Everly gets dumped by longtime fiancé weeks before their wedding day and returns home to heal.* The smirk on his lips didn't go unnoticed by me.

My blood boiled with anger. I knew it wasn't true, the fiancé crap and the wedding. Gossip magazines seemed to draw "breaking news" and "celebrity inside stories" from the local dumpster. Still, it didn't make me any happier to read the false words.

The cashier repeated the total to me, drawing my attention from the stranger and the magazine to her. Scowling, I pulled out my credit card and ran it through, tossing my bagged items back into the cart. I pushed it out to my waiting truck, loading the back bench with my new purchases.

The snow started to fall as I pulled out of the parking lot. I drove to the grocery store, grabbing much needed ingredients for the dinner I'd promised Everly and Cadence. I settled on spaghetti, since I'd bragged about it the night before. I knew it was the one meal that I could deliver with relative skill and ease.

I was in the produce aisle when I realized that the same stranger from Tap's and Walmart was *also* in the store. I finished my shopping, watching him out of the corner of my eye. He remained several carts behind me the whole time. Whenever he thought I wasn't looking, he would watch me with beady eyes.

I went up to the cashier, scowling when the dark haired stranger also joined the checkout line three people behind me. I paid for my groceries and left quickly, before my temper could cause a scene.

In high school, I wouldn't have hesitated. I would have gone right up to the guy and demanded to know his deal. I was a fighter back then, and I still was, but I'd learned to be more careful. There was a time and place for confrontations; the middle of the grocery store was definitely not the right place. Besides, I couldn't be positive that he was following me. It was a bit odd to encounter him at the Walmart in the next town over, but then again, it *was* the nearest Walmart.

I shook off my concerns, assuring myself that the next time I caught him doing anything suspicious, I would approach him. I had a lot to do before Everly and Cadence showed up at four, and it was nearly eleven. I didn't have time to play Nancy Drew.

When I got home, I put everything away—all except for the Christmas lights. I walked back outside, ready to start hanging them around the house. It didn't take long for me to seriously regret choosing the dangling blue icicle lights—they were a goddamn bitch to put up. I suddenly understood why so many people just left them up all year around.

Snow fell heavily for the better part of the morning and afternoon, and by the time I'd finally hung the last strand of dangling icicles, we'd gotten about two inches, with more on the way.

I climbed down the ladder, running the extension cord to an outlet. I plugged it in, stepping back to admire my handy work. The sound of tires crunching on the fresh snowy gravel alerted me to Everly's arrival. I turned around, watching as the car cautiously approached.

My heart started thrumming nervously in my chest as the car came to a stop beside my truck. I started walking towards them. Everly stepped out of the car, and I couldn't help but pause to drink her in. Her caramel hair was tucked under a gray Ushanka, her pale cheeks rosy from the biting November wind. She smiled shyly as she walked around the car, pausing with her gloved hand on the handle of the backseat door.

"Hey." I closed the distance between us, but fought my reaction to pull her into my arms. I didn't know if she'd want me to touch her like that in front of Cadence.

"Hey," she repeated, her smile spreading wider still. She opened the door, leaning forward to unbuckle Cadence from her seat. Cadence stepped out, holding on to Everly's hand for balance. She was wearing a matching Ushanka. Her blue eyes peered up at me with cautious curiosity. Seeing her in the flesh pierced my heart with emotion that I couldn't even properly name or describe. I swallowed, my throat suddenly feeling dry as all of my fears came rolling in front and center. "This is Grayson." Everly's voice was gentle and encouraging as she spoke to Cadence.

"Hi," Cadence mumbled, still staring right at me with eyes that mirrored mine. It was almost unnerving.

"Hey, I'm glad you were able to come tonight. I've never done this before," I told her, trying to keep my voice from shaking with the raw, heavy emotion I felt from seeing my four year old daughter for the first time ever. It was a difficult feat, and Everly could detect that. She reached out and gently took my hand, providing silent comfort and encouragement.

"Done what?" Cadence asked, peering around us. Her eyes focused on Everly's hand in mine before those blue eyes swept back up to assess me warily.

"Decorate for Christmas," I explained, a small smile teasing my lips upward.

"Oh. Are you Jewish? I have a friend who's Jewish. She doesn't decorate for Christmas either. She has a candle."

I chuckled lightly. Cadence was very articulate, and she seemed bright and worldly. Just like her mother. "No, I'm not Jewish. Usually I just go over to visit with family at Christmas. I've never decorated my place before."

"Why are you now?" Cadence questioned, her eyes piercing mine.

"I figured it was time," I answered, floundering.

Everly released Cadence's hand, bending over to grab a backpack from the floor of the car. "Let's go inside," she suggested, breaking the awkward silence we'd fallen into. I forced another smile, nodding curtly as I turned around to lead the way up the walkway to my front door. I'd already hung the wreath on the door and the garland and twinkle lights around it. I hadn't known what the hell to do with all the garland, so I looked it up online because I was so obsessed with wanting everything to be perfect.

I hadn't had time to set up the tree yet, but I'd brought in all the decorations and put them in the living room by the large window. Everly took off her jacket and boots and helped Cadence from hers. She gently removed the coat, careful of Cadence's casted wrist. She handed Cadence a little backpack, and Cadence eagerly opened it up, pulling out a very worn purple bear.

My heart momentarily stopped beating in my chest as I stared at the bear, my memories taking me back to the night all those years ago at the fair when I'd won it for Everly. Way back before I'd screwed up everything between us; back at the beginning of it all, when I realized that this girl had a hold on me.

That day wasn't the first day I'd met Everly. The year before that, I'd briefly attended the same middle school as her. The only thing I really remembered about that time was her.

My world was a dark, barren wasteland for so long until that day in seventh grade. I remember the moment I first glanced across the room and laid eyes upon her. She looked like an angel, something so pure and perfect; something I knew even then that I would destroy.

She had always been beautiful. Her soft, pouty pink lips were what first drew me in. The smooth cream of her porcelain complexion, her ethereal pale green eyes and thick lashes. She was a natural stunner, the first glimpse of breathtaking beauty that I had ever seen, and her beauty had never been matched. Or at least, it hadn't until I'd seen the little girl standing before me.

Everly intrigued me so much that I knew I was staring and I knew that she knew I was staring, but I still couldn't stop it. She had a pull on me.

Her looks weren't the only thing that I was drawn to; there was just something about her soul, her purity and kindness. I knew from the first time I saw her that she was special, that she was someone who deserved to be cherished.

I ended up leaving before I could screw things up, but when I ran into her again a year later, I couldn't stay away. She'd occupied enough of my thoughts for so long. She'd been the only person to make a lasting impression on me like that. I wanted to know why; why I thought about this girl and why I yearned for her.

So, when I saw her getting checked out by a greasy carnival worker, I couldn't stop myself from butting in and whisking her away...being the white knight that she had needed at the moment, but knowing that I'd ultimately fuck it up.

I still remember the way the warm September wind tossed her caramel hair around her face, and the way she had timidly smiled at me when she tried to feign indifference over my name. I knew she recognized me, and the way she looked at me was thrilling.

Our little moment was interrupted by Everly's friends. I sort of owed them one, though. If it weren't for Aubrey bumping into Everly, I never would have touched her. Even the casual movement of steadying her arms with my hands had my blood pumping south and my heart hammering in my chest. Touching her made whatever pull she had on me stronger. I wanted her, and I wanted her immediately. I had been with girls before, but never had I wanted someone so much over such a casual touch.

I wasn't impervious to what her friend was trying to accomplish, with the way she eyed me like a hungry cat, but I didn't even care. I only had eyes for Everly. I remember the look of astonishment on her pretty face when I'd handed her the purple bear after winning it.

But I knew from the first time her eyes locked with mine that I was all wrong for her. Or at least I'd *thought* that I was all wrong for her. From the moment I first touched her, nothing had felt more right and when I had foolishly let her go, nothing had felt more wrong. For years, I suffered through that sense of wrongness, of missing something crucial. I wasn't going to let any more time pass.

I swallowed hard, my gaze finding Everly's. She met my eyes with a vulnerable shy look of her own, confirming with a simple glance that it was the same bear I'd given to her. It was obvious that she had passed it on to

Cadence so that Cadence could have something of the father she'd never known—or *hadn't* known until now.

"That's a nice bear you have there," I remarked, smiling with warmth at her. "What's its name?"

"Violet," Cadence replied timidly, lifting the bear up to bury her face in it. "It means purple."

"Nice." I grinned. "Well, come on in. I've got all the stuff we'll need tonight." I led the way into the living room, gesturing to the pile of newly purchased decorations.

Everly arched a delicate brow, smirking. "You weren't kidding when you said you've never done this before," she remarked, eyeing the unopened boxes. "Everything looks brand new."

"That's because everything *is* brand new," I replied almost sheepishly. I scratched my head, the left corner of my lip curving upward. "You can thank Aubrey. I had no idea what I was doing," I added to clarify while Everly picked up one of the boxes of silver ornaments.

"I know." She smiled, setting it down. "Alright, let's set up the tree!" she added, rubbing her palms together.

Chapter Eleven

Everly

I HELPED GRAYSON set up the tree while Cadence sat on the couch, watching quietly. I chewed on my lower lip, wondering if I'd rushed things a little too soon. I knew that regardless of what happened between us, he had a right to know her, but I still couldn't help but wonder if I should have spent more time with Grayson first.

I still had so many questions that I wanted to ask. I wanted to know where he'd gone when he disappeared and what he had been doing in all that time. I knew, more or less, why he left. I knew that it was never about me; that it was about him. It didn't make the sting of it hurt me any less, but I took comfort in the knowledge that things hadn't changed for him either. It was detectable in each look he gave me. Hell, it was detectable in the air that I breathed.

"Could you grab the boxes of ornaments, Cadence?" Grayson asked, his voice muffled from behind the tree. He was separating the branches from one another, making them look more real and less clumped together. Cadence nodded, sliding off the couch. She picked up a box, clenching her bear under her arm as she hesitantly walked it over to us.

I smiled at her as I took it from her hand. I opened the plastic box, pulling out the sleeve of ornaments.

"Did you get hooks?" I asked. Grayson's brow furrowed with confusion. I smiled, resisting the urge to shake my head. I checked the plastic bags, finding the package of wire hooks that Aubrey had undoubtedly tossed in.

Cadence started to help us. She hung ornaments on the tree with Grayson's encouragement. She started to smile timidly, watching Grayson beneath her thick dark lashes. She seemed enthralled with him.

Like mother, like daughter, I thought, repressing a wistful smile.

It didn't take us long to set up the Christmas tree. Once the last ornament was placed on the last crowded branch, Grayson picked up the tree topper—a shiny star.

"So, I'm not tall enough to reach the top, but maybe if I pick you up, you could put it on?" he offered, crouching down in front of Cadence and handing her the star. He looked vulnerable and unsure of himself—a strange look for Grayson. He usually exuded an arrogant air of self confidence.

Cadence smiled shyly and nodded, accepting the star. Grayson effortlessly picked her up and placed her over his shoulders. She sat there, reaching forward to carefully put the star on top of the tree, the sweetest smile etched on her lips.

* * *

After dinner, we sat down to watch *Shrek*. Cadence sat between us, her head resting against my shoulder as Grayson hit play on the DVD player. She didn't even make it to the middle of the movie before she fell asleep.

"Do you want coffee?" Grayson whispered. I nodded, and he got up and disappeared into the kitchen. I shifted out from under Cadence, leaving her on the couch beneath a blanket so I could join him. I peered out, watching her while Grayson prepared our coffee.

She was still peacefully sleeping amidst the soft twinkling glow of the Christmas tree lights. I stood there, watching the gentle fluttering of her thick lashes and the small rise and fall of her chest as she breathed.

The lacerations on Cadence's face had nearly healed. Three pink scars marred her cheeks, but I knew they would fade with time. The psychological effects of the accident might linger for a while still.

I started taking Cadence to her weekly appointments with the child psychologist three days after the funeral. I wasn't permitted to sit in the room during Cadence's appointment. Since the psychologist needed children to express themselves, he evaluated them through recreational activities where family members could not intervene.

Cadence's night terrors had slowed, but they still occasionally happened. She still trembled when she got into a car. When her trembles faded, she would sit rigidly for the remaining time, as if her spine was forced in place with a metal rod. She still didn't talk as much as she used to, and when she did, she didn't talk about the accident or Julia at all. She even stopped telling us that she missed Julia, but I knew she still did.

"How is she doing?" Grayson's voice was gruff but gentle. I glanced over to him. He was standing behind me, holding two cups of coffee in his hands. I could see a yearning need in his eyes, but he maintained the same space he had all night long, keeping a respectable distance. I accepted the mug he offered, bringing it to my lips before I replied. I guess he noticed how I liked my coffee—drowning in cream and sugar.

"Better, I think. It's hard to tell," I replied, shrugging slightly. I was no longer wondering if it had been too soon to introduce Grayson to Cadence. They'd gotten along incredibly well, in fact. Cadence had opened up to Grayson and she had even smiled at him several times. Cadence's smiles were hard to reach these days. "She's sleeping now," I added apologetically.

Grayson closed the distance between us, his eyes landing upon Cadence's sleeping form on the couch. He smiled unlike anything I'd ever seen before. It was the smile that a father had for his child. It was impossible *not* to fall even more in love with him in that moment, and it was impossible to not feel absolutely terrified by that.

I swallowed, suddenly feeling emotional and claustrophobic. I walked away from Grayson, needing to regain my composure before I faced him again. My heart thumped painfully in my chest.

Grayson soundlessly approached me, taking the mug from my shaking hands. He placed both mugs down on the counter before returning to me, his arms wrapping around my body from behind. He pulled me toward him, holding me against his strong chest. He steadied the trembles, and I leaned back into him. I closed my eyes tightly.

I was angry at myself. My heart wanted to dive right back in to him and not look back at the painful past, but my mind reminded me what had happened to me before. Still, my body melted against his, and his arms felt so incredible around me.

"I will never stop apologizing for hurting you," Grayson promised, the pad of his thumb brushing away a lone tear that had managed to escape.

"I don't know if I can do this, Grayson," I said, unable to face him. I felt as if I was hanging on to my sense of self by a very small thread. "I don't know if I can give myself to you the way I did before...I don't know how to make this work," I whispered, gesturing to the both of us and to Cadence.

"We'll make it work," he assured me. The sincerity in his voice helped ease the panicked beating of my heart. "I don't know how, but we'll make it happen."

I walked out of his embrace, heading back to the kitchen. I placed my hands on the marble countertop, avoiding Grayson's intense gaze.

"Grayson, in two weeks I will be returning to LA."

I saw him stiffen out of the corner of my eye. "Two weeks?" he repeated, his jaw clenching. He thought we had more time.

I swallowed hard, wondering why the words were so difficult to get out. Grayson probably thought I was returning to LA to continue life as I had before. I shook my head, trying to clear it. "I need to get my assets in order and meet with the label...and my lawyer."

"Your lawyer?" He looked confused, as if he was having a hard time muddling through my choppy sentences.

"I'm not doing the tour. I can't, not with everything that's happened. I'll be taking a huge hit with the fines of canceling the tour, but I don't care. I need to return to LA next Friday for a meeting with my agent. He doesn't know yet. I've only told Kyle. I also need to put my house on the market."

"You're coming home?" The hope that exploded in Grayson's eyes nearly knocked me off my feet.

"I'm not leaving Cadence again. I can't. I almost lost her and..." I choked on the words, but he understood. "This decision was made before I saw you."

Grayson's jaw clenched at my words but he nodded with understanding. He folded his muscular arms across his chest and leaned against the doorway, giving me all the space I'd asked for.

"What does this mean...for us?" he asked.

I took a deep breath, exhaling harshly. "I don't know," I admitted, my heart aching. I was still afraid to let myself fall for him. I knew that Cadence had a right to know him, and he had a right to know her as well, but I didn't think I could ever release the hold that the sting of the past had on my heart. "Grayson, I loved you too much. I was the exact thing you didn't want. I became consumed by you and when you left, I…" Everything Grayson had ever said about his mother came rushing back. I loved him.

"Don't." Grayson's eyes darkened. "This was not...you weren't..." He couldn't find the words either. He looked up to the heavens for a moment, collecting himself. "I shouldn't have said that stupid shit that day. I was fucked up, and I'm sorry. I didn't know jack shit about love back then. I blamed love for my mother's problems, but it wasn't love that broke her. She was sick, and nobody realized how sick until it was too late."

I looked away from him. "I thought that I was strong, that I could handle you leaving—"

"You did handle it, Everly," Grayson cut me off, closing the distance between us. His hands came up to grip my forearms. His eyes were an intense storm of emotions that overwhelmed me. "Look at what you've done for yourself. You're fucking famous. You've got Platinum records. Fuck, Everly, I didn't even think I hurt you all that bad. Every time I saw you in an interview or on stage, the confidence and happiness you exuded justified my stupid thoughts about leaving in the first place. You were better off without me."

"I still broke, Grayson," I argued. "I can't let that happen again. I can't—"

Grayson's lips silenced me. He kissed me until every fear and insecurity washed away. He didn't stop until I melted against him, unable to stand. Then he slowly pulled away, his eyes fixated on mine. "I won't let you break, Everly. I won't hurt you again. I don't want to lose you...or Cadence."

"You just met her tonight; you don't even know her," I reminded him, not unkindly. "This may not be what you want and I can't risk that."

"It *is* what I want," Grayson argued; his brows furrowed in aggravation as he desperately fought for a way to make me believe him. He stilled, a sudden thought overcoming him. The broken look in his eyes made the air leave my lungs in a woosh. "Is this...is this not what you want?"

I closed my eyes tightly, unable to look at him. "My head is telling me to stop, to walk away before you hurt me, but I'm still here. Like an idiot, I'm still here, even knowing the outcome."

"You don't know the outcome." Grayson relaxed his hold on me. "I don't care if I have to prove it to you every day until you get it, Everly. I'm not going anywhere and I want to be here."

I turned my head away from him again, needing the space. "Grayson, we can't just turn into a happy functional family! Mommy, Daddy, a house with a white picket fence and a goddamn dog."

Grayson gave me a crooked smile, his eyes almost dancing with amusement at my little rant. He arched an eyebrow. "I didn't say that, did I? I said we'd figure it out. Not every family needs to be a cookie cutter June and Ward Cleaver. All I'm asking..." He hesitated, vulnerability replacing the amusement in his eyes. "All I'm asking is that you let me try. We could take things slow, just...let me try."

I swallowed hard, staring at Grayson with wide eyes. I knew that slow wasn't in our vocabulary. We were too explosive for slow, but I understood what he was saying. He wanted a chance; he wanted me to give him a chance, but how could I express to him how much that the very idea of what he was offering terrified me? That I was so scared to put my trust in him again?

It seemed that I didn't have to speak for Grayson to pick up on my concerns. His hands framed my face again, urging me to look at him. His eyes were full of torment, regret and promise. "Everly," he said, his voice husky with meaning. "I'm done walking away now—from anything I care about. Especially you and Cadence."

"How can I believe that?" I asked, the hole in my heart aching around the edges. I knew my words were cutting him to hear just as surely as they cut me to speak, but it had to be said. I could tell that Grayson was choking on the heady emotions that my question evoked. He swallowed hard, his thumb gently brushing the lone tear from my cheek.

"I'll show you," was all he could manage to say. His lips tenderly found mine, and he used them and his hands to seal the promise.

I got lost in the sensation of Grayson's hands on my body. His fingers gripped my hips almost to the point of pain. I whimpered, and he nipped my lip, grinding his apparent arousal against me and caging me against the counter. He used his knee to separate mine, and his fingers went to unclasp the button on my jeans.

Before he could free the button from its imprisonment, Cadence let out a blood curdling scream laced with terror. It was unlike anything I'd ever heard before. Grayson and I didn't even think; we both bolted to the living room to find her sitting upright and pointing at the window. Her face was ghastly pale.

"Cadence, what is it?" I demanded, falling to my knees by the couch. It wasn't always easy to tell if Cadence was having a night terror. Sometimes, her eyes were wide and full of fear while she was still asleep and dreaming.

"There's a man outside! He was looking in the window!" Cadence sobbed, her words barely understandable. Grayson was already throwing his boots and jacket on. He didn't even hesitate before throwing open the door and disappearing into the cold and snowy night.

I shivered against the intrusive gust of cold air from outside and pulled Cadence onto my lap. I still didn't know if Cadence was just having another night terror, or if she legitimately saw someone looking in. I rocked her back and forth and stroked her hair, gently singing to her. My voice lulled her off to sleep as it had so many times before.

Ten minutes later, Grayson returned gasping for breath. His cheeks were red from the cold and the running. He took off his jacket and kicked off his boots, quickly joining us in the room. "Is she alright?" he demanded, his voice barely above a whisper.

"Yeah." I nodded. "Did you find anything?"

Grayson nodded once, glowering out the window. He went over to the remote mounted to the wall that controlled his window shades and closed them abruptly.

"I chased him down the driveway, but he got into his car and drove away before I could catch him." Grayson sounded angry at himself. He disappeared into the kitchen to grab his cell phone to call it in. My heart thudded loudly in my chest and terror made my blood run cold.

I glanced at the clock on the cable box. It was nearly eight—well past Cadence's bedtime.

"I should go," I said, looking down at Cadence. She was fast asleep in my arms again. Grayson covered the speaker of his phone with his hand and shook his head.

He raised his finger, gesturing for me to give him a moment as he listened aptly to the phone. "Yes, I'd like to report suspicious activity outside of my house. I just chased a guy off my property. He had a camera and was taking photos of us. No, I didn't know who he was, but I've seen him around before. Yes, I'll be here." He hung up the phone after relaying his address and sent me an apologetic look. "They need to come here and fill out a report."

I nodded, my heart thumping in my hollow chest. In my experience, these things always ended up on the page of some gossip magazine or another.

"Wait, you've seen him around before?"

"Yeah, he was at the two stores I went to today...and he was at Tap's the other night..."

I frowned, not liking this situation at all. This was the one thing I wanted to avoid; people following those I cared about, people camping outside of my loved ones' homes hoping to get a picture. I looked down at Cadence, the fear I felt for her malleable in my heart.

"I should really get Cadence home, Grayson," I pointed out.

"He could still be out there," Grayson countered. "Besides, the roads are crap, Everly. That car won't be able to handle them; the plows haven't been by yet. I'd much rather you stay. They'll clear the roads by morning. I've got a spare room."

I sighed, biting my lip. Cadence was already fast asleep again, and Grayson was right. I didn't particularly want to share a road with the person who had lurked outside of Grayson's house. But this wasn't exactly taking it slow, and it was far outside of my comfort zone. Still, I didn't have much of a choice in the matter. The idea of driving in this scared me.

"Fine. Could you show me the way to the spare room?" I relented.

Grayson nodded, leading the way up the pine stairs and opening a door to the right of the stairs. It was dark in the room, but I could easily make out the bed through the light pouring in from the hall. He turned down the plain white sheets and I placed Cadence in the bed. I tucked her in, overly aware of Grayson behind me. The hairs on my arms stood up, as if charged by his electric presence.

His hand gently squeezed my shoulder, and we retreated back into the hallway. I closed the door, leaving a few inches so the bedroom wouldn't be completely dark.

"They'll be here within fifteen minutes. Let's go downstairs," Grayson told me.

We returned downstairs in time to hear my cell phone go off. I picked it up, reading the caller ID. It was my parents. I quickly answered.

"Hey, I was just about to call you," I said into the phone. "The roads are terrible, so Cadence and I are going to stay at Grayson's." I purposely left out the part about the lurker. I knew I should tell my parents, but I knew they'd freak out. I was worried it would be just another mark in the *reasons why Everly can't do this* category.

"Do you really think that's wise, Everly?" Mom questioned, her voice tense. She didn't even sound like herself at all. "You said you were just going over for dinner. If I had known you'd be out so late and that you'd end up staying over at his house, I wouldn't have agreed to this! It's too soon, Everly. You need to take things slow."

My spine stiffened at my mother's words. I understood that she was worried about Cadence, but I was an adult. I was Cadence's mother.

Grayson sent me a curious look and I turned away from him.

"Yes, I think it's wise. I'd rather not risk driving on these roads right now, and Cadence is already sleeping," I shot back gently. "And she deserves to know her father, doesn't she?"

I could hear my mother sigh with resignation. "Everly, I'm just worried... okay? For the both of you. We all know what happened last time he left. I don't want to see you go through that again...I don't want to see *Cadence* hurt."

"I know," I murmured, my spine still stiff and my eyes filling with more moisture. "We'll be home tomorrow morning," I added. "Goodnight, Mom." I hung up without waiting for her response.

Grayson came up behind me, wrapping his arms around my waist and pulling me against his chest. I knew he hadn't heard my mother's words, but he'd seen my response to them and that was all the tell he needed.

I turned stiffly into his embrace, and his arms wrapped around the small of my back, hugging me closer to him. It seemed like any time I allowed myself to move forward, a wave of insecurity would deliver a blow so severe, I'd stumble backwards. I was thankful he was here to catch me, but would he always?

Before he could say anything, a sharp knock sounded on his front door. Grayson regretfully pulled away from me and opened the door to two uniformed police officers.

I took a deep breath, preparing myself as Grayson welcomed them inside. They stood in the foyer, their incident reports out and pens poised.

At first, they hadn't noticed me standing in the living room. They listened to Grayson report what had happened. "My daughter saw him first," Grayson concluded. My heart nearly dislodged from my chest at his words. He hadn't intended on doing it; it had just come out. He quickly glanced over his shoulder at me, his eyes wide with astonishment and apology. I swallowed hard and pasted on a smile as both of the police officers' gazes followed Grayson's.

The younger of the two men did a double take. "Everly Daniels? From *Autumn Fields*?" he asked, his eyes widening with surprise. "I LOVE your music!"

I smiled shyly before Grayson cut in, glowering at the starstruck cop. "Now about this guy, are you going to put out a report for him?"

The man quickly tried to school his features and cleared his throat.

"Yes, we are," the older police man said, giving his partner a stern look as if to say *get it together*. "We're just going to have a look in the front there." He nodded to the front of the house. Grayson nodded, opening the door and allowing them to exit. Once the door closed behind them, he whirled to face me.

"Everly, I am so sorry, it just came out. I—" He shook his head, trying to clear his thoughts.

"It's alright," I told him, my voice sounding small. He had a claim on her, after all. Just because I hadn't been open with the public about my true relationship to Cadence didn't mean he had to follow suit. He didn't have to worry about his life story spread out on sleazy magazine tabloids.

Twenty minutes later, the two policemen knocked to inform us that they had all the information they needed and would keep an eye out for a person who matched the vague description that Grayson had provided. We watched as the police car pulled out of Grayson's driveway, almost sliding onto the road. The roads *were* messy, and the snow wasn't letting up.

I shivered and Grayson pulled me to his side. "So...I'm not sure if you want to sleep in the guest room or..." He arched a brow, smirking.

"Seriously? You're thinking about that in a time like this? What happened to slow?" I whacked him playfully on the shoulder and rolled my eyes, hiding the fact that his suggestive words had completely affected me.

"Of course I am." Grayson shrugged with apology. "And I could take it slow for you, angel...if that's what you need," he said, smiling dangerously.

Chapter Twelve

Grayson

COCOONED IN THE WARMTH of my huge bed with Everly's head nestled against my shoulder, the soft exhale almost tickling my chest, I felt damn near close to heaven. I thought I did a good job distracting her from the dark path her thoughts had started to take her.

I smirked at the memory of her beneath me...and on top of me. The way her lids would flutter as if she struggled to keep them open, the soft gasps she'd let out each time I pushed deeper inside of her. My cock jumped, celebrating the memory as well.

Everly sighed, nuzzling even closer against me and her hand splaying out across my chest. She felt so good in my arms, so right. Knowing that Cadence was down the hall just added to the warmth in my heart in ways I couldn't fully comprehend. This felt right, as fucked up as it was to admit. This was how it was supposed to be. How it should have been.

My hand came up to gently play with the strands of Everly's long hair while I thought about the night. It hadn't gone *exactly* the way I'd planned on it going—the whole lurker with his face pressed against my living room window was a clear indication of that. Plus, our heavier conversations.

I wasn't an idiot; I knew that Everly wasn't falling as easily into this as I was. I knew she loved me and I didn't doubt that. I knew she wanted me, but I had scarred her and she wasn't ready to trust me again. Not yet. The phone call from her mother only seemed to make things worse.

I had no idea what her mother said to her, but I knew it wasn't good by the defeated set to her shoulders and the slight tremble in her jaw when Everly hung up the phone. I knew that it probably had everything to do with me.

I couldn't blame her mother for wanting to protect Everly, but I was determined not to let the past repeat itself and I wouldn't stop proving it until Everly—and everyone around us—believed it. I would make this work, because the alternative just didn't cut it for me. I wanted this, and I wanted it every day. I didn't have to completely know the little girl down the hall to know that I already loved her and would do anything for her; that was apparent when I was chasing the intruder with blood thirsty eyes.

I'd never felt more rage in my life than I did in the moment I realized that the intruder had a camera lens aimed at my daughter. I'd nearly caught the bastard too, and I couldn't be too sure, but the jacket looked so damn familiar. He's *lucky* that I didn't catch him. I wasn't sure I would have been able to reign in the rage.

I had known, in that desperate moment as I watched the intruder escape in his crappy rental, that there wasn't anything I wouldn't do for those two.

Still, I had heard Everly's sharp intake of breath when I foolishly stated that "my daughter" had seen the trespasser first. I hadn't meant to say that; the words had just stumbled from my lips before I could even grasp the meaning of them. I knew that Everly didn't want anybody to know because she was worried about it getting out to the public. She didn't want paparazzi to stalk Cadence or her parents. She wanted to be left alone. After tonight, I understood that.

But saying the words felt right. *My daughter. Our daughter.* I swear to God, I nearly cried then and there and I am not an emotional guy. In fact, I'm the furthest thing from an emotional guy.

The first and only person that had ever really gotten any kind of positive emotion out of me had been Everly. I'd changed since knowing her—in a good way. Even when I burned what we had to the ground, even when I made the biggest mistake of my life, I was changed because of her. Because I put *her* needs before my own. She needed me to go, or she wouldn't have followed her dreams.

I hated that I'd left her, especially knowing what I left behind. But I couldn't change the past...I could only build the future.

I dozed off, my thoughts finally quieting enough for me to fall asleep, lulled by Everly's soft breathing.

* * *

The next morning, I awoke before Everly. She was still nestled in my arms, still fast asleep. At first, I tried to place what had woken me up. The house seemed quiet. Then I blinked and turned my head, seeing Cadence standing in the doorway of my room, her arms wrapped tightly around the purple bear.

"Hey...good morning," I said softly, trying to free my limbs from Everly without waking her. She slept on while I sat up. I was thankful that I'd thought ahead enough to put on some pajama bottoms. "Are you hungry?"

Cadence nodded, watching me with suspicious eyes while I quietly got up and grabbed a shirt from my drawer. I put it on and motioned for Cadence to follow me. She did, solemnly keeping pace with me.

I lifted her up and set her down in one of the island bar stools. "So, what do you like to eat?" I asked, gesturing to the kitchen. "I am *king* of breakfast," I told her, winking. Cadence gave me a small smile and shrugged, her feet swinging and knocking against the cabinet wood. "Not chatty this morning? That's alright. I'll just make a bit of everything," I told her, setting to work. I was thankful that I lived off of bacon, sausage and eggs. My refrigerator was always stocked full of those items, at least. I fried them up while I made toast, tossing a few pancakes on the griddle just to be safe. Cadence wasn't giving me any hints on what she wanted.

Cadence watched me work, her eyes wide. "I've never seen anybody do so much at once!" she declared, her tiny voice sounding bewildered.

I grinned over my shoulder. "I told you! I'm the king of breakfast," I reminded her, winking.

Cadence started to giggle. She pointed at the stove. "How come that's on fire then?" she asked innocently, reminding me so much of Everly that it took my breath away. I looked back, noticing that the bacon was indeed smoking a lot.

"That's alright. You can't mess up bacon. It's even better burnt," I told her, saving it from further destruction.

"That's actually true." Everly's voice made my head snap back toward the living room. She was walking into the kitchen, dressed in one of my t-shirts and a pair of my boxers. My throat dried and my blood started to surge. I shook my head, trying to clear out all the suggestive thoughts. "Bacon tastes so much better when it's burnt."

"You guys are gross." Cadence wrinkled her nose. "Why did we stay here last night?" she asked, turning her miss-nothing gaze to Everly. Everly seemed a little surprised. I remembered her mentioning that Cadence wasn't talking as much as usual.

"It was snowing a lot. Besides, you fell asleep!" Everly sat beside Cadence in the other free stool. She hugged her close. "How did you sleep?"

"Good," Cadence responded. "I had a dream about a man in a window though. It was scary."

Everly exchanged a look with me and I shrugged. There was no sense in scaring a four-year-old by telling her that what scared her hadn't been a dream. "I once had a dream that I had a pet grizzly bear," I supplied.

"Really?" Cadence giggled, a light smile on her face. "That's so silly!"

Everly was watching our exchange with a bewildered expression on her face. A smile teased the corner of her lips, and she shook her head as if she couldn't believe what she was witnessing. I turned back to the stove, turning off the burners and loading down three plates with food.

"She can't eat all that," Everly argued, seeing the massive pile of food I'd placed down in front of Cadence.

"She doesn't have to." I shrugged. "But if she does, I'll give her a prize."

Cadence seemed to perk up even more at my words. "What kind of prize?" she inquired, tilting her head as she patiently waited for me to respond.

"You'll get to pick," I promised. I stood on the opposite side of the island, facing the two most beautiful women in the world and feeling happier than I ever had before.

* * *

By the time we finished breakfast, the roads were freshly plowed and salted. It still didn't prevent me from following behind Everly just to make sure she got back to her parents' house safely. I already said my goodbyes, so I resisted the urge to stop and follow them up to the house. The thought of encountering either of her parents right now just wasn't all that appealing.

Instead, I drove to my dad's house.

There was no doubt about it, Dad was enjoying his early retirement. When I pulled into the driveway, he was sliding down the man-made hill of ice and snow on a toboggan with my half-sisters, nine-year-old Chloe and six-year-old Jocelyn.

"Hey, son!" Dad called, spotting me approaching them. Chloe and Jocelyn squealed, rushing towards me as quickly as they could manage in their bulky snowsuits and the deep snow. I allowed them to tackle me to the ground, like they always did. The snow felt cold against my jeans, but I didn't care. I was in an incredible mood.

I lifted them both up effortlessly as I stood, done with letting them have the upper hand. I carried them back to the snowy lot, depositing them into a thick pile of snow from Dad's snow plow. I pushed a bunch of snow over with my bare hands, burying their laps deep in it so they had to wiggle frantically to get out. The second they'd freed themselves, they started to roll chunks of snow into balls. Thankfully, the snow wasn't consistent enough and their snowballs turned to dust before they could even throw them. Still, their giggles were infectious, making an easy smile form on my lips.

It wasn't always like this, me with my sisters. I resented them at first— or at least...the idea of them. I refused to allow myself to get close to them, harboring the anger and resentment I felt after the demise of my parents' marriage instead of appreciating the fact that I had siblings.

I suppose in a roundabout way, I had Everly to thank. Before she showed me how to let people in, I didn't. I was like an abused dog, snapping at those who wanted to help me because I couldn't trust their intentions.

It didn't come easy, this change. I disappeared, and when I returned, I saw how much I'd confused and hurt Chloe. She didn't understand where I had gone or why I hadn't come home for a long time. All the kid knew was that she loved me, and I'd cast the love aside in a selfish attempt at self-preservation.

Reality was a cold stone bitch to swallow. I was still making up for the wounds I inflicted on those around me. My sisters had long since forgiven me—Dad and Vanessa too—but I still had a lot of work to do, particularly with Everly and Cadence.

"Let's go inside and get some hot chocolate," Dad said, calling off the fun as he rubbed his hands together and approached us. My dad was an older copy of myself. His dark hair had more gray in it these days and his belly was a little rounder than it had been in his youth, but his blue eyes were as piercing as ever. The girls groaned in unison. "Now girls, we've been out here for two hours already! My old bones are cold!"

"Alright." Chloe sighed before perking up. "You'll play Nintendo with me, won't you, Grayson?!"

"Hey, what about me!" Jocelyn pouted.

"You're too young for video games," Chloe said decidedly, giving Jocelyn a look of mock sympathy. "Sorry."

"She's not too young for Mario Brothers," I corrected, allowing Chloe to tug me up toward the house. Jocelyn took my other hand. "And I will, but I want coffee first."

Vanessa was already making hot chocolate for the girls when we came inside. Dad stepped up behind her, his hand creeping underneath the hem of her shirt. Vanessa squealed and slapped his arm, a good natured smile on her face. "Take these to your daughters. I'll put on some coffee," she said, shaking her head at him.

Chloe and Jocelyn barely sat still long enough to finish half of their hot chocolate. Wiggling with impatience, Chloe looked at me with wide eyes the same color as mine and Dad's...and Cadence's. "Can I set up the game now?"

"Alright, but I'm going to finish my coffee before I go up. Give me about ten minutes, okay?"

"Fine." Chloe sighed dramatically before flying out of the kitchen, Jocelyn trailing behind her. I heard the sound of their footsteps racing up the stairs followed by their argumentative voices. Chloe was always trying to boss Jocelyn around, and Jocelyn was always trying to stand up to her. It amused me to hear them bickering.

"So, what brings you for a visit?" Dad asked, cutting straight to the chase. He was sitting beside Vanessa with an arm causally and affectionately wrapped around her shoulders. It had taken me a long time to get used to this new version of my dad. He hadn't been the same way with my mom, and I used to resent it.

I smirked. "Do I need a reason to visit?"

"Usually, yes," Dad pointed out. "Problems with a job site?"

"Nope, not at all actually. We're all good there," I answered. I drew in a breath and sat back in the oak chair. "You're right, though. I came here for a reason. I have news."

Vanessa and Dad exchanged a look before focusing their attention back at me. "And what news is this?" Dad asked, his expression serious and dire.

"Well, you're a grandpa, I guess." I shrugged, taking another deep sip of my coffee.

Dad blinked at me without comprehension, and Vanessa let out a little gasp and covered her mouth to hide the surprised smile.

"Pardon?" he leaned forward, his eyebrows knitting together as if he was trying to make sense of a complicated math equation.

"I said you're a grandpa. I'm a dad."

"Grayson, you're going to give us a little more detail than that," Vanessa scolded, her hand lowering to her collarbone. "Who is she? When is she due?"

"She's not pregnant." I rolled my eyes. "Well, she was, five years ago. So, I have a four-year-old." I knew I was babbling, but I hadn't exactly rehearsed how I was going to tell my dad and step-mom about this. I'd hoped for a more eloquent speech, but my tongue wasn't cooperating with my brain.

Realization dawned across Vanessa's pretty features. My step-mom was a beautiful woman with fair hair and gentle brown eyes. I'd wanted to hate her at first, but it was impossible. She was so loving and caring that you couldn't.

"Everly?" she whispered. I looked up with surprise and nodded.

"Everly doesn't have a kid," Dad argued.

"Her sister did," Vanessa said, frowning.

I shook my head, sighing. I ran my hands through my hair while I tried to think about how I was going to explain this one. "Everly couldn't take the baby on tour with the band, so her sister stayed home to take care of her. The lie started when Everly was trying to protect them from the media."

Dad and Vanessa were both silent for several minutes, absorbing the news. They had absolutely no idea what to say to me. "So, what happens now?" Dad finally asked, peering up at me.

"I don't really know," I answered truthfully, thinking about all the reservations I still saw in Everly's eyes. "But I want to be a part of their lives. I have a little girl...her name is Cadence."

Vanessa gave my dad's hands a reassuring squeeze. He swallowed hard. "Do you have a picture?"

I fished out the photo that Everly had given me of the two of them on a hammock at her place in LA. I'd taken it out of the frame so that I could easily keep it close to me, in my coat pocket. They gazed at it for several long moments.

"She has the Dixon eyes. She looks just like you...and like Everly," Dad finally said, handing the photo back. "I can't believe I've been a grandpa all these years and haven't known it."

"I can't believe I've been a father all these years and haven't known it,"
I retorted dryly, putting the photo back into my coat pocket.

"Why didn't she tell you?" Dad asked, his voice accusatory.

"She came by," Vanessa interjected. "I didn't know she was pregnant...
but she came by looking for Grayson and I had no information to give her."

I bowed my head, accepting the wave of shame. "Yeah, well. My bad?"

"Grayson." Dad's voice was torn between supportive and accusatory.
He knew I'd received the shock of my life when I got that news, and that I
was burning with the need to fix it all.

"Anyway, I'd like for you to meet her, but she's been through a major
trauma and we're just going to play things by ear. See how she's doing and
what not. I was hoping I could extend the Christmas dinner invitation to
Everly and Cadence, if they're up for it."

"Of course," Vanessa said, quickly nodding. "We'd love to have them,
and we understand. She's been through a lot." We all fell silent, thinking
about the deadly accident that had taken Julia's life and nearly Cadence's.

"This probably goes without saying, but I need this to stay a secret a
while longer, so don't put out a congratulations notice in the newspaper
or anything like that." I sighed, rubbing my temple. "Oh...and Dad? I might
need some time off for a bit. You know, to get to know my daughter," I told
him, the corner of my lips teasing upward in a smile.

Chapter Thirteen

Everly

LOVE AT A FUNERAL...
Looks like Everly Daniels sought comfort from an old flame while home for a family member's funeral. We wonder what Kyle has to say about this!

The ice gathered in my chest as my eyes roamed the headline, breathing suddenly felt impossible.

I woke up to a hundred text messages and missed calls from Aubrey, Kyle, Marcus, even Cam. The guys had obsessively asked if I was okay, and Aubrey had been the only one to blatantly tell me that I was trending on Twitter.

I wanted to know what they were saying. I wanted to know how I needed to protect myself, so I pulled a rookie move. I sat down at the kitchen island and used my mom's laptop to Google my name.

I wasn't exactly sure what I expected to see, but it certainly wasn't a grainy photo of Grayson pressing me against my parent's car outside of my sister's old rental. The passion was evident on both of our faces.

The primitive moment of longing was definitely not meant to be caught on camera, nor was it meant to be on every gossip website on the Internet. I swallowed hard.

Worse still, were the supposed photos of Kyle looking completely gutted and destroyed. The article definitely painted the believable tale that I had moved on with another man, and that *maybe* my wandering eyes were the reason a brokenhearted Kyle called off our supposed upcoming wedding. The whole thing was laughable; Kyle and I weren't together and we'd never been together, but our fans didn't know that. My phone started to ring again. I picked it up, seeing Kyle's name on the screen.

"Everly, apparently I am supposed to say something about your relationship with another man or something?" Kyle's voice was full of amusement. "I say...congratulations and all that! Also, kudos to the media for retouching that photo of me from three years ago. Looks authentic, huh?"

Kyle meant to lighten the mood, but I barely relaxed at his words. Even though my close family and friends all knew the truth, the rest of the world didn't.

"Kyle, I'm tired of these articles. We need to address them."

"I agree completely. I can't very well propose to my girlfriend when I'm constantly reassuring her that the tabloids are full of shit," he added, the first hints of frustration lining his words.

"Wait, you were going to propose?" I'd known things were serious between them for a while, but I hadn't known that it was *marriage* serious.

"*Are,*" Kyle corrected. "Once I get the balls. Oh, and once we deal with this media shit storm. Plenty of time to clear the air when we go on the *Margo Morning Show,* right?"

"Yeah," I sighed, massaging my temple warily. Both the interview and the meeting with Brent had been consistently on my mind for days now. Luckily, Maddie had already handled all of that. All I really needed to do now was call Maddie and find out when the flight times were.

"Relax." Kyle chuckled.

I wilted with guilt, thinking about the bomb I was about to drop on the rest of the guys."I'm as relaxed as I can get, Kyle. I've been dealing with stuff here. Cadence has had a lot of appointments and—"

"Right, it's all good," Kyle assured me. "Listen, Everly…I'm mostly calling to tell you to chill out. If I know you like I know you, you're freaking out right now." I snorted with agreement. "Don't let it get to you."

"I'll try, boss." I sighed.

"Good. The guys and I are already back in LA. I've talked to them about everything, and they're…processing it but they do get it."

"Ugh, I wish I could have been there to tell them too," I exhaled. "I just won't have time when I fly in. It's the meeting with the lawyer and Brent, then the interview…which I'll see you guys at?"

"You definitely will, doll face," Kyle said with jest.

I rolled my eyes, smiling. "I might bring Grayson, Kyle…" I rubbed the bridge of my nose. I was not looking forward to dealing with that particular hurdle.

I could hear the disapproval over the phone even though Kyle hadn't made a sound. He waited a moment, likely collecting himself. I knew he wasn't about to lecture me on how to handle this complicated situation I was in, but I also knew his hatred of Grayson ran deep.

Kyle and I were friends and bandmates, and Kyle once carried a torch for me. I think he resented Grayson for years, for capturing my heart and then breaking it; leaving me in pieces. That was all water under the bridge now. Kyle was happily taken and apparently, about to propose to her any day now.

"Well, if that's what you need to do," he said shortly. "I've gotta go. Have a meeting with the label. I'll send your regards."

"Thanks, Kyle," I whispered.

"No problem. I'll call you later," Kyle said before he hung up.

I placed the phone down on the island. My eyes fluttered back to the computer again, to the open browser. The mouse hovered close to the exit button.

"What are you doing?" Mom's voice startled me.

I automatically clicked exit and closed the laptop. "Nothing, just checking some emails," I answered, my spine stiffening. After our terse phone conversation the other night, I hadn't really gotten a chance to talk to her alone. We usually had an audience, by way of Cadence or Dad. Right now, we were perfectly alone in the early light of dawn.

Mom walked the rest of the way into the kitchen, pausing to grab herself a mug down from the cupboard for her habitual morning cup of coffee. She measured out scoops of beans into the filter. While the coffee maker did its thing, she finally turned around to face me. Leaning back against the counter, she looked at me with her large eyes full of sorrow.

"I'm sorry for snapping at you the other night," she said, her lips drawn downward. My mom had changed a lot in the past few weeks. She'd lost some weight and her eyes had more lines around them. Both of my parents had aged with their grief. "I was just...worried."

"I get it, Mom, I do," I assured her. "But...you need to let it go. Things are obviously going to have to change. Grayson deserves to know her and she deserves to know him too. We're taking things slow..." Or at least, as slow as Grayson and I were capable of taking things.

"I just worry, that's all." Mom sighed. "And I guess not knowing what your plan is set me off too. You can't just play house anymore, Everly. Your sister isn't here anymore to handle everything that she handled..." Mom's voice caught on the pain.

"I know what I have to do, Mom," I said gently, not wanting to upset her further. "I'm meeting with my lawyer and the label Thursday afternoon. I'll be putting my house on the market and getting my assets handled there. It might take some time," I warned. "Then I'll start looking for a house out here...and I'll figure everything else out."

Tears welled up in Mom's eyes and her lip trembled.

"Why are you crying? This is good news, isn't it?" I asked.

She nodded, wiping away the tears. "I'm glad you're going to come home, that's all," Mom finally said, smiling through her tears. She took a deep breath. "Do the guys know?" Mom inquired. She knew how close we were with one another. They were like my brothers; I loved them and they loved me.

"I told Kyle and he told them for me. I wasn't going to get in town before the interview taping." I brushed my wayward hair out of my face, peering up at her. I watched as she took a small sip of coffee. "They're a little bummed out, but they get it. I think they're actually on the same page. We've all been touring and working so hard for so long...you get sick of it, you know? We all need a break."

My thoughts carried me back to the night in July when I finally spoke up about my exhaustion over the whole thing. We'd been at Kyle's house, hanging out after some awards show or another. For a rare change, it was just the four of us.

"I think I'm done," I whispered. "I can't do this anymore. I can't handle the guilt anymore."

Kyle, Marcus and Cam instantly knew what—or rather, who—I was talking about. Cadence. I didn't talk about her often because I didn't want to be the perpetual party crasher, but tonight I couldn't help it.

It was Cadence's fourth birthday, and instead of throwing my daughter a ridiculously over the top party, I'd been at an awards ceremony. Julia had thrown the party. They were going to fly out on the weekend to celebrate with me, but yet again, I missed a pivotal moment in my daughter's life.

"I don't want you guys to hate me." I sobbed, leaning into Marcus. He held me, comforting me while my tears fell.

"We can't thank you enough for what you've done, Everly. For what you've endured." Marcus' voice was pained as he leaned across the sofa to look me in the eyes.

"Yeah, Ever. We're okay with taking a break..." Kyle looked at Cam and Marcus knowingly. "We've actually been talking about it."

My emotions were running on high, so naturally, I assumed the worst. "You want to kick me out of the band?" I whispered.

"Hell no." Kyle's jaw dropped and his eyes widened with shock. "No! There's just some stuff that we all want to do too."

"Like what?"

Marcus shifted uncomfortably beside me. "You know, bang chicks and stuff." I looked at him with disbelief. Marcus still carried a torch for Aubrey. He loved that girl more than anything, but Aubrey hadn't been able to handle the distance and the lack of privacy that came from having a famous boyfriend. She still loved him, but she often said it was too complicated for her. So they'd taken the labels away from their relationships, and with it, the pressure to remain faithful.

Little did either one know that they essentially were still in a monogamous relationship, which was exactly why I gave Marcus the knowing look of disbelief. The only chick he'd bang was miles away...at home, with my heart and my lonely memories.

"Well, I'd love to settle down. It doesn't bother me to admit it," Kyle remarked. The silence that fell after his words was heavy like a thick cloud of smoke, but it was also...comfortable. A moment of reflection.

"So, after this tour...we're done?" Cam questioned, breaking the silence. He was the only one who didn't seem thrilled with the idea. Cam had loved everything that came with the fame. He hadn't been attached to anyone when we started, so he had no qualms with playing the womanizing bassist and living the party lifestyle. Even still, he seemed to understand where Kyle, Marcus and I were coming from. It was inevitable, this shift.

"I don't think we're ever going to be done," Kyle answered after a moment of thoughtful silence. "We work too well for that. But I think our music would benefit from a little break."

"I agree." Marcus sighed, his eyes wistful. "We need more life experience... preferably the good kind for a change, yeah?" he joked, nudging me. Most of our music was fueled by the heartache and pain I felt over losing Grayson, and the difficult situation of leaving my daughter.

"What about Grayson?" Mom finally asked, breaking the awkward silence we'd fallen into during my lapse down memory lane.

I started, surprised by her voice. "He wants to be a part of Cadence's life...of my life." I shrugged. "I don't think there's any more to say on that matter."

"And you forgive him?" Mom was desperately trying to understand my logic. I looked at her with pain filled eyes.

"I don't know if I can forget, but I forgive him. I understand what he did now," I added, thinking about Cadence and how I had left her too. I understood how painful it could be to leave someone you loved behind. "Mom, I'm not talking about going to pick out my wedding dress." I rolled my eyes. "We're just going to see where it goes. But I know he's serious about wanting to be a part of Cadence's life, and that's the most important thing," I said, thinking back to how easily they'd been in each other's company.

She gave me a bemused smile. "I know," she said. Her voice shook with emotion and her eyes welled with tears. Stubbornly, she turned away. "I just don't want to lose you guys too."

"You aren't going to lose us, Mom." I stood up, walking around the counter to put my arms around my mother. She felt even thinner than she looked.

She chuckled, tears pouring freely down her cheeks. The ache in her heart was palpable; it stretched and shot straight through mine.

"I miss her too," I croaked, choking on that suffocating pain, my vision blurring as I held her closer.

* * *

After the heart to heart with my mom, I called my personal assistant to get briefed on everything going on.

"Everly Daniels, next time you fall off the earth, please do a better job!" Maddie's tone was all business and seemed a little clipped, as if she was aggravated at me—which she probably was. Maddie wasn't just my personal assistant; she was also my public relations representative. She dealt with any media storms that concerned me, although that aspect of her job hadn't been required in a long time. The most the media got from me was a couple of photos of me hitting up Starbucks in yoga pants.

"Yeah, well...sorry. I guess. Only you know that the whole Kyle thing is complete bullshit," I said in defense.

"We know, but we like to avoid discussing that. The fans love the idea of you guys together, but in the last twenty-four hours since that 'article' was posted, your sales shot way up so I guess they love the drama a little more, eh?" she joked. "Bullshit aside, how are you doing? Who's the smokin' hot guy in the pictures? Oh...and how are...things?"

Maddie's words flew quickly from her lips. I got the impression that she'd been worried about me. It wasn't like me to shut her out; we'd spoken daily since I hired her. We weren't close friends, but we were friendly enough.

I still felt a wave of lingering guilt for having left her high and dry after she took the time from her busy schedule to come out to Julia's funeral. Maddie had met Julia a handful of times and genuinely liked her, but I knew how busy Maddie was with managing me—especially after I'd disappeared in the middle of a bunch of promotions.

"The guy is my...boyfriend, Grayson. Things are as good as they could be, in light of everything," I informed her. "Cadence is doing better in therapy, we've got my sister's estate sorted."

"That's good," Maddie said. I was relieved to hear the sincerity in her voice. When you lost someone, people tended to get a little awkward around you. I'd had my fair share of that over the course of the last week. I was glad that Maddie was still her collected and calm self. "You'll need to give me more details on this Grayson fellow when you get back to LA. Your meeting with Brent is booked for five on Thursday evening, and Haskell will meet you there. I've called the best real estate agent in Hollywood, and he'll be coming to assess the house on Monday morning. I know you need to be back for Sunday, so I'll handle that."

"Thank you, Maddie," I said sincerely. I was grateful to have her in my life, and grateful that she understood my need to return home to Cadence quickly. I knew it was too soon to bring her along with me. She would be staying with my parents, but I still didn't want to miss talking to her doctor or her child psychologist. "Can you send the jet to pick us up next Thursday morning?"

"Us?" There was no denying the question in Maddie's voice.

"Yeah. I'll be bringing a guest..." I trailed off. "Grayson." I didn't actually know if Grayson would even be interested in coming, but I needed to give the label a heads up. If worse came to worst, I'd just go alone. No harm in that, but I was focused on the best case scenario—Grayson coming to LA with me, the two of us spending the weekend getting to know each other again.

We had a lot to discuss before I could truly let go of the past...and my own guilt over it. I had no doubt that Grayson would be a wonderful dad after our impromptu sleepover the other night.

Watching the two of them had been incredible, in essence. I hadn't made my presence known right away. Instead, I'd watched while Grayson and Cadence easily interacted with one another. Cadence watched him warily at first, but then she started to warm up to him. Within five minutes, it was as if they were instinctively in tune to each other.

I knew without a reasonable doubt that *that* was real. That was a raw moment that Grayson hadn't even been intending on letting me witness, and it had been perfect. I hadn't seen Cadence smile like that in forever.

Still, we were on shaky ground and I knew that we needed to figure out a whole lot of details before I could let the insecurities go.

*   *   *

The next few days were a hurried rush of activity between Cadence's appointments. First came the orthopedic clinic to have her cast removed and x-rays done. The hairline fracture had completely healed, and the doctor gave the go-ahead for Cadence to resume regular use. The next day, I took her to her appointment with the psychologist.

"Cadence seemed lighter and happier this session," Dr. Livingston said after her session with Cadence, her thin lips lifting up in a smile. "Is she sleeping better?" Dr. Livingston was a really good doctor, and I liked her a lot. She connected well with Cadence and I'd noticed an improvement in her since we started to bring Cadence to see her.

"Much better," I said. "She's eating more too," I added, thinking about the day at Grayson's. Cadence had nearly cleared her plate completely, determined to win a prize. When she couldn't eat any more, she stared dejectedly at her plate until Grayson told her that she'd eaten enough to earn the prize anyway.

"What prize?" she had asked, flashing a wide toothy grin.

"A movie date with me," Grayson responded with a wink. In fact, we were going to meet up with Grayson that afternoon to catch an early viewing of *Rio*.

It sort of made me nervous to think about going out in public like that, but I was honestly more nervous at the prospect of not going. It wasn't that I didn't trust Grayson alone with Cadence; I just didn't want to miss it. I needed to be there.

I shook my head, clearing it from my distracted train of thought.

"I would like to know your opinion on something," I said, leaning forward.

"I'm all ears." Dr. Livingston grinned.

"As you know, Cadence's father has never been in the picture. He didn't know about her and I couldn't find him to tell him, but he's back now and he wants to be here for her..." I trailed off. "I just wondered if it was all too much or too soon for Cadence."

Dr. Livingston considered my words carefully. "It's difficult at this point to tell if this change would benefit Cadence or be detrimental to her. Has she met him before?"

"Yes, very recently. And she got along great with him. They have this connection..." I paused, smiling wistfully while I thought about it. "He's gotten her to eat more in one sitting than I had all week, and she smiled more in one afternoon than she has since...the accident."

"Well, based on what I've seen from Cadence today alone, I'd say go with your instincts. You're doing a pretty good job of it so far." Dr. Livingston smiled warmly.

I left the doctor's office feeling lighter and more confident in my decisions. I held Cadence's hand in mine. Once I'd strapped her securely into the car, I dug out my cell phone. I texted Grayson, telling him that we were on our way to the movie theater.

This would be the third time that Cadence would see Grayson. He'd only been able to stop by once since our sleepover on Saturday, when he came over for dinner. My parents had all but insisted that he come, and I knew it would ease their minds if I gave in. The dinner had started out tense, but my parents couldn't help but melt at the way that Cadence grinned at Grayson. She had all of his undivided attention, and she blossomed from it.

Watching them playing together on the floor after dinner healed the fissures in my heart, and I wished I could see it *more*. Every day, in fact. Of course, I knew my thoughts were getting ahead of me, but it was a sweet thought.

I asked Grayson to come to LA with me that night, shortly before he left for home. He didn't even think before whispering yes and pressing his lips to mine in the sweetest, most tantalizing kiss.

I took a deep breath. "Are you ready, Cadence?" I asked, peering into the backseat. Cadence had a huge grin on her face. She couldn't contain her excitement for her movie date with Grayson. She wasn't trembling or stiff, like she usually was when I put her in the car.

"Yes!" she squealed, a toothy grin flashing as her eyes sparkled.

Chapter Fourteen

Grayson

I WAS ALREADY at the movie theater pacing around, the tickets I had purchased for the three of us clenched tightly in hand. My eyes kept going to the front of the movie theater, searching the faces of those who came in, seeking two in particular that were tattooed in my mind.

When I suggested the movie date to Cadence, I hadn't exactly expected Everly to want to come—not that I was complaining. *Any* amount of time spent with the both of them was a God send. However, I couldn't help but feel nervous. Going somewhere alone with Cadence would have been easier; we could have flown completely under the radar. Everly was bound to attract some attention, and the unknown variables were making me anxious.

The air seemed to become denser as Everly and Cadence stepped into the movie theater. They were wearing the same Ushanka hats that they had worn the other night to my place. They held hands as they approached me.

"Grayson! Guess what?" Cadence exclaimed as soon as she caught sight of me. She broke free of Everly's grasp and propelled her little body into my arms. "I have a loose tooth! See!" Cadence used her finger to gently wiggle her left bottom tooth.

"Impressive! I guess that means the tooth fairy is going to visit soon?" I asked her, trying to swallow back the strange lump of emotion that became lodged in my throat at the sight of her running to me.

It was hard not to be affected by the harsh truth— I'd missed out on so much already. First steps, first words, first time riding a tricycle, first day of junior kindergarten. I had only myself to blame. Or at least, the idiot I'd been before.

Everly lowered her gaze as if she could read my mind.

"Oh yeah! The tooth fairy!" Cadence smacked her forehead with her hand. I noticed for the first time that the cast was gone.

"You got your cast off!" I grinned. "Awesome, only...I never got to sign it. Guess I'll just have to sign your arm!"

"You can't draw on people, Grayson." Cadence giggled. "That's bad. You can draw on my next cast!"

"You're planning on needing another cast?" I inquired, arching a brow.

"No." Cadence giggled again, her blue eyes dancing with merriment. "But if I do you can draw on it!"

"Alright, you two." Everly laughed. "Let's go find seats." I glanced up at her voice, noticing the uncomfortable edge behind her eyes. It almost wasn't detectable, because the winning smile on her face outshined it.

I stood up slowly and glanced around. The movie theater wasn't full by any means, but I could understand Everly's discomfort. She probably wanted to get into the dark theater before anyone took notice of her.

"Everly?" I inwardly cringed when I heard someone call out to her. Everly's face paled as she worked to keep the smile on her face.

"Lindsay! Hey..."

I turned around, noticing Lindsay approaching. She hugged Everly before turning her calculating gaze to me.

"Grayson...it's been a while," she said.

I furrowed my brow, completely confused by her odd behavior. "Yeah, I guess so," I frowned, shifting my gaze to Everly's face. "I've got the tickets already, if you want to head in."

"We need popcorn, Grayson," Cadence remarked, pointing toward the concession stands where the majority of people were.

Lindsay turned her calculating eyes to Cadence, giving her a huge smile. She leaned down. "Hi, Cadence! How have you been doing?"

Cadence gave her an odd look, her furrowed brow and slight frown mirroring my own. I wanted to laugh, but there was something...uneasy about the situation. "Mommy said never to talk to strangers."

"Did she now?" Lindsay said. "Well, that's very good advice. You *shouldn't* talk to strangers, Cadence. But I'm not really a stranger. Auntie Everly and I go *way* back."

"Auntie Everly?" Cadence's frown deepened and she looked at Everly for an explanation. Lindsay smiled slowly, as if all of her suspicions were confirmed.

"How about I grab the popcorn, and you guys go grab the seats?" I said, steering Cadence away from Lindsay and toward Everly. I handed her two of the tickets and watched as they walked off toward the theater that was playing *Rio*. I waited until they were out of ear shot before turning my menacing stare on Lindsay.

"I don't know what you're playing at, but you'd better stop," I warned.

Lindsay raised her hands in mock innocence. "I'm not playing at anything," she said. "I'm just saying hi to an old friend of mine."

"Bullshit." I took a step toward her. She backed up, shock flitting across her face before she could school it in. "I saw you with that asshole at the bar. The same asshole that was following me around *and* pressing his greasy face against my living room window."

"I don't know what you're talking about." Lindsay rolled her eyes. "I see some things never change though. You're still an asshole."

"Yup," I snarled. "You'd probably do good to remember that."

"Whatever," she said, shaking her head while she glared back at me. Her hands were clenched against her sides. "You'd probably do well to remember certain things too."

Before I could ask her what that was supposed to mean, she took off, disappearing to the other half of the theater.

I felt like she'd been hinting at something crucial, but I couldn't figure out what it was. By the time I got the popcorn and joined Everly and Cadence, the encounter had slipped to the back of my mind. I sat down on the other side of Cadence, baring the requested popcorn.

"Now, I'm not sure what the rules are on pop—"

"Mommy used to say pop will rot your teeth. Mama says to listen to Mommy because Mommy knows all about teeth," Cadence remarked.

"Right." I blinked, trying to hide the pained smile. "So, instead...I got you apple juice, which probably isn't any better than pop in the sugar department, but at least there's no caffeine." I winked at Everly.

"What's caffeine?"

"Something you definitely don't need," Everly answered, hiding a smile.

I couldn't focus on the movie at all. I was too busy watching Cadence and Everly's reactions. They smiled the same and they even laughed the same. I could see bits of me in Cadence too; or at least, me when I was a kid.

I need a million more days like this, I thought.

After the strange encounter with Lindsay, I was on my guard after the moment the credits started to roll. Luckily, we didn't run into anybody familiar, but Everly was stopped a few times by eager fans requesting a photo or an autograph. There wasn't a sign of Lindsay though, and I was thankful for that.

It was dark when we exited the movie theater. We placed Cadence in her car seat and I said goodbye. "I'll see you soon, kid."

"When?" Cadence pouted.

"Very soon," I promised. "We'll do something super fun too. I have a few plans in mind."

"Oh tell me! Tell me!" she pleaded.

"You'll need to be patient for a bit. Let me talk to your mom and see what she says. I ruffled her hair affectionately before closing the door. Everly was standing beside me, having watched the scene with watery eyes.

"Well, I chalk that up for a win." I stepped towards her. Everly placed her hand on my chest, stopping me, and glanced toward the car to remind me of Cadence's presence. "She'll get used to it," I challenged, my fingers coming around her wrist firmly. I gently pulled her toward me and kissed her until she shuddered in my arms. "One more thing..." I hesitated, giving her a shy smile as I pulled away to look at her.

"What is it?"

"Are you free Saturday night? Maybe we could do another sleepover at my place? We could rent a movie. I'll teach you the gist of cooking chicken?" I knew my voice was laced with vulnerability. I couldn't even be embarrassed or mad about it. Everly had been the *only* person to ever coax that emotion out of me. Before her, I'd never given a rat's ass how I came across. I didn't worry about having my feelings burned because I didn't invest much thought into anything other than being pissed and indifferent.

This though...this entire situation shook me to my core. I'd never felt more vulnerable or exposed. I had never had more to lose before.

"Of course." Everly's smile came easily; there wasn't any hesitation in her eyes. "What time?"

"Any time after three?"

"We'll be there," Everly promised.

"I was also thinking we could spend Sunday together. There's this indoor play gym that we could go to. It's pretty cool. I've taken my sisters." I studied Everly's face. I didn't want to push her, but I knew how much she worried about overwhelming Cadence too quickly.

"That sounds awesome," Everly answered.

I couldn't stop the massive grin from lifting the corner of my lips up. "Perfect," I responded, swallowing hard. My eyes dropped down to her mouth.

She hesitated, a slow smile spreading across her face as she leaned into me for another kiss. "See you later, Grayson."

I watched as she climbed into the car and drove away before I finally turned and headed to my truck. I slowed, seeing someone leaning against it, leisurely smoking a cigarette. It was a woman wearing a long black jacket with fur trim pulled up over her head. It was dark, so I couldn't make out exactly who it was at first; all I could see was the faint glow of a cigarette while she took a drag. Then she flicked it aside, chuckling.

"Grayson Dixon," she drawled, her face finally coming into view when she angled it just right beneath the street light. Lindsay Little sneered at me, shaking her head slowly. "Did you guys really think you could fool the world?"

"What are you talking about?" I scowled, growing severely pissed off at the amount of times I'd run into this person in the last little while.

"I'm not an idiot." Lindsay rolled her eyes.

"I beg to differ," I snarled.

Her calculating eyes narrowed at me. "It's plain as fucking daylight who the real parents of that kid are."

"It's plain as fucking daylight that you're a crazy bitch," I retorted. "Get the fuck away from my truck and stay the hell away from us."

"Easy," Lindsay tittered with a sly smile as she finally pulled away from my truck and approached me. I stood still, every muscle posed and ready to fight. She stopped walking and stood in front of me, her eyes roaming the length of my body. "Do you not remember?"

"Remember what?" I demanded, my patience so thin that it was scarcely there at all.

She laughed, a sound that grated upon my nerves and made my teeth clench together in annoyance. "Oh don't act like you don't," Lindsay almost purred. "Tap's? About a year and a half ago? *Dart night*?"

I frowned, trying to recall through hazy memories exactly what she was talking about.

"You and me...fucking in the bathroom stall." Lindsay smirked, her hand reaching out to toy with the zipper of my jacket. "Don't play dumb just because your little girlfriend is back. Although...I *guess* that would put a wrench in your perfectly calculated plan to win her back, huh?"

I grabbed her hand, wrenching it away from me as if her touch was acid. Anger surging beneath my veins. "First of all, don't fucking touch me. Second, I don't remember that at all. Probably because you were so insignificant that it wasn't even worth the space in my memory."

Lindsay's smile froze and her eyes darkened. "I'd be careful if I were you."

"Is that a threat?" I asked, leaning in slightly. My eyes flashed with contempt. "The last thing you want to do is threaten me, Lindsay. Stay the fuck away."

I didn't bother giving her a chance to respond. I stomped around her, slamming the door of my truck. I didn't look her way as I peeled out of the parking lot.

My heart was pounding in my chest, my nerves were on fire and I was fucking pissed. I fished my phone out of my coat pocket, quickly dialing Katrina's number. "Hello?" she said.

"Are you working tonight?" I demanded.

"No, it's my night off for a change. Why?"

"I'll be there in ten," I growled, hanging up on her. I threw my phone down on the bench seat, my hands tightening against the steering wheel as if I could strangle it. It took me less than ten minutes to get back to Newcastle and park outside of Katrina's; I hadn't paid attention to the speed limit at all. I stomped up the steps of her porch, my knuckles rapping loudly against the front door.

She threw it open, a look of concern on her face. "What the fuck Grayson?" I never randomly showed up at her place.

"I need to talk to you." My chest was heaving and I knew I looked frantically pissed off. She stood aside, the concern on her face only amplifying. "Please tell me I didn't fuck Lindsay Little."

Katrina arched a brow, confusion lining her face for a moment before she busted out laughing. She leaned forward, clenching her stomach. Tears of laughter welled up in her eyes like I'd just delivered the best stand-up routine she'd ever witnessed.

"It's not funny!" I growled.

"I'm sorry, Grayson, but that's fucking hilarious!" She wiped a tear from her eye. Normally, I would have found the situation funny too, but not with what was at stake.

"Did I?" My heart thudded painfully in my chest. I could recall a blonde in my alcohol soaked hazy memory—several actually—but I couldn't recall a timeline or an actual face. Hell, I couldn't even recall a place. "Dart night?"

Katrina's expression softened, as if she was remembering the night with clarity. She likely was; she hadn't been drunk off her ass. "I promise you that I would *not* let you sleep with that dirty skank," Katrina assured me. "I knew you wouldn't touch her with a ten foot long pole. Besides, the *only* time that Lindsay has ever set foot in Tap's while you were there was like a week or so ago, when you came in and asked me all those weird questions."

"Then why the fuck is she claiming that we did?"

"Think about it, you fucking idiot." Katrina shook her head and started moving toward her tiny living room. "She's always been massively jealous of Everly—especially after the band made it big. She's a destructive bitch that hasn't grown up. Plus, she knows about your reputation."

"How come I can remember a blonde?"

"Because there were probably a lot of blondes." Katrina shrugged. "I'm telling you, it wasn't Lindsay Little."

The fear in my chest dissipated slightly. My hands relaxed slightly at my sides. I honestly hadn't thought I *would* screw Lindsay Little; I hated that girl in high school. But I didn't trust myself either. I'd been a self-destructive asshole, drunk more often than not and it wouldn't be the first time that I'd forgotten the name or face of someone I'd screwed. There were many faceless women on that list, I was ashamed to admit.

Katrina tilted her head, eyeing me. "What's really going on here?" She sat down on her worn sofa, crossing her legs. Her foot bounced up and down as she waited for me to talk.

"I can't tell you."

"Grayson, I promise you. I'm not about to share your lame secrets with anybody. Just tell me what's going on so I can actually *help* you."

"You were enough help. All I needed to know is that I didn't completely fuck things up with Everly," I said quickly. A part of me wanted to tell Katrina the truth about Cadence, but that felt like a betrayal to Everly, and I wasn't about to betray her again. My heart ached just thinking about it. I'd nearly crashed the truck driving like a madman to ensure that I *hadn't* actually fucked things up with my stupid dick years ago.

"Fair enough." Katrina's eyes narrowed slightly. She knew I was keeping something from her, but she knew better than to push. "Maybe you should start asking for names, or writing them down somewhere or something."

"Very funny," I snarled, stomping out of Katrina's apartment.

* * *

I didn't know what game Lindsay was playing, but for the remainder of the week my stomach was twisted in anxious knots. I needed to talk to Everly about it. I knew she wasn't dense; she knew I'd slept with more than my fair share of women, but I had to tell her with utmost certainty that I hadn't touched that crazy bitch and had Katrina to back me if necessary.

I knew how disgusting it would all sound, and I was terrified of hurting her more, but it had to be done. Full honesty and all that shit. Yeah, I fucked a lot of girls and I didn't remember them because Everly's face was all I ever saw, but at least I could promise her that I *didn't* sleep with her ex-best friend from high school. Even drunk me wouldn't have done that. I should have known that Lindsay was just stirring the pot. Still, I had feared myself enough to wonder if I had *really* self-destructed to that degree.

Katrina's explanation made perfect sense. Lindsay was jealous of Everly; it was evident in the way she talked and carried herself whenever Everly was around.

Unfortunately, I didn't get an opportunity to tell her. Cadence had started back at school, and Everly was consumed with making sure that the transition was easy for her. I was tied up at work after some setbacks on the job sight, so we didn't get to see each other until Saturday afternoon. I planned on telling her after Cadence was asleep.

I was already in the kitchen, preparing dinner when Everly pulled up. I wasn't the best cook, but I was semi-functional and my results weren't overwhelmingly disgusting. She knocked tentatively at the door as I was drying my hands on a kitchen towel.

My heart hammered in my chest as I opened the door. Cadence had a megawatt smile on her face that matched her mother's. She flew inside, wrapping her arms around my legs.

"Guess what Grayson!"

"What?" I asked, unable to stop the smile from spreading to my own lips as I looked down at her. I ruffled her hair affectionately while she peered up at me with those big blue eyes.

"Mom let me bring *Shrek the Third*!" Cadence said.

"Awesome!" I grinned back. "Guess what?"

"What?"

"I'm going to teach your mom how to cook tonight!"

"Good luck," Cadence said so gravely that I couldn't help but burst out laughing. Everly blushed and smiled, shaking her head and crouching down.

"Thanks, kid," she muttered while she helped Cadence out of her coat and boots.

"One time, she tried to make pancakes and nearly set the entire kitchen on fire!" Cadence told me with wide eyes. I chuckled, completely bewildered by just how light and happy just being in their presence made me feel.

I'd always felt right in Everly's presence, as if I belonged there, but now that feeling was amplified. I felt as if I finally had a purpose and I knew exactly what it was. I swallowed hard against the sudden lump of emotion in my throat. My jaw clenched as I looked away, trying to rein it in.

It was so fucking strange to go from repressing everything to feeling again.

Chapter Fifteen

Everly

I COULD TELL that Grayson was struggling with something. The emotions that swirled around in those ice blue eyes were heady and they made my heart stop in my chest, but I didn't want to question him or push him in front of Cadence, even though I was desperate to understand the origin of them.

Instead, I took my coat off and ushered Cadence into Grayson's living room. The Christmas tree sparkled merrily, and there were several wrapped presents underneath. Like any other child, Cadence's eyes were instantly drawn to the gifts. She raced over to them while Grayson wrapped his arms around me in greeting. He kissed me chastely, his eyes promising so much more later. I couldn't help but swoon in his arms when he looked at me like that. I knew he'd deliver his promise, and I knew I would enjoy every minute of it.

"This one says my name!" Cadence squealed suddenly, looking up with wide, astonished eyes. I furrowed my brow, looking at Grayson for an explanation. He shrugged, looking extremely sheepish. He gave me a lopsided smile and ran his hand through his hair.

"Does it now?" he asked her. He lowered his voice, placing his lips right beside my ear. "I didn't know she could read."

"Of course I can read, Grayson." Cadence rolled her eyes. "Why did you get me a present?"

"Why not?" Grayson shrugged, squeezing my hand before he released me and joined her in the living room. He crouched down. "Don't you deserve a present or two?"

Cadence thought about it for a moment and bit her lip, looking down at the present. Neither Grayson nor I missed the sadness that passed over her eyes. Cadence was young and she couldn't exactly communicate all the complicated thoughts running through her mind, but I got the impression she felt guilty. I'd had that feeling for some time now, despite the fact that Cadence didn't talk about the accident. My heart squeezed painfully in my chest.

"Do you want to open it now?" Grayson asked. He was struggling to control the emotion in his own voice as he smiled at her.

"Don't I have to wait for Christmas?" Cadence asked, peering up at me. Her brow was furrowed the same way Grayson furrowed his brow when confused.

I smiled at her. "If Grayson says it's okay, you can open it," I told her. Christmas wasn't for several more weeks, but Cadence needed this.

Grayson picked up the biggest present and handed it to her. It was wrapped expertly in silver paper with a golden ribbon tied around it. He helped her untie the ribbon and then gently pushed the present toward her, coaxing her. Cadence hesitated, her finger beneath the fold of paper.

"Go on." Grayson smiled. My heart stuttered in my chest, and it got a little harder to breathe while I watched this moment between the two of them. Cadence finally ripped into the present with the childlike joy and lack of constraint she would have shown prior to the accident. The paper fell, revealing the massive Barbie Dream House. Cadence's eyes widened with approval.

"I LOVE it!" she said with excitement. I didn't have to instruct her on manners; Julia had drilled them into her right away. She flew around the house and threw her arms around Grayson's neck, knocking him over from his crouched position. He laughed a laugh that I'd never heard before. "Thank you, thank you, thank you!"

"I guess you need to open a few more to have fun with it, huh?" Grayson asked, his eyes twinkling. He reached over and grabbed two more. "What's a Barbie house without any Barbies?"

Cadence ripped into them eagerly, revealing a pink convertible. She also got a Barbie, Ken, and Kelly doll. The emotion in my chest almost hurt. He'd chosen dolls that looked as similar to us as he could. The male Ken doll had dark hair, as did the child doll.

"Thank you!" Cadence squealed, jumping up and down while Grayson started the tedious task of removing her new toys from the boxes. He ended up having to carry the majority of them into the kitchen to use a knife, his brow furrowed as he muttered about the seemingly impossible task.

Once all of her new toys were out of the boxes, Cadence sat down in the living room to play with them. I had remained by the foyer, watching the scene unfold in front of my eyes like some kind of dream. Grayson approached me warily, as if he was afraid of getting in trouble. I smiled at him and he relaxed, his arms coming around my waist to pull me against his chest.

"How did you know?" I asked, gesturing to the impressive Barbie set up. He grinned, his eyes roaming my face.

"I do have sisters her age..." he reminded me. "I'm kind of awesome at the whole present thing."

I smiled, my lips seeking his out for a quick kiss. Cadence was so enthralled in her new toys that she didn't even notice.

"Now...can I give you your present?" Grayson asked almost shyly. The corner of his lip curved up in a smile.

"It's not Christmas yet," I pointed out.

"Well, it's not *really* a Christmas gift, angel." He shrugged, grinning wickedly at me as he pulled a small box out from his back pocket. "It's just something I saw that I needed to get for you."

I stared at the tiny box. It was clearly a jewelry box, wrapped in the same silver wrapping paper and golden ribbon as Cadence's presents. I swallowed hard, the color draining from my face.

"It's not that." Grayson smirked, seeing where my thoughts were going. He gently took my hand, flattening my palm and placing the gift in my palm.

I opened it slowly, overly aware of Grayson's eyes on me.

"Oh, Grayson...it's beautiful," I said, bringing my hand up to my mouth as I stared at the stunning white gold necklace. It was a simple, yet elegant and had a beautiful tear-shaped solitary diamond.

"I saw it and I needed to get it for you." He shrugged as if uncomfortable with my emotional response. He took it from me, removing the necklace carefully from the box. He studied it for a moment, his eyes wistful and almost sad. "I put you through so much pain in the last five years. The things you had to endure because of my stupidity...I could never make up for that, Everly. When I saw this in the display case, it reminded me of that; of the sadness and the longing that we both went through. To me, it represents the beauty in pain." He was speaking low enough so that only I would hear him. He swallowed hard, brushing aside my hair as he moved behind me to clasp it around my neck. It rested just above and between my breasts.

"It's beautiful," I said again, my eyes misting.

"Yeah...it looks fucking hot sitting there." He smirked, his fingers reaching out to brush the teardrop diamond and the tops of my breasts. I smiled, shaking my head and brushing aside his wandering hands before he could attract Cadence's attention.

"So..." he drawled, cocking his eyebrow up as if challenging me. "Shall we go teach you how to cook?"

* * *

"See? That wasn't so bad, was it?" Grayson asked several hours later, after Cadence was fast asleep in the spare bedroom. She'd fallen asleep halfway through the movie again. This time, Grayson had carried her up to bed and tucked her in with me watching from the doorway, several emotions clashing against one another at once. Happiness, hope, and love.

I shrugged, trying not to smile. It *hadn't* been too bad. In fact, it had tasted delicious despite the fact that Grayson had made me cook the chicken on my own. He'd selected the spices and garlic and stood aside with a proud smile on his lips, telling me to add a little bit of everything.

We were standing in his kitchen, having just finished tidying it up. I was leaning against the counter, my arms folded across my chest. I was having a difficult time sifting through all the emotions. Grayson seemed to notice; he tilted his head while he looked at me. His own eyes were a clashing storm of emotions as well— love, happiness, hope, regret, and desire.

"It was good," I agreed finally, my voice sounding strange even to me. Grayson's eyes locked on mine as he stalked toward me. He put his hands on either side of me, clenching the counter and caging me in, all the while his eyes fixated on me.

I exhaled, tipping my head back so our lips were separated by mere inches.

"Do you remember the first time you kissed me, angel?" Grayson asked, his voice husky with desire. His hand came up to gently stroke my jawline, his thumb brushing across my lips before dropping back down to grip the counter.

I smiled. "On Kyle's porch."

"You were drunk as fuck." Grayson chuckled, shaking his head. His eyes danced while he drank me in. "I took one look at you and just knew I was screwed."

"Why?"

"Last time we drank together, you got brave," he whispered, gently pressing his hips against mine. I could feel his arousal growing as he brushed it against my thighs. The action left a tingling sensation in its wake, instantly leaving me wanting more. "You dragged me out to the dance floor and started doing sinful things with those hips, giving me that seductive look that almost undid me. I had to run away before I had my way with you then and there."

"You wanted me?"

"Of course I wanted you." Grayson seemed surprised. "I've always wanted you, Everly. That was the problem."

"The problem?" I frowned, confused.

He nuzzled his lips against the side of my neck. His words vibrated against my skin, making my nipples harden in response. "I wanted you more than I've ever wanted anything in my life, and it fucking scared me. I got out of there because I was a coward. But when I saw you on Kyle's porch, I knew I didn't have the strength to walk away again. I knew I'd let you do whatever the hell you wanted to do to me, and I'd enjoy it."

He was impossibly hard against me now, and I was equally throbbing and aching for him too. I pressed my pelvis into his engorged cock, the sound of his tortured groan against the sensitive skin on my neck spurring me on. My hands tugged at his jeans, pulling him closer.

Grayson's hand gently gripped my wrist, pausing me in my quest to undo the stubborn button of his jeans. He pulled away slightly, his eyes brushing across my face.

"I need to tell you something before I let myself get lost in you," he murmured, his eyes dropping down to my lips.

"What?" I wondered if he could hear my heart thudding loudly in my chest. My question stirred his attention from my lips. He locked eyes with me again, his other hand tentatively reaching out to touch a wayward strand of hair. He fingered it for a moment, never breaking eye contact.

"After the movie, I ran into Lindsay again."

"Oh?" The combination of the look in his eyes and the tone of his voice had me on edge. I was dancing on his energies, and he knew it. He smiled, trying to ease my mind a little.

"She made some threats, and tried to stir the pot."

"How so?" I demanded.

Grayson sighed, his hand falling back against the counter. "Maybe we should sit down for this conversation." He sighed again and took my hand, leading me out to the living room. The TV was on, with CP 24 relaying breaking news. His eyes didn't even flutter to the screen as he sat down heavily on the couch.

My heart pounded frantically in my chest as I sat down beside him. I drew my knees up and wrapped my arms around them, as if doing so could protect me from the heavy conversation I knew we were about to have.

It had been a perfect evening, but there had been something hanging over the both of us. My unasked questions and his unasked questions looming above us like a heavy, dark cloud. I knew we had to have this conversation if we wanted to move forward, just as I knew it was going to hurt me.

"What did Lindsay say?" I knew that Lindsay was only a portion of the problem, that something else was haunting him, but I didn't know how to ask him so I started with that.

"She knows that Cadence is our daughter." He frowned, shaking his head. "Guess it's pretty fucking obvious, but I don't like that she knows."

"How did she try to stir the pot?" I asked, my voice tiny. Of course, I'd seen the look on her face at the movie theater. I knew she had guessed it.

Grayson swallowed hard. I watched his Adam's apple bob as he did so. He closed his eyes for a moment while he considered his answer. "She tried to make me think I'd slept with her."

"What do you mean?" I was confused by his vague words. They didn't make any sense to my ears. Dread overwhelmed me at the idea of them together. "Did you?" he shook his head vehemently, and I relaxed a mere fraction.

"There's something you need to understand about that...time between then and now," Grayson said, his voice raw as if the memories pained him. I felt my heart squeeze painfully in my chest and I knew that whatever he was going to tell me would test the fragile ground of our relationship. I took a deep breath, trying to steel myself against the impending heartache.

"Just tell me, Grayson," I begged. The unknown was making the air harder to take in.

"Everly..." His voice was like a plea—or a prayer. I could hear the pain in it, pain that he was desperately trying to reign in.

"I get it Grayson, you weren't in a good place...but please, be honest with me." My heart was pounding in my chest, mostly from Grayson's gutted reaction to my question.

"Once I got to Alberta, I threw out my phone. I worked, and basically... that was all I did." He winced. "When I wasn't working, I was either drinking my weight at the local bar, or..."

I knew why he didn't continue on. The regret that lined every one of his handsome features was enough of an indicator of that.

"I could never drive you from my mind," he admitted, burying his face in his hands. "I tried to, Everly. I thought it was for the best. I drank to try and forget; I bedded so many faceless women, I didn't even bother to ask names. I just wanted to try and erase it, to forget the fact that I fucked up the best thing to ever happen to me. But it never worked—none of it. I heard you everywhere. Hell, I saw you everywhere. It was no good trying to run from my past, from my mistakes...and leaving you was the biggest one. As selfish as that sounds, I didn't even think about my dad or my sisters until I came home. Then I realized the gravity of what I'd done to them."

My heart ached at his words. Of course, I'd known that Grayson likely hadn't been celibate all those years. It still stung to picture him with anybody else, but I understood. *I* hadn't been celibate either. What was I supposed to do? I thought he was gone forever. Moving on is the natural progression of things, even if it feels shitty

"Did you sleep with Lindsay?" It hurt to ask the question, but I had to know. I could maybe deal with faceless women, but not Lindsay.

"Fuck no." Grayson laughed bitterly. "She almost had me convinced, because honestly, Everly...I don't remember a single fucking thing about any of them. But then I realized that she was playing off that. Stirring the pot because she's jealous of you. But it still doesn't make me feel any better about the others."

"How do you know that?" I whispered, needing more reassurance.

He winced. "Katrina works at Tap's. She said the only time Lindsay has ever been at Tap's when I was there was a couple weeks ago...when you were already home."

"Oh." I exhaled, the relief palpable.

I tentatively reached out to touch his shoulder. He didn't flinch away from my contact; he just breathed deeply and looked at me with red-rimmed eyes. It was the closest he'd ever been to crying.

"I can't fault you for trying to move on...I tried too." He winced at my words, not seeking comfort from them. I didn't know if I intended to do that or not.

"I know I have no right to ask," he said, his tormented gaze locking on mine. I knew what he was asking, even if he couldn't let himself finish the question.

"There were just two." I looked away. "Nobody you know."

"Fuck." Grayson dropped his head back into his hands, tugging at the roots. I knew exactly what he was feeling; the same twisted jealousy and hurt I was feeling.

"Sometimes you have to lose it to understand it," I offered helplessly, my voice breaking. "We can't undo what was done between then and now. We just need to find a way to move past it." I sounded unsure because I *was* unsure. Grayson and I had both hurt each other so much that it was terrifying to try and think about how we could move past that hurt and build a strong foundation for a healthy relationship.

He gave me a lopsided smile laced with pain and hope. "When I realized that I could never forget you, that you were it for me, I told myself that *if* you came back...I'd tell you everything. I will hide nothing from you, Everly. Even if it tears me apart to admit it. I don't want secrets. I don't want you finding out about...that shit from someone who would tell you with the intent to hurt you. I hate that I did that. I hate that I have to tell you this, but I needed it to come from me." I nodded in understanding, my breath coming out in uneasy spurts.

This was a huge step for Grayson. In high school, I could count on one hand the number of times he talked about his feelings or explained his actions: almost never. He still wasn't the most articulate person when emotional, but at least he was showing it. He was stripping himself bare.

The tears welled in my eyes, and I couldn't help but cry for the heartbreak I had felt at seventeen—or the heartbreak *he* felt. I couldn't help but cry for all the years we had lost.

Grayson's hands cupped my face and he tried to brush away my tears. His eyes were tormented and I knew he would give anything to go back in time and change this so I didn't have to feel this pain. He pulled me against his chest, his arms wrapping around me.

"I'm so fucking sorry." His voice broke. "I want to be the man you deserve, Everly. Nothing has ever felt more right than being with you...and with Cadence. I want this but every time I turn around, I fuck it up some more."

"You're not fucking it up." I hiccupped, thinking about how he'd been since I got home. "It's just the past that hurts. Seeing you with Cadence, being with you now, that feels right too. But..." I trailed off, the emotion cutting off my ability to speak.

This *hurt*. It hurt in the most raw and painful way. It hurt because it couldn't be undone. It hurt because it was a part of the past and therefore, a part of the future. It hurt because I had no idea how I was supposed to let go.

"I wish I could take it all back," Grayson murmured. His lips were pressed against my hair. He took a shuddering breath. "I promise you, Everly, I will never hurt you again. I will never push you away. I should have realized this a hell of a lot sooner than I did. I was a fucking idiot."

"At least you realize it now," I said.

He snorted in agreement.

Chapter Sixteen

Grayson

IT HAD BEEN INCREDIBLY hard to look at Everly when I was laying all my ugly secrets out on the table. I knew it pained her to hear about the faceless women, the drinking—hell, even the fighting. She'd openly wept when I told her about returning home and realizing just how badly I had hurt Chloe.

I was stupid, though. I allowed myself to fester in the resentment and hatred that spilled from my mother. I allowed myself to believe that my new family didn't care, because how could they? They were happy with each other; they didn't need me. I was a black hole that made them miserable.

I bared my soul to her, every last ugly part of it that I hated. I knew in doing so that I was hurting her. Clawing at her damaged heart; the heart that *I* had damaged through my own carelessness, and that ripped me in ways I'd never felt pain before...and I'd felt *a lot* of pain. It was in my nature to be self-destructive, but this? This came from the need to purge it out and seek forgiveness.

This came from me no longer wanting to self-destruct. It came from me wanting to throw open a new chapter, not just for us, but for me too. It was a long time coming, but it was inevitable.

And she knew that. I knew by looking at her that Everly *knew it*. She saw all my ugly colors, all of my mistakes, and although they hurt her, she understood them. She understood *me*.

With all my pieces in front of her, Everly just as easily could have given up on me. She could have told me to fuck off. How easy would that have been? Pretty easy. I'd given her more than enough reasons to back away from me, to take Cadence and run. But she knew that this time I wasn't saying these things out of spite to hurt her. I was telling her because she had to know.

Everly listened almost silently, her eyes full of tears, never removing her hand from my shoulder. When her arms wrapped around me, I almost lost it.

"Where do we go from here?" My voice broke. The light kept catching on that beautiful teardrop diamond, reminding me that everything was coming full circle. I hadn't meant to spill it all out then and there; it just happened...and it had to happen.

"We move forward," she whispered into my ear. "I won't hold the past against you, Grayson...and I hope you won't hold my past against me."

As if I could ever hold the past against her. Every decision she made after walking out that door was *because* of me. Because I had forced her. Because I was gone.

My hand encompassed the back of her neck, tucking into her long layers of hair. I twisted the soft strands around my fingers, using it to guide her face to mine before I possessed her lips. I had to feel her beneath me; I needed her in the most achingly raw way.

She whimpered against me. I could feel her heartbeat increasing beneath my lips as I kissed her neck, her chin, her lips and anywhere else my lips landed. She tugged on my shirt, trying to pull it over my head without breaking the kiss. I inched away, ripping it off and casting it aside. I slipped hers off too in one quick motion, letting it fall wherever it landed. I saw nothing but Everly and her perfection. Our lips came together in a desperate tempo. Her teeth sank into my bottom lip as she pulled me back on top of her.

"Your pants need to come off now," she panted beneath me, trying to struggle with the button while I pressed my pelvis against hers.

"I couldn't agree more, angel," I almost growled. I was straining in my jeans to the point of pain. Before I handled that particular roadblock, I focused on finishing undressing her. The skin of her thigh was like ivory beneath my hand. Her eyes fluttered closed as my hand roamed upward, teasing her through her lacy thong. She whimpered again, a tortuous sound of need and pleasure. I couldn't help the smirk that accompanied such a beautiful noise.

I'd missed hearing her whimper with pleasure. I missed the way that she reacted to me. It was a stroke to the ego and the most erotic thing I'd ever experienced. When I was with her, I was completely with her. I didn't miss a single thing. I felt, rather than saw, every flutter of her lashes; every soft sigh of pleasure.

And I didn't ever want to lose that again. I couldn't.

"Grayson..." she pleaded with those luminous green eyes. "I need you now."

I didn't need to be told twice. I pulled her thong off, tossing it over my shoulder before I abandoned my jeans and boxers in a heap on the floor and dove into the greatest, most satisfying addiction I'd ever had.

* * *

Falling asleep with Everly in my arms and waking up with her warmth still encasing me like the best kind of blanket was unspeakably incredible. I couldn't help but just lie there, quietly holding her with my hand on the small of her back while I stared up at the ceiling.

I honestly never thought things would go this way. I thought I'd fucked it up so badly that the moment she saw me again, she would throw things at me and demand that I get out of her life.

And I would have; I would have done whatever Everly told me to do without question. I was lucky enough that Everly could see past her heartbreak and let me in...even a little. I knew she still hesitated—how could she not? But the way that she melted against my touch was enough for me. More than enough; it was more than I deserved.

"What are you thinking about?" Her voice was gentle, but it still surprised me. I hadn't realized that she was awake yet. I was too locked in my head as I laid there, enjoying the feeling of her against me, the feeling of her finally being in my arms once again.

"About us," I answered, my voice rough from sleep, lack of use and emotion.

Everly smiled slowly. "What about us?" she whispered.

"About how lucky I am," I answered, the lump in my throat getting bigger as my other hand came to brush against the necklace I'd given her yesterday. It rested between her breasts, glinting in the early morning light. Last night, it had served as a reminder of the pain I'd caused. Today, I was looking at it with new meaning. Hope.

"I'm hungry," Cadence's voice came timidly from the hallway. I lifted my head up, grinning at her. She was rubbing the sleep from her eyes, almost pouting. At the sight of our daughter in the doorway, my grip tightened around Everly. It was still surreal to me.

"Okay, go on downstairs and check on your Barbies. We'll be right down, alright?" Everly smiled. Cadence nodded, shuffling back out of our room and disappearing. I could hear the soft gentle fall of her feet descending the stairs. Everly stretched against me before sitting up, a vulnerable look on her face.

"What?" I asked, almost amused.

"We need to tell her. Today." Everly bit her lip, looking down at the sheet that she had pulled up over her breasts.

"So, let's tell her then." I sat up and shrugged, feigning confidence as if the mere idea didn't terrify me when it absolutely did.

"You make it sound so simple." She smiled sadly, shaking her head.

I caught her chin between my forefinger and thumb, gently lifting her face so that her eyes locked with mine. I brushed the pad of my thumb over her lips, enticing a shiver of pleasure from her. "There isn't a single thing about you or me that has ever been simple. I don't know about you, angel, but...I like that about us," I drawled.

She inhaled sharply before my lips brushed against hers. I kissed her slowly, savoring it and smiling against her lips as she sighed in blissful response.

When I pulled away, I left my fingers on her chin, drawing power from the affected way she bit her lower lip. Any other time, I would have given in and ravaged her then and there—and I knew she was thinking along the same lines I was—but I could hear the distant sounds of Cadence playing in the living room, and I wasn't exactly skilled at my stealthy moves when it came to Everly. I liked to take my time with her.

"Well, we might as well do this." Everly sighed again, this time with apprehension. I knew she was terrified of confusing Cadence. I squeezed her hand reassuringly before I pulled myself out of bed.

"Cadence is definitely important," I remarked, ruefully shaking my head and almost chuckling as I stood before my dresser, searching for clothes.

"And what do you mean by that?"

My eyes found hers from across the room. "Because nobody else would have been able to get me out of that bed with you."

Everly laughed lightly and blushed. "Well, it's a good thing we have a personal alarm clock, then. We wouldn't want to miss going to that castle place today."

After dressing, we went down the stairs together. Everly had her arms crossed, giving me a tentative smile before she sank down on the floor beside Cadence. Cadence was playing quietly with her Barbie dolls and house.

I didn't bother asking what they wanted to eat; I just set to work making a breakfast of epic proportions like last week. I called to them when it was ready to go, and they walked in as I set three heaping plates on the kitchen island.

"That's *a lot* of food," Cadence remarked, her eyes wide as Everly helped her up onto the stool.

"Yeah, but you did so good last time, I figured you'd be interested in another challenge." I smirked.

"What kind of challenge?" Cadence questioned, her brow lifting in the same way mine perpetually did. My smile widened and my breath caught in my lungs. It was still surreal to see so many signs of myself in such a perfect being. It was impossible to carry around any hate for myself when I looked at Cadence.

"If you eat *all that*, we can go somewhere fun today."

"Where?" Cadence inquired, still not touching her food.

"Do you know of *Fairytale Palace*?" Cadence's face lit up as if I'd just told her she had won the lottery. "If you eat all of that, we'll go there."

She didn't need to be told twice; she dove in with the biggest grin on her face. Everly's eyebrows were raised, and I could tell that she was impressed.

"It's a talent I have." I shrugged.

"Oh, I know that talent." She smirked. "You could sweet talk the Statue of Liberty into giving you her torch."

I snorted, shaking my head at her analogy.

We ate in silence for the most part, with me standing on the other side of the island, Everly and Cadence sitting on the stools. Everly kept watching me, taking sensual bites of her sausage with a deadly serious look on her face. I knew she was just kidding around, but it didn't stop my pants from straining uncomfortably. I lowered my eyes at her, promising retaliation for her teasing later, and she grinned.

"I can't anymore." Cadence pouted, pushing her halfway finished plate away and dropping her head down on the counter.

I grinned. "That's good enough. We can still go," I told her, clearing the plates from the counter as she cheered.

"Now, Cadence...there's something we need to tell you," Everly said.

Cadence turned her blue eyes to Everly's face. "I promise I'll be good! I'll listen when you say it's time to go and I won't talk to any strangers!" she said solemnly.

Everly smiled. "That's good, but that's not what we need to talk to you about." Everly's voice wavered as she looked at me. I came back to stand before the counter. "So, you know that you came from my tummy, right?" Cadence nodded, her eyes quietly assessing Everly. "Well, I had to have help to make you, right?"

"I guess so." Cadence's face squished up with confusion.

"Well...Grayson helped me make you." Everly smiled, looking at me nervously.

My heart was pounding frantically in my chest, and emotion choked me, but I didn't show it. I kept a passive yet friendly smile on my face as Cadence's eyes slowly swept over to me. She studied me for a moment.

"So...is Grayson my daddy?"

I swear my heart stopped hearing those words coming from her. I swallowed hard, the minutes standing still.

"Yes," Everly answered.

"I always wanted a daddy. Everyone else has one—except for Lily. Her daddy went to heaven but she still has one I guess..." Cadence frowned thoughtfully. "Do I call you Grayson or Daddy?"

"You call me whatever you're comfortable calling me," I said, my voice raw. "If you want to call me Grayson for now, you can. If you want to call me Daddy...well, you can do that, too."

"What do you want?"

"Cadence, I'm happy with whatever makes *you* happy. I don't want you to feel pressured either way." I leaned forward when I spoke, making sure that my eyes never wavered from Cadence's face. It didn't matter what I wanted, and I basically already had it. I had the opportunity to get to know our daughter, to start anew with Everly. That was more than I could have ever asked for and more than I ever imagined five weeks ago— that was for damn sure.

I used to tell myself I'd tell Everly how I felt if I ever saw her again, but I never truly imagined a positive outcome. After all, she was a successful star, and I was the idiot who burned her in high school. Telling her would have just been a way for me to know that I'd truly done everything I could have to make things right, no matter what her answer was.

But this...this went beyond a happy ending. It was exactly what I needed and hadn't known I wanted.

"I'll have to think about it, but I'm glad I have a daddy now," Cadence said. Everly brushed a tear away quickly before Cadence turned to look at her. "Where was he before?"

This was the question we were both dreading. Everly took a deep breath, her eyes rising to meet mine. "He didn't know, or he would have been here."

"Why didn't he know?"

"You'll understand this bit when you're older...but you don't know right away when you make a baby. It takes time, and Grayson had to go away for a while...for work." Everly was almost stuttering, but she was doing a better job than I was. I couldn't even form words.

"Like you?" Cadence's eyes fixed back on Everly. She winced a little.

"Yup, but now we're here and we aren't going anywhere," I told her, finally finding my voice. "So, let's start today off with a trip to *Fairytale Palace*, shall we?"

"Okay." Cadence nodded. "That sounds good. Can I play with my Barbies for a bit?"

"Of course." Everly smiled, standing up to help her down from the stool. We watched her head out to the living room before turning to face each other. "Well, that went better than I expected."

"I told you there wouldn't be a problem." I shrugged, forcing a smile. I turned back to the counter, needing to busy my hands. I scraped the plates, rinsed them off and loaded the dishwasher, all the while feeling Everly's eyes on my back. I felt her move in behind me then her arms came around my waist.

"Are you okay?" she whispered against my back.

"Yeah." I took a shaky breath, swallowing hard as I turned to face her.

"Was it a mistake to tell her?" Everly asked, the vulnerability detectable in her eyes and face.

I cupped her face with my hands. "No, angel. It wasn't. I'm just..." I searched her eyes as if I could somehow find a way to convey my feelings. I swallowed again. "You know that intense feeling you got the first time you held her? The first time it truly sunk in that you were her mother?" she nodded. "Well, that. I guess."

She smiled, her eyes welling with tears. I brushed them away from her cheeks with my thumb. "Is it a good thing?" she whispered.

"Of course it is. It's the best thing ever." The words came out without me having to even think about them. I was sure that this was the best thing that I had yet to experience. I kissed her slowly, pulling her against me. "You really are my angel, you know that?"

She laughed lightly with disbelief.

"No, you are," I insisted, turning her chin upward so that she had to look at me. "You've brought light into my life, and hope. Even when I did nothing to deserve it...you're my savior."

Everly didn't respond; she just melted into my arms, her lips parted slightly with open invitation.

Chapter Seventeen

Everly

WE WALKED ACROSS the snowy parking lot of *Fairytale Palace* with Grayson's hand on the small of my back and me holding Cadence's hand. She was practically skipping with excitement. I felt jittery, almost like I was about to go on stage and perform, when I was really just going to take my daughter to an indoor play structure that supposedly looked like something out of a fairytale.

"Maybe this wasn't a good idea." I worried my lip, looking at the building as if there was really a fire breathing dragon inside.

"Come on, Mama, can't I play for a little bit?" Cadence pleaded.

Grayson arched his brow up, grinning. "I don't think you have anything to worry about," he said mysteriously, opening the door for me. I narrowed my eyes at him, not trusting the look on his face in the slightest. I didn't have much of a choice, though; Cadence was tugging on my arm hard enough to dislocate her own. I followed her warily inside.

"It's empty." I frowned, peering around the entrance room. There were several cubby shelves for boots and hooks for coats, all of them vacant.

"I know." Grayson grinned, winking. "I rented out the space. I hope you don't mind, but I invited just four other people. Two of them are your age, Cadence. They'll be here any minute."

"Yay!" Cadence squealed, releasing my hand and rushing to take off her coat and boots. She carefully put them in an empty cubby and attempted to reach one of the coat racks. Grayson took her jacket off her and hung it up with ease, grinning with just as much excitement as Cadence was vibrating with.

"Who are the other people?" I asked, slowly slipping out of my coat.

"My dad, my step-mom, and my two little sisters." Grayson shrugged. "I knew coming here wasn't going to be a good idea unless I booked the whole thing, but I still wanted Cadence to have fun with other kids and, well...they're the only other kids I know." Grayson frowned, scratching his head as if it suddenly occurred to him that I may not be okay with that.

I forced a smile. I was nervous—of course I was nervous. I'd never met Grayson's family before, and I knew they knew about Cadence and me. I wasn't entirely sure how warm their reception would be toward me, but I could see Grayson's point. He just wanted to do something fun for Cadence while still avoiding anything similar to the movie theater situation.

"Okay," I said, shrugging out of my coat and boots as a young girl bounced into the room. She was wearing a *Fairytale Palace* t-shirt and a mega-watt grin.

"Welcome to *Fairytale Palace*!" she said, crouching down to look at Cadence. "Have you been here before?"

"No but *all my friends* have!" Cadence said, practically jumping up and down.

The girl smiled. "Well, you're in for a treat! I'm Becky...what's your name?" she asked. Becky was around sixteen years old with long brown hair braided over her shoulder. She had a soft mannerism about her, and gentle brown eyes that smiled warmly at Cadence.

"Cadence!"

"Okay, Cadence, do you mind if I get you guys wrist bands? The wrist bands are for the food and beverages. You get scanned every time you want something so that you don't need to pay until the end," Becky explained, stepping behind the reception counter.

"Sure." Grayson stepped forward first, holding out his wrist. She expertly placed the band around it and moved on to Cadence, then did mine.

"Perfect!" Becky grinned, avoiding looking directly at me. I knew she recognized me by the way she averted her gaze. Her hands kept shaking while she put the band around my wrist, but she was working her hardest to appear unaffected, which I found admirable. Most teenage girls couldn't help but do the ear-piercing screech when they noticed someone famous out in public. "Why don't you come on back and I'll give you a little tour."

"Sounds great." I nodded, smiling warmly at her. She smiled shyly back and took Cadence's hand to lead us through the doors that separated the entrance room to the food area. Grayson gently guided me by the small of my back. The food area had plenty of tables and comfortable looking sofas for parents to sit, and a concession stand with empty warming ovens and several coffee makers. The room was empty, naturally, but I got the impression that it was pretty uncommon for a Sunday afternoon.

"Brock will get you any food or drinks, so just see him if you want a coffee or anything. There are cold beverages in the refrigerator and some snacks for the kids. We also have fresh muffins and croissants. We have pizza delivered around noon, and we'll be putting on hot dogs soon as well," Becky explained, gesturing to the room.

"Wow, this is incredible," I said, my eyes widening as I took in the space. It truly did look like something out of a fairytale book.

Becky grinned happily. "Thank you! My parents built this place for me, actually," she gushed, turning a bright shade of red. "I was obsessed with Disney princesses growing up, and prior to this, there weren't any indoor play areas locally. It made for long and boring winters. I wasn't able to play outside like the other kids—I had a terrible immune system. I was premature at birth and my lungs were under-developed. I'm better now though, but I do have asthma...anyway, my parents got the idea and I sort of got to pick out what I wanted for it..." Becky's face grew redder with each word as she realized I was listening raptly to her explanation.

"So this was your vision?" I arched a brow, deeply impressed.

"Well, I guess so." Becky seemed uncomfortable with the attention. She forced another bright smile and looked down at Cadence. "Who's your favorite Princess?"

Cadence bit her lip shyly. "Fiona!"

"Fiona as in Shrek and Fiona?" Becky prompted, grinning. "I like her too! My favorite is Belle though. I like to read."

"You look like Belle," Cadence remarked, blinking up at her with wide blue eyes. Becky grinned.

"Aww, thank you! That's very sweet. Do you want to go check out the playroom?"

"Maybe we could wait a little? The other girls will be here any minute," Grayson interjected hopefully. We both knew that if we lost Cadence to the playroom, we likely wouldn't get her back any time soon. He was excited for his family to meet her, so I nodded my agreement.

Cadence nodded as the door chimed, alerting us to the arrival of the rest of our little party. We turned, seeing two fair-haired little girls approaching.

"This is the coolest thing EVER!" the taller one yelled. "It's practically empty! The girls caught sight of us and raced up to Grayson with excited expressions on their similar faces. They all but tackled him, each grabbing hold of Grayson's legs.

"Ah, speak of the devils. These are my sisters, Chloe and Jocelyn. Girls, this is Everly and Cadence." Grayson grinned, affectionately hugging them with one hand each before gesturing to us each in turn.

The taller girl, Chloe, gazed up at me with the same piercing blue Dixon eyes and that miss-nothing stare. "So *you're* Grayson's girlfriend?"

"I guess I am," I answered, trying to hide a smile.

"Do you kiss him and stuff? Because that's *gross*," Chloe said, crossing her arms and frowning.

"No way! That *is* gross. Besides, I wouldn't want to get cooties." I winked, earning a smirk from Grayson.

Chloe giggled, turning her gaze to Cadence. "Hi, I'm Chloe. This is my sister Jocelyn. She's six and I'm almost nine. How old are you?"

"Four," Cadence responded shyly, dropping her gaze to the floor.

"I've never seen it this empty," a woman's voice said. I looked up to see a taller version of the girls approaching us with a friendly smile. I froze, my smile stuck in place as I watched Grayson's dad and step-mom approach.

I'd met Grayson's step-mom, Vanessa, once. It was shortly after I'd found out I was pregnant, when I'd gone to Grayson's house to try and find out where he was. I felt like I had to tell him. Vanessa had been sympathetic and sweet, but hadn't had any information to give me.

Grayson's dad looked like an older version of him. The same dark hair, the same ice blue eyes, the same Adonis features and sinewy build. The only differences between the two were that Grayson was taller and his father had gray lining his dark hair. His middle was rounder with the accompanying pouch that came with age and comfort. It was obvious he had once been every bit as fit as Grayson. It was easy to see where Grayson got his good looks; his father was quite the attractive specimen.

From the resentment and hatred that Grayson had once carried for his father, I expected him to put me on edge. I expected him to be an angry individual—the villain, more or less. But there was a warmth behind his eyes that set my nerves at ease. He carried himself with quiet dignity, confidence and the self-assurance of a man who was happy with his life's decisions and where they had brought him. His arm was wrapped affectionately around his wife's shoulders, and the love he felt for her radiated off them both. It was magical to witness.

More surprising was how he looked at me. I expected Grayson's father to be angry at me for keeping Cadence a secret. After all, Cadence had lived one town over for the last five years, and he hadn't known about her. Instead of anger, he looked at me with gentle understanding, and he smiled at me as if he didn't hate me for keeping his granddaughter a secret all these years.

His eyes welled up a little as he looked down at Cadence, but he cleared his throat quickly, not wanting to frighten her with a huge display of emotion.

Grayson cleared his throat, his hand pressing firmly against my back as if he needed to ground himself. I could feel the nervousness rolling off him in waves, although he did his best to act indifferent to the awkward situation. "Everly, this is my father, Dale Dixon, and my lovely step-mom, Vanessa," he said. "Dad, Vanessa...this is Everly and Cadence."

"Hi," I murmured, feeling suddenly shy, awkward and completely inadequate. I could perform in a stadium in front of thousands of screaming people. I could carry myself like the shining star I'd been combed over to be on the red carpet, but apparently, I couldn't meet my boyfriend's family without turning into a knobby kneed thirteen year old.

"It's nice to finally meet the girl that has captivated Grayson's heart," Dale said, stepping forward to shake my hand. He had a gentle yet firm grip, and I could sense no animosity coming from him. "And you. Aren't you a pretty little thing!" Dale added, grinning down at Cadence fondly. Cadence peered up at him shyly, whispering a soft hello.

"Can we go play now?" Chloe almost whined, her patience slipping away as she gazed with obvious longing toward the playroom.

"I can take them back if you want," Becky offered. She grinned when we nodded our approval. "Come on girls!"

"Have fun!" I said, squeezing Cadence's hand before Chloe and Jocelyn ushered her into the play room, followed closely by Becky.

"The coffee here is pretty good," Vanessa said. "I take the girls here once every couple of weeks, or I pawn them off on Grayson." She seemed to sense that I needed a moment, and gently tugged on Dale's sweater to make him follow her over to the concession stand after giving me another warm, encouraging smile.

Grayson stepped closer to me, his arm coming around my waist again. "Are you okay?" he whispered, his lips close to my ear.

"Yeah, I am." I smiled, surprised at how true that was.

* * *

"I feel like I haven't seen you guys in forever." I sighed, relaxing into the sofa. My parents had gone out for the evening, leaving me and a sleeping Cadence home alone. Tomorrow morning Grayson would be picking me up for the airport and we would be going to LA for four days so I could tie up ends there.

I'd been so busy the last three days with Cadence's schedule. Between school, her after school activities, and our quick dinners at Grayson's house, I'd barely had time to sit down and process anything.

Like how incredible things felt with Grayson, for example. Or all of the things that I'd learned about him. Or the Lindsay thing.

Luckily, Aubrey had heard about the trip to LA and insisted on doing a girls' night before I left. I happily obliged. I hadn't really gotten a chance to see them in a while, and it would be nice to gain some insight from them.

"I know," Aubrey murmured in agreement. She took a sip of wine, her eyes appraising me carefully. "So, what's happening lately with the whole Grayson thing?"

"A lot, actually." I sighed, eyeing her warily. I knew it was just like them to dive straight into the hottest, most challenging topic. I absently touched the necklace at my neck. "We've been talking a lot...and honestly, I'm still a little scared."

"That's normal." Aubrey nodded. "I sense a but?"

"But he's never been like this with me before," I trailed off again, glancing at the TV. We had some cheesy romantic comedy on that none of us were paying attention to. "I knew in high school that he cared about me... a lot. I would even say he loved me then, but he wasn't committed to me. He was too busy keeping the walls up, too busy focused on his problems and his demons. There were moments—tons of moments—where I felt he wasn't holding back at all, but there were also tons of moments where I knew he was...where he was purposely pushing me away."

"Mmmhmm." Alicia raised her eyebrows and pursed her lips. She knew exactly what I was talking about, and so did Aubrey.

"But this time...he isn't holding anything back. He's still not the best at talking about it, but he's *showing* me. He's stripped himself bare so many times to show me all the pain and regret. He looks at me like I'm all he sees."

"He always did that, the looking at you like you were all he sees thing," Aubrey pointed out with a dismissive wave of her hand. "Probably because you *are* all that he sees. But go on..."

"He's been honest…" I sighed. "Brutally honest, to the point where it hurt me physically. He told me what he did the last five years and..."

Aubrey and Alicia exchanged a look, as if that didn't surprise them. I swallowed hard. "I mean, I wasn't celibate in his wake either."

"I know." Aubrey said. "You can't exactly punish him for his stupidity. I bet he didn't think you'd come back, and he certainly didn't think he'd stand another chance."

"Nope, he definitely didn't," I shook my head ruefully. Grayson had made it clear time and time again that he'd hoped for another chance, but hadn't counted on it happening. I raised my eyes, meeting both my friends' gentle gazes. "He told me that Lindsay is trying to stir the pot."

"Doesn't surprise me," Alicia muttered darkly. "What's she doing now?"

"She tried to insinuate that she was one of the...girls." The thought of it still stung.

"And do you believe that she wasn't?" Alicia wasn't asking to be cruel; she genuinely wanted to know.

"He says she wasn't, and he seems sure of it. If I really wanted proof, I guess I could go to Katrina..."

"Why Katrina?" Aubrey asked, her eyes narrowing. I'd told her exactly what I'd walked in to all those years before, and she definitely didn't have the highest opinion of Katrina Underhill.

"Because she works at Tap's." I shrugged.

"I'd have to agree with Grayson," Alicia muttered. "I saw her at the funeral, and I saw him in passing too. Lindsay didn't look at him the way she looked at the people she's been with. Trust me, I know how she looked at those guys. She stared at him in her calculating, deceitful way. Remember the way she'd get before she'd do something dramatic?" Aubrey and I nodded. "Well, she had that look about her. I didn't think anything of it because it's Lindsay."

"What's the worst she could do?" Aubrey wondered aloud.

"Quite a bit." I sighed dryly. "At least when it comes to the media and stuff...she knows about Cadence."

"How?" Alicia and Aubrey said simultaneously.

"She ran into us when we went to the movies that night and she told Cadence that she was a friend of 'Auntie Everly'." I massaged my temple, feeling the beginning of a migraine coming on. I had tried my absolute hardest to *not* stress about Lindsay, but the seeds of worry kept creeping up on me when I least expected. I hadn't stopped looking over my shoulder for the last several days, convinced that something was going to happen.

"Shit." Aubrey shook her head. "What a conniving twat." Alicia chortled in agreement.

"It doesn't matter." I sighed. "The truth is bound to come out sooner or later. I just need to get through this week...and this LA trip. I have to get my house on the market and tell the label I'm not doing the tour."

If the media caught wind of my early retirement before the label found out, I was in for it. But I knew that my secret was safe with Aubrey and Alicia. They'd protected much more serious secrets for me before.

I couldn't help but smile. It was good to have friends that I *knew* had my back, even if I'd let them down in the past by being too consumed with my own life to inquire about theirs.

"Then you'll be home for good?" Aubrey asked. I nodded in response, holding my wine glass up. "Well good. Home suits you. You look happier."

"*Grayson* suits her," Alicia corrected, smirking a little. I shot her a look and she shrugged. "It's not a bad thing."

"You used to think it was," I pointed out, recalling all the warnings Alicia had given me in high school.

"True," Alicia said thoughtfully. "But that was before. This is now. He's changed, you've changed. You've experienced life without him and now I think that you're choosing him because you want to, not because you feel you need to."

Aubrey and I both gaped at her. "Holy shit, Alicia. That's deep. Where the hell did all that wisdom come from?"

"I took a couple of psychology courses." Alicia shrugged again, taking a sip of her own wine. "It helps with the whole 'art therapy' thing if you actually know a little bit about the human mind and all that. Plus there's the fact that he came back and told you everything. He gave you every reason to walk away, not because he was trying to push you away but because he wanted you to know the truth when you made your decision. He didn't have to do that."

"Touché," I responded, frowning thoughtfully. "Well, you're right. Of course, the prospect of not forgiving him has come up—*several times* I might add—but that just felt wrong. Forgiving him felt right. For so long, I've felt like a crucial part of me has been missing, and I *hate* saying that because it sounds so helpless. I mean, it's not like I couldn't function without him—I did function. But I just missed that part. It was like... missing a limb. You can make do without it, you can learn to walk again or use a prosthetic limb, but you still *miss* it. You still long for it...and given the chance, I don't know one person who wouldn't choose to have it back."

Aubrey made a funny face and picked up the wine bottle, turning it around to read the ingredients.

"What are you doing?" Alicia asked, trying to stifle a giggle.

"There must be something in this shit. It's making you guys all wise and it's seriously beginning to wig me out," Aubrey responded, setting her glass down on the end table after giving it a distrustful glance.

Alicia and I looked at each other and exploded into a fit of giggles. After several long minutes, I was finally able to calm down enough to wipe the tears of laughter from my eyes and give Aubrey a stern look. "What about you?" I demanded.

"What about me?"

"Marcus, duh," Alicia clarified, rolling her eyes.

Aubrey grabbed her glass again, taking a deep sip and looking everywhere but at us. "I don't know, okay? He's just...we're just...we've both changed."

"Change isn't exactly a bad thing, you know," Alicia pointed out.

"Thank you, oh wise love guru. How is Mandy doing?" Aubrey responded dryly.

"Ouch." Alicia pouted. "Okay, that's not my fault. She wasn't ready to tell her parents the truth about us. I'm tired of living in closets. I don't live in my own anymore, and I don't want to live in someone else's either. Don't try and pass the buck on to me, Missy. You and Marcus need to have a serious re-haul."

"She's right, you know," I said, using my best Morgan Freeman voice, which admittedly wasn't very good. Aubrey threw a couch pillow at my face to shut me up. I deflected it with my forearm and continued on. "Seriously, I spend a lot of time with Marcus and I know he's not over you.

You're not over him either, and the only thing keeping you apart is apparently his status as a 'celebrity' and the whole touring thing, which probably won't be a problem since I'm bailing on the band."

"Oh shut up." Aubrey rolled her eyes, irritated by the pitiful dig at myself. "You know they're fine with it, and you aren't bailing out. You had a family emergency."

"Whatever, the point is...what's the excuse now?" I asked.

"What's yours?" she retaliated, smirking.

"That doesn't even make sense." I rolled my eyes.

"Doesn't it?" she countered coyly, taking a slow sip of wine.

* * *

The next morning came quickly, and with it, a wine headache of epic proportions. It probably wasn't my best decision to drink a bottle of wine before I had to get up at three in the morning, but still.

Grayson pulled up to my parents' house at the ass crack of dawn. I stepped out onto the front porch, closing the door behind me. I carried a small luggage bag and my purse. My tired eyes lifted, noticing the vehicle he'd chosen to drive. My jaw went slack then I let out a dazzling smile as I stared at the green truck.

He stepped out, opening the passenger door for me. I climbed in, my eyes quickly finding the halo that still hung from the rear view mirror. I grinned, shaking my head. I couldn't believe he had held on to it all these years.

"I would have never pegged you for the sentimental type," I commented, my finger gently reaching out to brush against it as the memories of that night flooded back.

"I'm not." he shrugged. "At least, not usually." He sent me a meaningful grin before his hand caught my chin and directed my gaze back to his face. My heart pounded in response; I loved it when he took control like that. He stared into my eyes for a moment before he tenderly kissed me.

I kissed him back, my hand coming up to the back of his neck. My lips parted slightly, allowing his tongue entrance. I could feel his growing arousal as he pulled away regrettably, leaving me wanting so much more. From the carnal longing in his eyes, he was fighting the same disappointment, but we were on a schedule and if we didn't get to the highway soon, we'd get stuck in traffic.

"Plenty of time for that later," I agreed, playfully shoving him away so I could regain my composure. Suddenly, my wine headache didn't feel so bad.

I was quiet during the drive to the airport. I was worrying about Cadence, wondering if she'd have any issues while I was away. I was excited to spend the weekend with Grayson, of course, but that worry set heavily in my stomach and I knew that it wasn't going to go away any time soon.

"She'll be alright, right?" Grayson asked, needing the reassurance himself. I knew the whole daughter thing was new to him, and it was probably shocking just how much worry came with it.

"I'm sure she will be," I answered with confidence I certainly didn't feel. "She hasn't had a nightmare since she met you—I'm not counting the window lurker; that obviously wasn't a nightmare. Besides, I know my parents can handle her. She used to stay over there every weekend."

"Aren't you worried?" Grayson's brow furrowed as he attempted to understand these new found feelings.

"Of course I'm worried, Grayson." I looked at him as if he were obtuse. "The worry never goes away. It gnaws on my stomach whenever I leave her." I didn't say it, but I figured that I deserved it.

He reached across the bench seat, taking my hand in his and squeezing it gently. "She'll be okay," he said, trying his best to be reassuring.

We didn't say anything else for the remainder of the drive. Grayson's attention was diverted when we started merging into the busy city of Toronto.

Finding parking was a struggle, of course. The tiny airport parking lot was a joke for its actual size. Somehow, Grayson expertly managed to park the truck in a tight parking spot, making my eyes widen with shock.

"I don't know how you do that," I remarked, shaking my head.

"What, park?" He chuckled. I rolled my eyes and he sent me a wicked grin before he jumped out. He met me beside his truck and took my bag from me. His eyes made me take pause, and his free hand came up through my open jacket to squeeze my hip. He pressed me against the side of his truck, the playful, carnal look in his eyes taking my breath away. "Are you thinking what I'm thinking?" He asked, gently pressing his pelvis against me before his lips crashed against mine. He kissed me like he had all those nights ago, and it was almost like we were back in Zoe's drive way. He finally released me, leaving me panting.

"You're a jerk." I rolled my eyes at the smug look on his face. "Have fun getting through security with that," I added, gesturing to the noticeable bulge in his pants.

He laughed as I frantically made sure that all of my hair was tucked under my gray beanie and put on a pair of thick sunglasses. He eyed me with amusement. "Do you think that'll help disguise you?"

"Usually does," I responded, attempting to grab my bag from him. He moved it just out of my grasp, grinning wickedly.

"Maybe...for Prince Eric," he snorted with amusement at his own joke then raised an eyebrow at the confused look on my face. "You know? *The Little Mermaid*?"

"Right." I smirked.

"What?" He shot me a look. "It was my favorite movie growing up. Ariel is hot." He shrugged as if it couldn't be helped. His eyes danced with amusement. My breath caught in my throat as I stood, captivated by him. "What is it?" he asked, his smile fading slightly.

I took a moment to consider my words before I replied. "In high school, there was a storm brewing behind your eyes more often than not. Torture, pain, anger, passion...and very rarely the carefree happiness and lightness that I see right now..." I trailed off, shaking my head.

"It's because I have you back, and I'm not going to fuck it up this time." He swallowed hard and stepped toward me. His face was like an open book to all the emotion he felt. All the need, all the love and the vulnerability he felt in that moment was written as clearly as if they were words on a page.

Chapter Eighteen

Grayson

IT HAD BEEN A LONG, slow and tedious process to let go of the bitter resentment and hatred I carried around with me for so long, and I hadn't even realize how much progress I had made until Everly came back into my life. Maybe it was because of her, or maybe something just clicked in me, realigning everything so it all made more sense. Whatever it was, I was thankful for it. It felt good to be free; it felt good to embrace the goodness with her...and with Cadence.

She stood staring at me for several long minutes, a bewildered look on her face as if she had realized that I truly *did* mean everything I said, and it wasn't just her trying to romanticize things. I tilted my head, curious. "Is everything okay?"

"Everything is fine," she said after finally dropping her gaze, but not before she gave me a secret smile. "Let's go."

I followed her through the confusing maze of the airport, my eyes constantly coming back to her perfect ass in those sinful tights.

"The label sent the company jet," she told me, turning to speak to me over her shoulder while she continued walking. She caught me checking out her assets and grinned slowly. "I think you'll love it," she added mischievously. I smirked, eagerly lapping up that suggestion.

One bonus of the company sending their jet was that our wait time was significantly shorter than the wait time of any other travelers that morning—within ten minutes, the flight attendants were letting us board. Once inside, I could easily see the multiple bonuses that came from flying in a company jet.

It was absolutely nothing like flying commercial. There were about eight full swivel seats and so much leg room I couldn't help but relax into the seat as the pilot prepared for takeoff. The flight attendant showed us where the exits were and gave a run down on what to do in case of an emergency. I completely tuned her out, not needing to add any more fuel to the fire when it came to my anxiety toward flying.

"Please keep your seat belts on while we take off," the pilot instructed as the flight attendant disappeared to wherever it was flight attendants went when they weren't roaming the cabin showing us how to buckle up.

I gripped the armrests of the chair tight enough to turn my knuckles white and send a shock of pain up through my nailbeds. I gritted my teeth, trying to ignore the unpleasant lurching sensation in my stomach. It felt as if I had left my stomach on the ground when we took off.

"Is everything okay, Grayson?" Everly's voice was lined with concern.

"Yup," I croaked in response. I knew she didn't buy it for a minute. A moment later, the most ridiculous Cheshire-cat smile spread on her face. "Are you enjoying this?" I grunted, closing my eyes as the jet hit turbulence and rocked back and forth.

"Of course not." Her strange smile faded quickly and she bit her lip to keep it away. I couldn't argue with her; I was too busy trying not to throw up the empty contents of my stomach. I didn't know what was worse, the sensation of leaving it behind, or the sudden sensation of it shooting back to me like a goddamn boomerang.

Half an hour later, the jerking movements stopped and the pilot informed us that we were now free to move around the cabin. The flight attendant quickly stopped by to offer us refreshments and after fetching us a glass of water each, she left us on our own again. I couldn't speak until I'd had several sips of my water. My throat was too dry.

"I thought you were afraid of heights. How do you fly so calmly?" I demanded, finally finding my voice.

"I am still afraid of heights," she admitted. "I just don't think about it. Flying is just a part of the job." She shrugged. She couldn't seem to stop the smile from touching those plump lips again. "Cadence is a calmer flyer than you."

"Well, how many times has she done it before?"

"A lot." She smiled. "Julia would bring her out several times every year. She loves the plane."

"She definitely doesn't get that from me," I remarked. Before Everly could respond, we hit turbulence again. It only lasted a few minutes, but my body was rigid with anxiety.

"Besides," she added, leaning forward so that she was closer to me. My eyes slowly opened, heat rolling beneath them as I noticed the playful glint to hers. "It's much easier to join the mile high club. The bathroom in this jet is a little bigger."

My eyebrows shot up, almost disappearing into my hairline. My fear of flying seemed to fade almost completely, drowned out by the way Everly was suggestively looking at me and biting that bottom lip.

"Are you a part of that club already?" I asked, scowling against the intrusive thought of her tangled up in someone else.

"No." She smiled slowly. "Not yet, anyway. Hopefully, you can change that for me. I've never been a part of a club before..." She winked.

With that bold statement, she stood up and ran her hands along the tops of her thighs before slowly strutting over to the bathroom. I waited for a few minutes, my hands gripping the arm rests. I glanced around the cabin, convinced someone would see me and tell me to get back to my seat. The cabin remained empty though.

"Fuck it," I declared, unbuckling my seatbelt and going after her.

The door was unlocked, and she was leaning against the sink with a teasing smile on her face. Her jeans and t-shirt lay in a discarded rolled up ball against the rather large counter. It was clear from her lack of clothes and the seductive smile on her face that she'd been anticipating this moment.

I swallowed hard, taking in the sight of Everly before me in only a matching pink lace bra and panties.

I closed the door quickly, sliding the lock into place. My heart was hammering in my chest and my pants were straining from the desire I felt for her.

She approached me slowly, her hips swaying enticingly with each step. Her arms wound around my neck, and she pressed her body against mine.

My hands gripped her hips and I pulled her against my pelvis, loving the feel of her body against mine.

Part of me wanted to tell her to slow down, but the primitive part within was stronger in that moment, and I silenced my own thoughts by crashing my mouth to Everly's, feeding upon her like the starving man I was.

I wasn't an idiot; I knew what Everly was doing. She was trying to help me relax—she was trying to distract me. She knew I hated flying, and she was trying to give me something I'd enjoy about the experience. I fucking loved her for it.

It was the same tactic she'd used when we were together before. Any time my hangups started to get in the way, she'd work her body just right to make me let go of everything. All my fears, my doubts, my self-hatred and my insecurities disappeared in the wake of the magical spell her presence evoked.

People say that relationships shouldn't be all about sex, but sex was the one thing that I always got right. It was the one thing that came easily to me and always had. I didn't have to talk, I didn't have to think. I could just lose myself completely, let my body take over and do whatever felt right.

Her hands dropped down to unbuckle my jeans, freeing me from my boxers. She shoved them down over my hips, taking my hard long length into her soft hand. She squeezed and slowly pumped her fist. My eyes rolled into the back of my head from the agonizing throbbing pleasure of the motion.

I tried to tell myself I'd go slower with her the next time, but it wasn't possible in this moment. Not with where we were, not with how sexy she looked in that lacy thong. I didn't even bother trying to take them off her. I lifted her up, pushing her thong to the side before I sank deep into her. She was tight and wet, as ready for me as I was for her.

*   *   *

I couldn't wipe the stupid grin off my face for the remainder of the flight. I was absolutely sure that the flight attendant knew exactly what we were up to in there. Thankfully, she had enough tact to pretend she didn't.

The grin didn't fade until the pilot announced that we needed to remain in our seats during landing. The jet started to shake as it made its descent to the runway at Los Angeles International Airport, and the color instantly faded from my face.

Everly giggled behind her hand, taking delight from my anxiety.

"What?" I all but growled.

She dropped her hand, still smiling. "It's nice to see that *something* unnerves you."

"A lot of things unnerve me." I frowned, not understanding what she was insinuating.

She shook her head, her smile changing into one of sadness. "You've always appeared so calm and in control."

I blinked at her. She couldn't be further from the truth. I'd always been a swirling mess of emotions, mostly anger and resentment or sadness and self-loathing. But regardless, I definitely wasn't calm and in control of everything. I suppose I was good at putting on a stoic mask and just not expressing myself, but still. She had to have known just how out of control I'd always felt when it came to her.

"Well, I'm not," I said, the words sticking in my throat. She met my gaze and a somber, knowing look passed across the green depths of her eyes.

Once we'd made it through customs and security, Everly lead the way over to her personal assistant. The girl had dark hair and sharp bangs, and a polished look about her. She arched an eyebrow appreciatively at me, but I ignored her, my attention instead focused on the two massive men flanking either side of her. Everly had told me there would be security guards waiting for us at the airport, but I hadn't really anticipated them being crazy amped up muscle heads. I couldn't help but feel a little threatened. I knew it was customary, but still. Didn't she feel safe enough with me?

"Welcome back to LA," the girl said as we approached.

"Thanks," Everly responded, stretching slightly to work out the kinks in her neck while I stood awkwardly at her side. I almost felt out of place, and I definitely didn't like it. "This is Grayson Dixon. Grayson, this is my personal assistant Maddie and these two scary looking fellows are actually harmless teddy bears named Creed and Landon," she said, gesturing to the two men. The first one, Creed, chuckled while the second one seemed to glower at Everly's assessment.

"Alright, now I know you've had a lot going on, but I wanted to keep you updated on things with the tour and the new album," Maddie started, wincing slightly. She appeared uneasy with the mention of work. Everly smiled at her encouragingly. "The numbers for *Autumn Fields'* new release, *In Tandem*, are through the roof, Everly! The song blew up faster than anything you guys have done before."

"Awesome," Everly remarked, forcing a smile to her lips. I knew she was excited about the band's success, but I couldn't miss the obvious hesitation any time someone reported back with numbers and stats. It was obvious that she was dealing with a lot of feelings of guilt over her decision to walk away.

"I know, right? Anyway, your meeting with Haskell and Brent is at five tonight. We'll head straight there; the traffic is *nuts* today, but we'll get there in time." Maddie fired out her updates in rapid succession, barely looking up to register if we were listening as our party of five started walking out of the airport.

I was suddenly aware of *why* celebrities needed security guards. So many people in the airport turned to stare and snap photos, and many of them tried to come closer. Creed and Landon pushed through the crowds with professional precision.

"A car will be there to pick you up at six tomorrow morning for the Margo Show—you know the routine. The guys will all be there too. Margo wants you to perform *In Tandem* during the halfway point, before she brings out Deegan Redford."

"Deegan Redford?" I interrupted, impressed. Everly sent me a patient smile and I shrugged apologetically. Deegan Redford was a blockbuster hit actor who mainly starred in action and thriller movies. He was a couple years older than we were, but I was a fan of his movies. Then again, most guys were considering that the main plots generally consisted of blowing shit up and showing off hot women.

"Yup. So Margo wants to interview you guys, then you'll perform, then we can get out of there. Your flight has been booked for Sunday morning at seven, but it will be on a commercial flight as the label needs the jet," Maddie continued on, barely sparing me a look. Neither Everly or Maddie seemed phased by the potential of running into one of the biggest actors in Hollywood. I suppose it was because they were used to seeing famous people. Everly was one, after all.

"Alright, that's fine," Everly said as we stepped outside. The warm LA sun was beating down on us. Taxis weaved in and out with ruthless maneuvers that intimidated even me. It was a completely different planet than our small hometown in Canada.

"Perfect! Try not to sweat your meeting with Brent, okay? Haskell will be there, so there shouldn't be any problems." Maddie gave Everly a sympathetic look that set me on edge. Why would she be worried about a meeting with her agent?

"Fine," Everly gritted out. I sent her a questioning gaze. Everly shook her head, forcing a smile to convey that she didn't want to get into it at the moment. I nodded once, my jaw locking in aggravation.

"I'll be there too," Maddie assured her. We came to a stop in front of a nondescript black car. The driver had already jumped out of his seat and came around to hold the door open for us. I went to put the bags in the open and waiting trunk, but the driver quickly stepped forward to coax them out of my hands.

"I'll see you at the studio," Maddie added, hesitating momentarily before she threw her arms around Everly. "I'm glad you're doing okay... given everything."

Everly nodded her thanks, pulling away so she could climb into the car. I followed behind her, my jaw still working.

"So, what's this Brent guy's deal?" I demanded, scowling.

"He's just an asshole. I hate dealing with him." Everly sighed. She forced another smile. "I only have to worry about it for a little longer though, right?"

"I guess so..." I said doubtfully.

"How do you like LA so far?" Everly questioned brightly, trying to divert my attention and change the topic.

"It makes me feel emasculated," I responded with a smirk, gesturing with a nod of my head towards the driver.

"Questioning your manhood already?" Everly arched a brow. "You're really going to hate LA then. The guys wear tighter jeans than me and everyone has a toy dog."

I winced and Everly couldn't help but laugh at the expression on my face.

"I guess I shouldn't buy you skinny jeans just yet, huh?"

"Nope. Hold that order," I replied dryly as the driver merged the car into the flow of traffic, and we left the airport.

Chapter Nineteen

Everly

THE MEETING TOOK nearly two and a half hours. Brent Woodstock's tight tanned face, the subject of many Botox treatments and vigorous tanning sessions, had appeared pinched as he glowered at me over the solid black walnut desk in his office. His hard, black eyes focused intently on my face and I wanted to disappear. Dealing with Brent on a regular day made my stomach twist with disgust, but today it had been exceptionally difficult given the reason for the meeting.

My lawyer, Tim Haskell, made the meeting go a lot smoother. Brent was on his best behavior, and there was really nothing he could say or do about it. We'd come to an agreement about paying the fines, but I still knew how pissed he was from the animosity rolling off him in waves.

He wasn't ready for his star puppet to cut the strings. Even though our contract was up for renewal, he was expecting us to sign back on.

I was beyond relieved when the meeting was finally over and everything was handled. I still had to do the interview with *The Margo Show*; now we'd have to break it to the fans that the tour was off. People would likely be pissed about it, if Brent's reaction was any indication of that, but I was desperately hanging on to the thread of hope that the fans would understand.

The drive to my house was almost silent, allowing me some time to mull over the meeting and everything else while Grayson took in the scenery along the way. I just had to get through the interview, sell the house, and then I could leave all this behind me.

I wasn't sure how I felt. It was definitely what I wanted; I wanted to focus on Cadence—I *needed* to focus on her—but I couldn't help but feel sad about the end of an era, the end of a dream I'd been chasing for years.

When the guys and I first started making waves, the record label bought us a house to live in when we weren't on tour. It was located near the studio, ensuring that there would be no excuses for late arrivals on recording days.

I lived with them for two years. Living with the band was just as aggravating as traveling with them. I loved Kyle, Marcus and Cam. They were great guys who loved music and worked hard and they never let me down when it came to music, but I grew sick and tired of living in what felt like a fraternity house. Watching them bring home girls and party all the time got old really fast. I was constantly walking in on things I didn't want to see, constantly irritated by anything that they did. I was grumpy and horrible to live with. I decided the best thing for me to do would be to buy my own place, and I did.

I had money, and lots of it. I covered *all* of Cadence's expenses and then some, but that wasn't even a portion of my income. I knew I could easily afford a house in Los Angeles, and I knew that the investment would be a positive one for me to make. I knew that when I eventually sold this place, I'd bring in almost double what I'd paid for it, strictly on the grounds that I had lived there.

I had a financial advisor and a lawyer to help me handle my finances. I wasn't about blowing the money I earned on the party lifestyle; I wanted to make smart decisions with my income because I didn't know how long I'd be able to do this—being away from my family and putting in 80 hours a week, living with the guilt I felt for all but abandoning Cadence on my sister.

I still loved music, I still loved singing and writing, but the exhaustion was getting to me. I wanted to settle down. I wanted to finally play a bigger part in Cadence's life...and now with Julia gone, I was about to do just that.

My house was located near the beach in Brentwood. I had fallen in love with this particular Los Angeles neighborhood upon seeing the historic coral trees on the beautiful grassy median in the San Vicente Boulevard. I didn't even really need to see the house to know that I wanted to live there, close to the beach. It was about as different from my hometown as I could get, and I needed that if I was going to stay focused.

Fortunately, the house was just as beautiful as the drive in had been. It was four thousand square feet and had a modern contemporary design— a lot like Grayson's house. Being a builder himself, I was sure he'd like *that* part about it.

I loved my house. It was the only reason I hadn't minded living in LA. The master suite had a large deck with a beautiful view of the ocean. I could sit on my deck and enjoy the beautiful taste of ocean with my morning cup of coffee as I watched the waves roll in. My deck also overlooked the beautiful in-ground pool beneath. It was Cadence's favorite part about coming to stay.

I couldn't stop wringing my hands together as I nervously watched Grayson take in the upscale neighborhood that was Brentwood. I was both excited and nervous about the prospect of showing Grayson the house. I was worried that he would think it was over the top, and it was. It was a mansion in a gated community where a bunch of other celebrities lived. Black cast iron gates and a security guard prevented just anybody from coming up to my house.

I also had security cameras trained on every entrance to the house, manned by the security guard. A year ago, I'd had a creepy "fan" that had tried to break in to convince me that we were destined to be together. I was extremely lucky that my housekeeper had been there at the time and called the police. I gave him a lovely parting gift—a no contact order.

The driver, Jim, turned into my driveway and slowly rolled down the window to speak to the security guard. I couldn't hear their exchange, but the gates swung forward a moment later, allowing us entrance. Jim parked the car in front of the four-car garage. Jim had been my unofficial driver for the last three years, and true to Jim's nature, he got out and opened the rear passenger door for us with a cordial smile before disappearing to the trunk to grab luggage.

Grayson's eyebrows arched as he took in the beautiful house and grounds. He stepped out of the car, letting out a low whistle. "Jesus...this place is huge," he remarked, holding the door open for me. I climbed out, my hands trembling slightly. "You seriously lived here alone?"

"Kind of. Friends and family are welcome to come and stay whenever." When I first bought the house, I entertained the daydream of having Julia and Cadence move in with me. But Julia didn't want to leave Newcastle, and I realized how terrible of an idea it was after my stalker-fan tried to break in.

"Why didn't Julia and Cadence just move in with you?" he questioned.

"Because Julia wanted to be where it was familiar. Besides, I was hardly ever home anyway. Julia and Cadence would have been alone here more often than not. It made sense for them to stay in Newcastle," I answered as I glanced back at Jim. He was preoccupied with getting our bags out of the trunk. "And I didn't want to take her away from Julia."

"Take her away?" Grayson's expression darkened. His brows knitted together while he tried to make sense of my decisions. I sighed, trying not to feel defeated. I couldn't blame Grayson for trying to figure it all out. *I* didn't even understand my choices completely, I still questioned if they were the right move. "It wouldn't have been taking her away...she's your daughter. Our daughter."

"I know that," I snapped.

Grayson's eyebrows shot up, it wasn't like me to lash out, but he wisely didn't say anything further as Jim approached us with our bags. "That's fine, I got it," Grayson said gruffly. He took the bags off the smartly dressed driver. Jim inclined his head slightly with acknowledgment as he passed the bags off to Grayson's outstretched hands. I hoped he wasn't offended by Grayson's behavior. I probably shouldn't have snapped at him, but I was so sick of people trying to dissect my decisions; it was another reason why I'd kept quiet for so long about them.

"The car will arrive at six tomorrow morning, Miss Daniels," Jim said, reminding me for the hundredth time.

"Thanks, Jim, see you then," I told him, offering a thankful smile. Jim nodded, the corners of his lips perking up in response.

"Have a good evening," he said before climbing back into the sleek black car.

I turned to face Grayson, my shoulders deflating slightly. "I'm sorry I snapped, Grayson," I said, heat flooding to my face. "I know what people would say if they knew...that I'm a terrible mother...that I abandoned her... and I just couldn't bear for you to feel that way too."

"Angel, that is not at *all* how I feel," Grayson murmured as he stepped toward me. His expression was one of pain and regret. "I understand what you did. I do. Sometimes, it's not easy to wrap my head around, but I don't feel like you abandoned her. You've given her a hell of a lot more than I ever did."

"You didn't know about her," I pointed out. I tried to blink the moisture from my eyes. This was *not* how I wanted to start out our weekend together.

Grayson's hand tentatively came up to brush across my cheek. "We've both made mistakes...lots of them...but we can't move on from them if we don't let that go. Clean slate, remember?"

"Is that what you did?" I inquired, looking up at him.

"More or less." Grayson shrugged, a sad smile appearing on his lips. "I seriously didn't have my shit together before I saw you again that day. All I knew is that if I ever had the chance with you again...I wouldn't throw it away. I'd do everything in my power to be the person I believe you deserved. I just didn't think I was going to get the chance to prove it to you."

I smiled at him, closing my eyes against his touch and savoring it for a moment.

"We should go inside," Grayson suggested. I opened my eyes to see that devilish smirk that usually brushed across his kissable lips and took a shuddering breath. I turned and led the way up the stone walkway, my keys gripped tightly in my trembling hands. I unlocked the door and punched in the security code quickly, standing aside to allow Grayson in.

I could tell that Grayson had his architectural hat on as he surveyed the beautiful pine floors, stone accent walls, and beautiful built in bookcases that housed a variety of different decorations, photos, and books.

"Impressive. They know how to build in LA," Grayson finally said, breaking the silence with his declaration of approval. He set his large hands down on the smooth marble coffee colored countertop.

I shyly smiled in response, mentally holding up a truce flag. "Are you hungry?" I asked. Grayson's eyes quickly found mine, heat flickering behind the icy blue of his eyes. He absently bit down on his lower lip, and I could tell he was clearly thinking suggestive things. My heart stuttered in my chest and I smirked. "For food...Lydia probably left us some of her delicious homemade lasagna." I turned around, needing to break the spell. I couldn't think when he looked at me like that. It was almost enough to undo me completely.

I distracted myself by opening up the refrigerator and peering inside. Lydia knew that I'd be back, and she had clearly gone shopping at some point today. My refrigerator was full of groceries; fresh produce, fruit, yogurts, and deli meats lined the shelves. In the middle of the refrigerator was her delicious chicken lasagna; my mouth started to water at the very prospect of it. Lydia's cooking surpassed my mother's, and *that* was definitely saying something—not that I'd ever admit that to Mom.

"Who's Lydia?" Grayson asked, remaining at the island as he watched me bend forward to grab the Tupperware container.

I closed the refrigerator, setting the container down on the counter before I turned to face him. I tucked a strand of my hair behind my ears. "She's my housekeeper and my cook..." I trailed off, feeling awkward.

Lydia was a soft-spoken Latina woman in her late thirties. She did all the shopping for me, she took care of the house when I wasn't home, and she cooked me meals when I was. She was a single mom of two teen girls that she'd had very young. She was warm and trustworthy.

I looked over my shoulder at him, watching as he smirked.

The look in Grayson's his eyes immediately set my skin on fire. The air suddenly felt heavy in my lungs, so I turned away from him, needing to distance myself a little.

"I need to eat before you get any ideas," I warned. I hadn't eaten since before we boarded the jet, and that had only been a banana. I didn't enjoy flying; it still made my stomach feel weird and I always found it best to avoid eating before and during a flight. Now that I was back on the ground, my stomach was rumbling impatiently, demanding attention. I pulled off the lid, setting the container in the microwave.

"Yeah, you're going to need your strength for tonight," Grayson retorted, coming up behind me. His arms landed on either side of me, his hands gripping the counter as he caged me in. He pressed his pelvis against the small of my back, gently pushing me against the counter. I pressed back against him, grinding against his stiff arousal.

"You're going to need your strength too," I said coyly, dipping my head backwards. Disappearing into each other sounded like a perfectly good idea to me, especially after that terrible meeting with Brent. I knew Grayson could easily melt away all of the tension I was carrying.

His lips found the sweet spot against the side of my throat, just below my earlobe. He kissed me there, his lips softly promising more things to come, and I instantly felt some of the tension roll away.

The microwave dinged, interrupting Grayson before he could make good on my threat. He allowed me to break away and grab plates, realizing that I really was too hungry to focus on anything else. I dished out the steaming lasagna onto two plates. I grabbed forks and offered Grayson his plate. He took it eagerly.

"Smells good," he commented as he followed me over to the table. He sat across from me, barely sitting down before he started to shovel in the lasagna. I followed suit, too hungry to care that I was scarfing back food in front of Grayson. Normally, I was shy about eating in front of people.

It wasn't fun to have your photo snapped of lettuce stuck between your teeth.

"Do you want a glass of wine?" I offered once we'd finished. I rinsed the dishes, placing them into the empty dishwasher before I grabbed two wine glasses from the cabinet.

"Sure." Grayson shrugged.

"Red or white?" I asked. He looked at me blankly. Amused, I grabbed the bottle of thirty-year-old red wine from Italy. I'd been saving it for a special occasion and I figured this was as good as any. I poured two glasses, putting the cork back in before I handed Grayson his glass and led the way into the living room. I sat down on the couch, using the remote to turn on the small fireplace that separated the entertainment room from the living room.

Grayson joined me, setting his glass down on the black walnut coffee table. "So...are you ever going to tell me what happened during the meeting?"

"Oh." I frowned, my mood darkening slightly at the mention. I sighed. "It went about as well as any meeting with Brent could have gone. He's a total asshole, but he was on his best behavior. I honestly don't have anything to worry about. My lawyer is going to take care of everything."

"Why is he such an asshole?" Grayson inquired. I chewed over my answer. I had to be careful with Grayson on *how* I answered him. Grayson wouldn't take kindly to hearing the truth.

Brent Woodstock was a genius who did deserve credit for helping us achieve all the success we had, but he was also a slimy, greedy possessor. He was oily and distrustful. He was the fuel behind the Kyle and Everly engagement rumors, and he had a perpetual habit of tipping off the media so they could get incriminating photos of his clients.

He'd also come on to me during our first year in LA. He was used to the female clientele allowing him to act in all the disgustingly sexual ways he wanted to act. He had requested a private meeting with me in his office, wherein he sat close to me on his greasy sofa and tried to touch my upper thigh while implying that he could really make me big if I "just cooperated with him". I had freaked out about it; I'd caused such a scene that Kyle, Marcus and Cam had burst in from the waiting room.

It wasn't difficult to see exactly what had happened, and the guys wasted no time telling Brent exactly what would happen if he tried a move like that again. Then they were extremely careful of ensuring that I would never be left alone with Brent Woodstock again.

Telling Grayson all this would just piss him off, though, and considering nothing *had* actually happened, I didn't feel like rocking the boat.

"Because he works for a record label and is a ruthless prick." I shrugged. "It's really not a big deal. I won't have to deal with him directly anymore, and for that I'm thankful."

"Amen. Here's to shitty bosses," Grayson remarked, winking. We clinked glasses and took another deep sip of wine, looking at one another over the tops of our glasses. "This is a really nice house, Everly," he added, his eyes still on me.

"Thanks. I'll be sad to see it go. I bet I won't be able to find one like it in Newcastle," I said, folding my legs up beneath me. I avoided Grayson's eyes while I tried to sort through the thoughts racing in my mind.

"Maybe..." He shook his head. He looked up at me, giving me a rueful smile. "Never mind. It's stupid." I could hear the vulnerability in Grayson's voice.

"What?" I pressed, a small smile finding its way to my lips. I took a sip of wine, listening to the comforting sound of the flames licking against the fake wood in the electric fireplace while I kept my eyes fixated on him. He saw something there, and moved forward.

"Why don't you and Cadence just move in with me?" His voice was low and intense. The emotions swirling in those glacier blue eyes made my breath catch in my throat.

Grayson's words had my thoughts running a thousand miles a minute. It would be so wonderful to wake up every morning in his arms, to get to see him interact with Cadence every single day. It would be the best kind of wonderful to do mundane things with him...like cooking dinner and watching TV together once Cadence was asleep. If I closed my eyes, I knew I could easily envision it all: a family. I wanted it so bad that it almost hurt.

On the other hand, a part of me felt as if that would be rushing things. We'd only just gotten back together, and he'd only just found out he had a daughter. We had had little to no time to adjust to those huge shifts, and even though things were moving smoothly, I couldn't help but fear that diving in and investing everything I had would just leave me heartbroken in the end. I was afraid even though my heart told me I shouldn't be. After all, I hadn't stopped loving him. He'd always been it for me, and I desperately wanted to make up for all that lost time.

As if he could see the doubt fluttering through my mind, Grayson's expression changed to quiet understanding laced with disappointment. His hand reached out and tentatively found mine. He was about to speak, but I beat him to it.

"Grayson...it's not that I don't want to," I told him, my eyes locking with his and pleading with him to understand. "I want that more than you could ever imagine. I'm just...scared. Things have been going so well, and I'm afraid. I'm afraid to lose it. I'm afraid to push it before it's ready. Before *you're* ready...before *I'm* ready. If it were just you and me, I'd do it in a heartbeat. It would only be myself at stake, but it *isn't* just you and me. I have to think about Cadence too..." I trailed off and looked toward the fire, trying to blink away the stubborn tears that decided to flow.

Grayson's hand gently cupped the underside of my chin, urging me to look at him. His eyes flickered with pain, longing and understanding. "Angel, it's okay if you don't want to rush it. Please just know that the offer is there, whenever you want to take me up on it." His voice was gravelly with emotion and longing, but I knew he understood the place I was in.

"I just need to be absolutely sure that we're *both* ready for that..." I trailed off again, swallowing the lump of emotion that seemed perpetually lodged in my throat.

Grayson winced as if my words physically hurt him, and I knew that they had. He was likely recalling what had happened last time we moved too quickly. We hadn't both been on the same page, and the result hadn't been good. I was afraid of that happening again, even though I knew we were both in different places.

"I understand," he assured me, his lips gently descending on mine. He kissed me in a scorching way that made me feel as if I were melting from the inside out. I tipped my head back, offering him more. My hands automatically went to his buckle, and he groaned with my lip caught between his teeth when my hand grasped around his hard length. He stilled my movements, his heat filled eyes opening to lock on mine. "I do understand...for the record," he clarified, a smirk teasing the corners of his lips upward.

Chapter Twenty

Grayson

THE NEXT MORNING, I awoke to the sound of the shower turning on. I blinked, disoriented for a moment or two. I hadn't really taken notice of my surroundings the night before, given the carnivorous activities we were engaged in.

I followed the sound of the shower to the ensuite bathroom. Everly's shower was made up of glass almost all the way around, and the glorious sight of the water beading and disappearing down the small of her back made my dick stand fully erect.

It was my fault we were running late. We raced out of the house fifteen minutes after six, and earned a scathing look from Maddie when we finally got to the studio where they filmed *The Margo Morning Show.*

"Look, you're running behind. They're waiting for you backstage in makeup. Grayson, you're going to need to follow me...you can't go with her."

"Why not?" I challenged, arching a brow.

"Because you're a distraction." Maddie rolled her eyes as if she didn't have time to explain. "Carly, take Everly to makeup. I'll accompany this guy to join the others."

"Others? What others?"

"The other guests of the band," Maddie exhaled, closing her eyes momentarily. I didn't have to know her to know that I was completely rattling her patience.

Everly kissed me quickly before she followed the other girl that had been standing beside Maddie.

"Come on, Romeo." Maddie sighed. She led the way down a hallway and paused outside a red door before opening it. I walked in cautiously, my eyes assessing the room.

There were several black leather couches set up facing each other, along with a long coffee table that was loaded down with pastries and fruit. A counter to the left of the room housed a coffee maker and a refrigerator. There was a large TV on the far wall with *The Today Show* on.

There were five other people in the room. I didn't recognize the two girls, but I knew Kyle, Cam and Marcus well enough.

Marcus was lounging by the coffee maker, animatedly talking to Cam about something. Kyle sat on one of the couches, his arm wrapped around the shoulders of a pretty girl with short blonde hair and cornflower blue eyes. Beside her sat a girl with shockingly red hair and a massive grin. Had her hair been braided, she would have borne a remarkable resemblance to Pippi Longstocking herself.

When we walked in, all eyes looked up at us. Kyle's easy smile dimmed several notches as we eyed each other warily.

The last time I had seen Kyle, prior to our brief encounter at Everly's house, I had knocked him out cold after a school dance for merely speaking the truth. Well, that and for touching my girl.

I'd gone to the bathroom and when I had returned, I saw Kyle across the dance floor, grinding up against Everly. When she realized it wasn't me behind her, she started to tell him off.

At that point, I was seeing red. I knew that Kyle wanted Everly. I hated him for it, even if I couldn't blame him. I likely would have walked away when I saw them kissing on the dance floor of a Halloween party months before—if the second she left he hadn't started making out with some other girl. Kyle didn't deserve her any more than I did.

"Kyle, if you touch her again, I'll break your hands," I said. I couldn't even recognize my own voice, so twisted with anger it was.

"She deserves so much more than the scraps you throw at her," Kyle spat angrily, glaring back. My eyebrows shot up, and I saw Everly wince out of the corner of my eye. The verbal punch hit where it hurt, just like Kyle intended. He was right I wasn't giving Everly nearly enough. It was nobody's fault but my own, but hearing the truth and seeing her wince enraged me. I didn't want it to be true. I wanted to be worthy...I wanted to feel worthy, but I wasn't and I didn't. Even Everly's hand against my chest couldn't stop the rage from flying out.

The punch happened so quickly that it took even me by surprise. One moment, I was subdued with Everly's hand on my chest, and the next minute, my fist was slamming against Kyle's jaw with a shocking intensity. Kyle's head flew back on impact and he stumbled. He stepped back a few steps before he regained his footing. My blood was roaring.

Kyle slowly ran a hand across his mouth and wiped away the blood from the split in his bottom lip, glowering at me. People formed a half circle around us, gearing up to watch a fight. Someone turned the volume of the music down.

"You're fucking unhinged, man," Kyle said, shaking his head in disbelief. "Your reaction when I call you out on how you treat her is to punch me? Guess the truth hurts."

I snarled, my lip curling cruelly.

"Kyle! Stop it," Everly exclaimed, trying to pull back on my arm. I felt like a caged animal, and Kyle's words were only egging my uncontrollable rage on. Everything resurfaced in that moment—my parents' divorce, my mom's suicide, every insecurity I had ever had because of it...and the startling realization that Kyle was right.

"Tell your fucking boyfriend to stop it, Everly!" Kyle retorted, glaring hotly at Everly. "He treats you like shit and you know it. We know it. He fucking knows it!"

"You think you're better for her?" I scoffed, staying still only because her hands were pressing hard against me, tethering me to her.

"I guess that doesn't really matter, does it?" Kyle asked. "Because she's with you...for now. But she'll open her eyes. Sooner or later, you'll let her down one too many times, and I'll be here."

Everly's hands were no longer able to keep me in place. I darted out and around her, my fist colliding with Kyle's jaw again. This time, Kyle fell against the coffee table, completely knocked out...

"...help yourself to coffee and some breakfast," Maddie was saying, gesturing to the tables. I blinked at her retreating back.

"Well, this just got interesting," Kyle remarked dryly after the door had closed behind Maddie. The blonde girl he had his arm around gave him a warning look while the redheaded girl stood up eagerly and approached me, her hand stretched out in greeting.

"Hi! I'm Crimson! It's nice to meet to you. You *have* to try the chocolate croissant; it's to *die* for!"

"Hi..." I shook her hand.

"Where are you from?" Crimson asked, not picking up on my discomfort as I shoved my hands back into my pockets.

"He's from Newcastle," Marcus answered before I could. "We went to high school together."

"Oh my God! That's awesome! So you guys are friends?"

"Not particularly," I said, trying my best not to scowl at Kyle.

"He's close with Everly," Kyle responded automatically, his lip curling up in a near snarl.

"Awesome!" Crimson didn't seem to notice the hostility in the room, or maybe it was just her way of trying to neutralize it. She led me to the vacant couch across from Kyle and the blonde girl. I sat down obediently, still eyeing Kyle.

"So, you know Kyle, Marcus and Cam, and now me...this stunning lady is Jenna! We're from Ottawa, actually. Jenna met Kyle at a concert five years ago, and they're kind of a hot item so she gets all these tickets and invites to the fun stuff the band does and she brings me because I *love* the band!" Crimson said brightly, plopping down beside me. She picked up a chocolate croissant and offered it to me.

"No thanks." I wasn't hungry. Part of me felt like dragging Kyle outside and punching him again, just because I didn't like him. Another part of me wanted to apologize for that night in high school, but it wasn't really the place...and the only person I'd ever successfully managed to apologize to Everly, so it probably wouldn't have mattered. I likely would have ended up punching him regardless of my intentions.

Instead, I settled for distractedly listening to Crimson while she talked... and damn, that girl could *talk*. I couldn't even follow half of what she was saying because my mind was whirling with memories of high school and the person I was back then and the person I was struggling to be today, in this moment, sitting across from Kyle.

The tension between us was blatantly obvious to everyone except it would seem...Crimson. Finally, Kyle couldn't take it anymore.

"I need a smoke," he declared, standing abruptly. He kissed Jenna quickly on the lips before stomping out of the room.

The room was silent; Marcus and Cam were eyeing me suspiciously.

"Sorry about that," the blonde girl said, leaning forward. Her hand came up to rest against the nape of her neck as she stared at the closed door as if waiting to see if it would stay shut. After a moment, she looked at me again. "Kyle really cares about Everly and...well, you know."

I got the sense that the blonde girl was referring to Cadence. I tried to be impassive, but it was difficult to hear the reminder—Kyle hadn't left. Kyle was there for Cadence's birth, or at least afterwards. He knew Everly's secret before I did, and that pissed me off.

The girl smiled at me with compassion. "I'm Jenna, by the way. I didn't catch your name."

"Grayson."

"Oh! A color inspired name!" Crimson grinned, grasping my arm with innocent excitement. She must have felt my muscles stiffening, as she quickly released me and gave me a little space. "So...are you and Everly together?"

"Yes." I knew I sounded short and unfriendly, but I couldn't seem to help it. My mind had gone to a slightly dark place and the last thing I felt like doing was making small talk.

The door opened, saving me from further conversation, and Maddie poked her head in. "Alright, they are starting to fill the audience now so you guys can go to your seats," she said to the three of us. Crimson jumped up with excitement, her eyes shining. Jenna calmly stood. I followed the three of them to the audience, trying to take in my surroundings.

There were hundreds of chairs in the audience that reminded me of a brightly lit movie theater. People were starting to take their designated seats, their excited chatter echoing throughout the large studio room. On stage, there was a comfortable looking seating area and a large projection screen TV. I sat down in the seat that Maddie pointed to, in the front row near the center of the stage. I'd have a perfect view of Everly.

Crimson sat down beside me, and Jenna took the chair beside her. She grinned widely at me, the freckles that dotted across her upper cheeks and nose dancing with merriment. She had the kind of face that was innocent and pretty in an understated way.

"I seriously *love* Margo so much. She's hilarious," Crimson said, shaking her head ruefully. "I wonder if we'll get to meet her?" she added to Jenna.

"Probably not." Jenna frowned slightly, seemingly put off by her friend's eagerness; as if she worried that Crimson would get up in the middle of the show and head up on stage to introduce herself to Margo.

On second thought, I wouldn't put it past her.

I tuned out the girls for twenty minutes, closing my eyes against the harsh lights directed on the audience, and waited until all the seats were full. It was another twenty minutes after that before the lights in the studio started to dim. Flood lights were trained on the door that led to back stage. Catchy dance music blasted through the speakers, and suddenly Margo Harwood was bouncing across the stage, shaking her ass in rhythm to the music and waving at the audience. Crimson cheered exuberantly with excitement, ignoring Jenna's attempts at hushing her.

The music faded as Margo sat down in her chair. Her short, pixie-like auburn hair was styled in crazy spikes and she was dressed in a snug pant suit. Her bright blue eyes twinkled as she chuckled at the audience's continued welcome.

"Good morning!" Margo's voice made the audience fall silent, the last of the claps fading off in the wake of her booming voice. "Today we have some special guests, the lovely people in *Autumn Fields;* Everly Daniels, Kyle Russell, Marcus Muller, and Cam Roberts. After we chat for a bit, they're going to sing for us and then we will be joined by actor Deegan Redford! If you don't know who he is, you must be living under a rock. He's been in pretty much every movie that's been released in the past three years!" the audience chuckled at Margo's commentary on Deegan Redford. Even I let out a small smile. The guy was literally in *everything.* "But first! We need to do our usual phone call."

Margo picked up the old school phone that was next to her mug on the coffee table. She always started her television shows off by calling a fan and saying hello and offering free tickets to her show tapings in LA. The conversations were usually amusing. Not only was Margo was an extremely entertaining woman, but her fans often said the funniest things to her too.

After Margo hung up the phone, she showed the audience her top tweets of the week. My fingers tapped against the arm rest; I was growing rather impatient. I didn't find tweets funny, and I was eager to get this done with so we could get out of the stuffy studio and preferably back into Everly's bed.

"Stay tuned! After this quick commercial, we'll be welcoming our first guests!" Margo grinned into the camera. The cameras stopped rolling and a couple of stage directors came out to tidy up the stage and prepare for the first guests. At the mere thought of Everly, my lips perked up in an unrestrained smile.

"How long have you and Everly been together?" Crimson asked, peering at me with curiosity. She tucked her hair behind her ear, and I noticed for the first time that she was wearing a clear hearing aid.

"Crimson, shh," Jenna warned, glancing around to make sure that nobody had heard her.

"It's complicated," I responded, frowning. I was not accustomed to random strangers questioning me so bluntly. Usually, people were put off by my scowling, dire mood. Although, I suppose I hadn't exactly been scowling or in a completely dire mood, for that matter. Now that I was back with Everly, I was smiling more and scowling less. Which probably made me look friendly and approachable. I clenched my jaw.

"Oh." Crimson nodded wisely, her brows arching with understanding. I didn't know exactly what she thought she understood, but I didn't care enough to find out. Surprisingly, the girl kept talking. "I have a complicated relationship with my boyfriend too. His name is Cole and we have been together for *years*. We met during our first year of University. I just graduated with my BA in Psychology. I'm from Simcoe originally, but I moved to Ottawa for University. Best decision ever! That's where I met this beauty and our other bestie, Harlow. She's not here because she hates flying. Anyway, so...things with Cole are complicated because he's got a lot of issues he's trying to work through."

I opened and closed my mouth like a fish. I just didn't know how the hell to respond to that. Jenna gave me a sympathetic look as if she understood how overwhelming Crimson could be, and quickly distracted her attention.

"And now! Please give a warm welcome to the geniuses behind *Autumn Fields*! *Everly Daniels, Kyle Russell, Marcus Muller* and *Cam Roberts*!" Margo's voice was full of warmth and welcome as she introduced each and every one of them. I straightened up, watching as Everly walked out onto the brightly lit stage followed by Kyle, Marcus and Cam. As always, I only had eyes for her.

She was waving at the audience and smiling in that dazzling way that made my blood surge with desire. The band was getting an insane reception from the audience. Many of them, including the girls beside me, stood up and loudly cheered and clapped.

Everly looked stunning in a tight pair of jeans, a red low-cut top and a black leather jacket similar to the one she usually preformed in. She almost seemed to glide across the stage over to Margo Harwood, continuing to wave and smile at the audience as she went. They ate it up, cheering loudly when she blew a kiss.

Margo was standing in front of her arm chair in the middle of the room, clapping along with the audience. Everly reached her first and Margo threw her arms around her in a massive hug while the audience cheered louder still. Margo turned her lips close to Everly's ear and whispered something. Everly grinned and nodded, responding quietly so the audience couldn't hear. The crowd fell silent as Everly lowered herself into the long sofa across from Margo. Margo hugged Kyle, Marcus and Cam in turn before they sat on the sofa. Everly sat closest to Margo, with Kyle sitting beside her and Marcus beside him. Cam sat on the far side, sending flirtatious looks to the girls closet to the stage.

"It's so great to see you guys again! You've all done so much since the last time you were on the show. Why don't you tell us a bit about your projects?" Margo grinned, looking from Everly's face to Kyle. It was obvious that they were still the main stars of the show. Marcus and Cam seemed completely content with that.

Everly looked at Kyle and he nodded as if encouraging her to take this one.

"Yes!" she responded, running her delicate hands along those designer jeans that I wanted to peel her out of. The other guys seemed content enough to let her take the reins. "We finished our latest album, *Free From Blame* in September."

"Your last two singles, *In Tandem* and *Gutless*, both topped the charts *the days* that they were released and are still sitting at the top now. It's been a month for *Gutless* and two weeks for *In Tandem*. That's pretty impressive! Will your fans be just as happy with the rest of the album?"

"I think so," Kyle responded this time, flashing his award winning grin at the crowd. They lapped it up. "I think a lot of people will be able to relate to it. We worked harder than we've ever worked before to make sure that it's our best album yet." As the last word fell from Kyle's lips, the audience hooted and clapped.

"I'm sure you don't say that lightly," Margo remarked, smiling. "Your last three records have gone platinum and you guys have won several Billboards!"

Everly smiled in response, shaking her head as if she couldn't believe it herself. Her wavy tresses moved with her. "It's been incredible..." she managed, choking a little on her words. Kyle gently put his arm around her, squeezing her to him. I scowled slightly, but it was a typical Kyle move. In every interview I'd ever watched, he was always touching Everly in some way.

"We've grown so much, both individually and together...we're like a family," Kyle added. Marcus and Cam nodded in agreement.

"It's easy to see that!" Margo said, grinning. "Now you guys got your big break performing at a Battle of the Bands in your final year of high school, isn't that right?" Margo asked.

Everly nodded.

"Yep! The guys and I already had a band, but back then we called it something else...probably *Hairy Balls* or something equally revolting, and Marcus and I sat across from this stunner one day and her friend mentioned she could sing. When we heard her, we talked her in to performing with us!"

Margo smiled, shaking her head with amusement at Kyle's exuberance. "Did you guys imagine yourselves making it *this* far? Accomplishing all that you have?"

Kyle, Everly, Marcus and Cam all exchanged a look with one another as if they were communicating without words. The kind of intuitive relationship that comes from people who spent a lot of time together, who knew each others' weaknesses and strengths.

"No, I didn't." Everly's answer was the first to come and it was honest as she demurely smiled, her lashes lowered as if she felt bashful. "I dreamed of performing, but I didn't know it was possible for me."

"We knew it was possible," Marcus replied, nudging her shoulder with his.

"You're not modest." Margo laughed, and the audience chuckled along with her.

Marcus grinned and shrugged in response. "I know talent when I see it!" he argued.

"Maybe your next calling is a talent agent." Margo winked before moving on to her next question. "What do you attribute your success to?"

"A lot of luck...and Kyle's hair, probably," Everly responded, grinning cheekily at Kyle as the crowd hooted and whooped with agreement.

"Kyle *does* have some incredible hair." Margo chuckled, her eyes dancing across the audience.

"Why thank you!" Kyle pretended to blush. "The secret is I barely wash it!"

"He's not kidding," Cam interjected, leaning forward slightly. The audience laughed again. Even I wanted to smile at their easy banter. The way they bounced off one another had the audience feeding out of the palms of their hands.

"So, what's next for *Autumn Fields*? Your tour is set for February?" Margo asked, her eyes sparkling. She was thoroughly entertained by them, even more so than some of her other guests. Yeah, I'd seen a few of her shows before. Usually unintentionally.

Everly and Kyle looked at each other again, and he smiled encouragingly at her.

"We were supposed to go on tour for this album, yes. But due to personal circumstances, I've had to bow out. We'll be taking some time off..." Everly answered hesitantly, looking at Kyle as if seeking permission. He nodded, squeezing her closer to him again. Everly swallowed hard, her jaw trembling slightly.

Pretty much all of the people in the audience groaned loudly in protest, but fell silent when Everly started to speak again. "The death of my sister has been difficult for my entire family, and I need to be with them."

Margo's hand reached out to gently squeeze Everly's. It was an emotional moment. Everly's eyes welled with tears at the gesture and the look on her face sliced into my heart. "I'm sorry to hear about your loss, I'm sure we all are. You do what you need to do girl, I'm sure your fans— and your band family—will stand behind you!" The audience hooted with agreement.

"Our fans are incredible." She nodded earnestly. She tried to blink away the water from her eyes. Her pain gutted me. I wanted more than anything to be the one holding her right now, but I wasn't completely pissed at Kyle for being there; I was surprised to feel thankful for his presence. It was obvious that he had done a lot for Everly...and for Cadence. Still, I wished I could be the one to take her pain away, but I couldn't. Not in that moment. All I could do was watch as Kyle held her closer to him and Marcus and Cam tried to lean forward to hug her as well. She took a moment to collect herself before speaking again. "It was an incredibly difficult decision, one that I do not take lightly, but the guys are in full support of it."

"We definitely are," Kyle remarked, smiling at Everly with affection. "We've been working hard the last five years, and we need a little break... otherwise our material will dry up!"

"So does that mean you guys *aren't* splitting up?" Margo arched a brow, a secret smile on her face.

"We'd never split up," Kyle answered assertively. "We're a family. We're interwoven into each other's lives. Even if we aren't touring or in the studio together for sixty hours a week, we'll still be a band. We're still a family."

"I think you reach a point when you need to take a step back, get some new inspiration...experience life a little bit more," Marcus added quickly. Kyle, Cam and Everly nodded with agreement.

"Speaking of new material...would you guys care to perform for us?" Margo inquired, her voice getting completely drowned out by the cheers of the audience.

My eyes hungrily lapped up Everly as she moved across the stage. Somehow, during the interview, when my attention had been captivated by the banter between Margo and the band, three microphones and the band's instruments had been set up.

Everly approached the middle one, with Kyle beside her. He picked up his guitar. Marcus settled in behind the drums and Cam picked up the bass.

Everly's lyrical perfection rang out, making the hairs on my arms stand up. She was so beautiful and talented that I honestly ached to see her on stage knowing that she was stepping away from it. I closed my eyes, listening to the rhythmic sound of her voice as it washed over me.

I never meant to be gutless
I never meant to be thoughtless
I just wanted all of this
and I know what I've missed....

Chapter Twenty-One

Everly

THE AUDIENCE GAVE US a standing ovation as the last notes faded off. I smiled, bowing along with my bandmates. The adrenaline rush hit me the moment I stood in front of the microphone; the moment that Kyle started strumming on his guitar. My heart was still pounding as we left the stage, Kyle's large hand on the small of my back as he directed me. He dropped it once we'd reached the back stage section.

"That was incredible," he said, like he said every single time we performed. He shook his head as if he couldn't believe how talented we were. I smiled, Kyle's energy easily affecting me.

"Sure was." Marcus winked, jumping on Cam's back for a piggyback. It was amusing to watch; Kyle was two times bigger than Cam. Cam was taller, but lanky. He spent more time hanging out with his female admirers than Marcus did in the gym.

"Seriously? You're a heavy shit. Get off." Cam laughed, trying to shake him off. Marcus laughed and left him alone, shaking his head.

"You should probably focus on leg day a little more," he joked.

"Oh I focus on leg day, they just aren't mine...but they're usually wrapped around me," Cam joked back, winking.

I was going to miss moments like this; the easy banter between my friends after a performance. The excitement, the wonder.

As if sensing my thoughts, Kyle threw his arm around me while we continued our walk to the dressing rooms. "It's not forever, you know," he reminded me.

But it could be, I thought. I chose to smile my reply instead. Kyle didn't know where my head truly was. *I* didn't even know where my head truly was.

We hung out in the dressing room until the audience had cleared out and it was safe for the band to exit the studio without getting assaulted by a bunch of over energetic fans.

I was eager to see Grayson again and eager to get home. Maddie suddenly pushed open the doors, granting me my desire to see Grayson. She'd gone into the audience to grab him and the other guests of the band. Jenna was the girl that Kyle was almost ready to propose to. She was followed closely by her nice but sometimes overbearing friend, Crimson. I smiled at Jenna warmly. She was really sweet, and I enjoyed her company immensely.

Back then, we would play anywhere so long as we played for someone. When Cam's cousin called about a local charity fundraiser in Ottawa, we had jumped on it. It was my first performance after giving birth to Cadence, and I was a mess. Luckily, it hadn't shown—or so I'm told, anyway.

After the show, Cam's cousin had joined us, bringing along the girl he'd just started seeing. Lucas was a year younger than Cam. They'd essentially grown up as brothers, back when Lucas' family had lived in Kirby. I hadn't personally met Lucas, but I'd heard a lot about him from Cam. He reminded me of a hipster, but he was friendly enough.

The girl he brought was shy but kind. She'd had a beautiful smile and cornflower blue eyes. We'd naturally fallen into conversation with one another while the guys were busy being rowdy and ridiculous, the post-show energies at an all-time high while I suffered silently, longing for home; longing for Cadence and for all the other things I couldn't have. My arms felt empty, and my heart was even emptier. Unbeknownst to me, I'd been suffering from a severe case of postpartum depression. Jenna had looked at me with a certain recognition.

I didn't share my story with Jenna right away. That would have been foolish, and I was anything but. I was guarded, protective of my secret and the burdens I carried.

We didn't see Jenna again until years later, when Kyle invited her to another local show and she came. I didn't know it, but Kyle and Jenna had stayed in contact throughout the years. She was no longer with Lucas and the chemistry between Kyle and her had been...intense. It made me ache to see it, with remembered longing of what it had felt like to be with

Grayson. Kyle and Jenna had been together ever since, seeing each other whenever possible and constantly being each other's rock.

I didn't tell Jenna outright about Cadence; I think she sort of guessed. She came to visit Kyle one summer when Cadence and Julia were down. She took one look at the three of us and guessed the whole thing. Although she knew, she never admitted it. It was more or less that I had a feeling she knew, especially after she shared her story with me.

I shook my head, smiling at Grayson as he approached. It was obvious that he had only eyes for me. He paid no mind to anyone else in the room; he just walked up to me with those ice blue eyes appraising me wantonly and that dangerous smile upon his kissable lips.

"You were incredible," he said in a low voice when he reached me. His arms came around me, pulling me to his hard chest. His hands roamed the small of my back, igniting my skin in sparks of molten fire.

"Thank you," I murmured, bringing my own hands up around his neck. He kissed me in a way that made my toes tingle and a blush creep up to my cheeks. I couldn't even muster the ability to push him away and scold him for making me forget all the extra eyes on us.

Grayson chuckled, pulling away as if he'd known all along that I was helpless against him.

"Are you two going to stand there all day exchanging saliva, or would you like to come out for lunch with us?" Kyle asked begrudgingly, eyeing Grayson with distaste.

"You *need* to come with us!" Crimson pleaded with her wide, innocent eyes. "I haven't seen you in forever, Everly! Besides, we're going to Heavenly Slices!"

My mouth started to water at the mention of my favorite restaurant in LA. It was an understated mom and pop pizza shop that the guys and I had accidentally discovered after spending the day in the studio recording. They had the best pasta and pizza I had ever tasted, and better still—they weren't known by other celebrities so the paparazzi didn't camp out front like they did in other establishments.

"It would be nice to catch up," Jenna added, giving me a hopeful smile.

"Only if you two keep your tongues in your own mouths while I'm eating." Kyle frowned. "Seriously. Soft-core porn is great and all, but it's slightly nauseating coming from you two."

In response, Grayson tugged me against him, his lips feasting upon mine in a more explicit manner than they had before. My mind almost melted into a puddle of goop, and had he not stopped it when he did, I was pretty sure I would have let him have me then and there.

* * *

We took two cars over to Heavenly Slices, accompanied by the label body guards Creed and Landon. Maddie tried to insist that we take a limo, but I wasn't the only one completely opposed to that idea. If we had shown up in a limo, we likely would have attracted the attention of the paparazzi and ruined our quiet lunch.

Maddie had pursed her lips at my refusal, but accepted it for what it was, especially after Kyle backed me. I knew that she wanted me to be seen around LA, preferably in the company of Kyle even if we weren't actually *in* the company of one another.

I was happy she relented. I didn't mind being spotted out in public, but I definitely preferred the quiet luncheon to the celebrity hot spots. It was easy too, with Grayson by my side. He had this wordless way of making me feel safe. That, coupled with the body guards that I knew were outside waiting, I felt pretty optimistic that we could have a semi-normal lunch without anything dramatic happening.

The restaurant wasn't full, but it also wasn't empty. Luckily, the locals were accustomed to seeing celebrities around town, and aside from a few whispers and a lot of looks, we were basically left alone.

The tension between Kyle and Grayson was still detectable, but through the grace of Crimson, Jenna, and the other guys in the band, conversation around our table still flowed. We talked about the most memorable shows, the most embarrassing moments on the road, and what we were going to do with our time once we went on break.

Kyle and Jenna had exchanged a secret knowing look then told us that they were going to do some traveling. Marcus confessed that he would likely head back to Newcastle to spend some time with his family—I knew Aubrey was also included in that equation. In fact, I was pretty sure she was the main reason. Cam told us that he still wanted to stay in LA for a bit, maybe try and get some acting under his belt.

As lunch wore on, Kyle's scowling tapered off as his attention focused more and more on Jenna. He sat beside her, his knees angled to face her and his eyes constantly on hers and shining. Soon, he forgot all about scowling at Grayson.

Grayson seemed to ease up a little too. He held my hand when we walked in and pulled my chair out for me. Then he put his arm around the back of my chair, brushing against my shoulder and discreetly touching the nape of my neck every now and again, as if to reassure himself that I was still there. The electric current that shot through my body at every brush of his fingers against my skin made my lashes flutter every single time.

The public displays of affection made my heart swell. Grayson wasn't like that in high school. He was closed off and guarded, afraid to show his true feelings. I had been deeply in love with Grayson back then—so much so that even when I walked away, every part of my body and mind had continued to crave him with the same intensity as the very day I left. Now though, I was falling even more in love with him, and I hadn't at all thought that was possible. But it felt different, this time. This time...I truly felt as if he'd catch me. I didn't feel consumed by my love for him; I felt hopeful, on the same page. I knew that he would catch me because he was allowing himself to fall, too.

Everything was perfect until we went to leave, and then *everything* changed. Reporters swarmed the front of the restaurant, cameras poised and flashes exploding before my eyes. They rushed us in a swarm. Creed and Landon were nowhere in sight.

"Everly! Is that the mystery man? Can you tell us about your new man! Kyle! How do you feel about Everly moving on so quickly, aren't you reeling from the breakup? Everly, tell us why you lied about your daughter!"

The questions flew out at us in a rush, but the last one knocked the wind out of me. "Pardon?" I inquired, my face turning an almost sickening pallor.

"Enough questions," Kyle demanded, trying to push past the crowd of paparazzi so we could get to the street. I finally caught sight of Creed and Landon, stuck on the other side of the swarm and trying to push their way through to us. I felt Grayson squeezing my hand, tugging on my arm as he tried to lead me away from the spot where I was firmly rooted.

"I said, why did you lie about your daughter? You told your fans that she was your niece!" The speaker was a man in his early-thirties. "A source close to you says that you are her mother and that he is the father," the man added, pointing at Grayson with a smug look on his face. There was something about him that I vaguely recognized. The other reporters fell silent, eyes wide and cameras poised and trained on me, waiting for my response. I swallowed, my throat suddenly as dry as sandpaper.

Grayson growled, releasing his grip on my hand as he stomped over to the man. The anger rolled off his shoulders in waves, he looked downright menacing.

"You!" he snarled, grabbing a fistful of the man's dress jacket and yanking him forward. The man dropped his camera and his eyes widened with shock at the sudden contact.

"Grayson, no!" My hand shot forward, trying to grab him. Everybody in Hollywood knew that acting out violently toward the paparazzi was a big mistake. Of course, Grayson wasn't a part of the Hollywood scene; he didn't have a career to worry about or a manager to contend with...but I did. I also knew how easy it was for the reporter to turn around and press charges.

"Stay the fuck away from us, got it?" Grayson roared, his eyes hard as stone.

Kyle, Marcus, and Cam all rushed forward to grab Grayson. He put up a good fight, determined to get back to the man. Kyle and Cam held his arms back while Marcus tried to grip his waist. Creed and Landon were still shoving their way through the bodies, trying to get through.

"You're going to regret that! I'll get you. I'll ruin you!" the man shouted, rubbing his neck and glaring at Grayson.

"Not if I get to you first," Grayson growled. He ripped his right arm free from Cam's grasp, his fist connecting hard with the reporter's face. His nose crunched and he fell back, blood exploding out. Grayson had broken his nose with one, almost effortless hit.

Cameras flashed left right and center. The chaos that ensued was mind numbing. Creed and Landon finally broke through, putting themselves between the guys and the reporters.

"I'm calling the police!" someone shouted.

"Grayson, what the fuck?" Kyle yelled, his eyes sharp with anger.

Grayson looked even more enraged. "What the fuck what? That fucking asshole deserved it. I've seen him around town and I chased his ass after he fucking took pictures of Cadence through my living room window and terrified the shit out of her!" Grayson's voice was raised, drawing the attention of several bystanders.

Kyle's expression changed from angry to confused. He looked at me for confirmation. I was shaking so hard that I didn't think Kyle could even tell that I was nodding, remembering the night at Grayson's when Cadence had woken up terrified after seeing a man in the window. I looked back at the man on the ground. His nose was still bleeding profusely and several fellow reporters were trying to help stop the flow. I had a sickening feeling that I knew him from somewhere, but I couldn't remember from where.

"I didn't see him, but Grayson did..." My hands were trembling, my whole body was trembling. Jenna stepped up, wrapping her arms around me. Crimson's face was pale, and for once, she was silent. Her usual steady stream of words was blocked by her shock over the situation.

Sirens were roaring and blue and red police lights were flashing, reflected in the windows of the shops behind us. A police cruiser and an ambulance pulled up haphazardly in front of the restaurant. I noticed for the first time that the remaining people inside the restaurant were watching from the windows, and the crowd on the street had grown to include more curious bystanders. I swallowed hard, keeping my chin up. I knew the situation we were in was bad, but I wasn't about to break down in front of all these watching people.

Grayson was standing several feet away from me. His face paled when he heard the sirens, and his fists were clenched at his side. I could tell the gravity of his actions was finally starting to seep in through his anger. I approached, coming to a stop in front of him. His eyes were swirling with anger, torture, and regret. He gazed down at me, looking every bit the burning man he'd been five years ago, on the day that I'd walked away.

I couldn't be mad at Grayson for snapping. He'd only known about Cadence for just over three weeks, and he certainly wasn't prepared for what came with fatherhood and fame. He looked at me as if he finally understood why I'd lied about Cadence, why I had kept her parentage secret from my fans. Not all paparazzi were dangerous, but the few that were—the few that stalked your home and pressed their cameras against your living room window, hoping for a picture of you with your kids— were the ones you had to worry about.

I put my arms around him, pressing my body to his. I was still shaking, trembling. His arms came up to hold me. Every muscle in his body was tense, poised for fighting, and yet he was trying to comfort me. I closed my eyes, burying my face against his chest and breathing in the scent of him, trying to tell myself that everything would be okay. *It had to be.*

The two police officers approached us, eyeing the bleeding man on the ground. "What happened here?" the first one asked while his partner stood silently and imposing beside him. The first cop looked to be in his early forties and had a thick dark mustache, friendly eyes and a patient expression on his weathered face. His badge read *Officer Thomas*. The second cop was in his thirties and almost as big as Creed. His muscles seemed to ripple as he crossed his arms, his sharp eyes not missing anything about the scene. The way he was staring at us intimidated me. Grayson was still holding me, and I didn't think he'd let me go any time soon.

"I punched him," Grayson answered rigidly.

The cop raised his brow, half of his mustache turning up in a smile. "We see that. Why?" the second cop, Officer Roebuck according to his badge, asked in a near bored tone.

"Several reasons," Grayson answered, his eyes hard. "One, he annoyed me. Two, he's been following me for a while. And lastly...I caught him outside my house taking pictures of my sleeping daughter. He had it coming."

Thomas nodded with understanding. "I've got two daughters of my own," he remarked, exchanging a look with his partner. "We're just going to take some statements from witnesses. Hang tight, alright?"

All any of us could do was nod obediently as Officer Thomas pulled out a notepad and approached the crowd of bystanders. I remained in Grayson's arms, still shaking with fear and uncertainty. Kyle, Marcus, Cam, Jenna and Crimson all stood nearby, flanked by Creed and Landon.

"I'm calling Maddie," Kyle responded shortly. He pulled his phone out and walked a little bit away from us. He started speaking animatedly into the phone, a scowl on his face. "Well, find a way to fix this mess!" he barked before ending the call.

"What did she say?" My voice shook. Maddie hadn't joined us for lunch; she'd claimed that she had business to attend to. It made me suspicious the way that things had gone down. Maddie was my friend, but she also worked for the label first. If Brent demanded she tip the paparazzi off about our lunch date, she would have done it thinking no harm would come to anyone. After all, we were used to being swarmed by reporters. But what she likely hadn't counted on was Grayson's temper.

Kyle looked at me, his jaw clenching and releasing while he considered just how much to tell me. He sighed. "*Stellar Magazine* released a special issue report detailing that your late sister's daughter is really *your* daughter. Photos of you and Grayson and Cadence are compared with an 'expert' saying it's 'beyond possible'," he finally answered after realizing that I was bound to find out eventually. All I had to do was open my cell phone up and search my name.

My knees buckled, but I remained held in place by Grayson's strong arms.

"Fuck," Grayson spat.

"I need to call home," I said.

"I'll call Aubrey," Marcus promised, pulling his phone out and scrolling quickly through his contacts. "Aubrey? Yeah. We know. Are you with them? Is everything okay there? They aren't swarming the house, are they?"

It was killing me that I couldn't hear Aubrey's answers, but Marcus looked relieved at least. One of the benefits to living in Canada was that word traveled a bit slower. Had my family lived in the states, especially near Hollywood, the house would have already been inundated.

All I could think about was Cadence and Grayson. Nothing else. My mind was numb. I didn't care if I'd pissed off our fans by my lie. I didn't care if the label would be furious. I didn't care about anything but making sure that *my* family was okay, and it was impossible to do anything in this instance while we waited to find out exactly what was going to happen next. I had a terrible feeling that it wasn't going to be good.

I watched soundlessly as Roebuck checked in with the paramedic and talked to the reporter. He crouched down, speaking words that I couldn't hear. The man replied venomously, pointing at Grayson with a shaking hand. His nose was no longer bleeding; it was set and bandaged, but his eyes were already bruised and swollen.

"I've spoken to the witnesses, and they've confirmed your story. Most of these reporters are scum. Can't say I wouldn't have done the same thing in your shoes, son," Thomas said, shaking his head while Roebuck approached with a solemn look on his face.

"He still wants to press charges," Officer Roebuck said, confirming my fears. I felt a sensation similar to that of my heart dropping into my stomach.

"Sorry, son, you're going to have to come with us to the station." Thomas sighed heavily, as if this hadn't been the outcome he wanted. He pulled a pair of handcuffs out from his utility belt.

"Is that necessary?" I demanded, swallowing hard. Grayson's hands came up to my forearms, gently squeezing. My arms stayed locked around his waist. I didn't want to let him go.

"This is the fun part of the job." Thomas grinned, winking. "It almost makes up for the massive amount of paperwork we'll have to do. Don't worry, he won't be held for long...but I still get to cuff him!"

Officer Thomas was attempting to be funny, but I couldn't find the humor in the situation. I looked up at Grayson with panic-filled eyes.

"It'll be alright," he assured me, pulling me against him for a moment. His lips found mine quickly before he released me. I felt empty without his arms around me.

Officer Thomas cuffed him after sending me an apologetic look. I watched as the police officers lead Grayson to the cruiser. Officer Roebuck put his hand over Grayson's head, helping him into the back of the cruiser. I swallowed hard, the tears finally spilling freely down my cheeks.

Jenna and Crimson both stepped forward to stand beside me, trying to provide comfort. "It'll be okay," Crimson said. "He might get charged with assault, but he won't go to jail...unless this isn't his first offense?"

I thought back to that night after the semi-formal in high school, when Grayson had punched Kyle. While Kyle hadn't pressed charges, I had no idea what kind of activities Grayson had gotten into after. He could very well have a record already, in which case there was a high likelihood he could end up in jail.

I let out a strangled whimper.

"Get her home," Kyle instructed after taking one look at me.

Chapter Twenty-Two

Grayson

I DON'T KNOW HOW MUCH time had passed since the incident with the reporter outside the restaurant. After bringing me into the station for questioning, Officer Thomas deposited me into one of the holding cells and hadn't been back since then. There was a clock on the wall across from the bars, but I couldn't read it. *It has to be broken,* I thought, convinced that the hands hadn't moved an inch since my arrival.

It would be just like the police officers to let the batteries die on the only clock within view; I know I would have laughed if I were them. God knew you had to get your laughs in somewhere when dealing with the criminals and trash of society. Good people didn't end up on the cold metal bench. Misunderstandings were not really misunderstandings.

I sat on that cold metal bench, my feet tapping impatiently on the tiled floor. The holding cell stank of vomit and piss. I wasn't the only one in it, either. A couple of other people were waiting there, most of them slumped on the floor and leaning against the bars of the cell. Almost every last one of them looked blitzed out of their minds; glassy eyes, rotting teeth, the permanent stench of despair. It was enough to almost choke me.

Despite how much I was freaking out on the inside, I remained calm and stoic. Cooperative. I'd answered every question, gave a thorough account of what had happened at my house a week ago, and even provided the names of the officers that had filed the incident report.

I didn't have any previous charges against me, despite all the fights I'd gotten in throughout my life. My juvenile record had been wiped clean at the age of eighteen, and I hadn't been caught since. Still, I deserved to be in this stinking cell, and I knew it.

I should have controlled my temper. I shouldn't have let that fucker's gloating smirk taunt me to no return, but all my rage from the other night when I had chased the same fucker came flooding back and all I could picture in my head was Cadence's terrified expression when she woke up to see a strange man pressing his face against the window.

It was a primitive, Neanderthal move on my part, but I can't say I regretted it. Even knowing that I probably fucked things up in some way for Everly.

Everly. My heart twisted at the thought of the look on her face when that fucker started running his mouth.

"I said, why did you lie about your daughter?"

My fists clenched with the strong desire to punch him again. As if it was any of his fucking business. The only people Everly hadn't told the truth to were people who didn't need to know it. Just because she was a successful singer didn't mean that she had to lay out all the intimate details of her life for public consumption. The public's obsession with the rich and famous was nauseating. I didn't understand why they couldn't just accept the talent these people brought without needing to know who they were dating or where they lived or what kind of workout clothes they wore to the gym.

"You told your fans that she was your niece! A source close to you says that you are her mother and that he is the father."

I couldn't get the reporter's smug tone out of my head. *A source close to you.* Who could that have been? Suddenly, the blood in my veins turned to ice. Lindsay Little.

"Dixon, get up." Officer Thomas' sudden appearance startled me. He was standing in front of the jail cell, holding it open and waiting for me to get up off my ass and walk over. The other people in the cell watched with bored eyes as I stood up and crossed over. Officer Thomas locked the jail back up behind me then motioned for me to follow him down the hall.

He led me to an interrogation room and told me to make myself comfortable in the metal chair across the table from him. The chair legs scrapped against the tile floor as I pulled it out. I sat down, my eyes never leaving Officer Thomas' face.

Thomas leaned back in his own chair, regarding me with quiet authority. He sighed heavily, running his index finger and thumb across his mustache, as if making sure every little hair was properly in place.

"You remind me of myself when I was younger," he finally said, breaking the silence. "I had a temper like you wouldn't believe."

I didn't exactly know how to respond to that, so I settled for pursing my lips and nodding in acknowledgment. My feet tapped against the tile floor with impatience. I wanted to get out of here and back to *her*. I wanted to figure out just how much I'd fucked up.

The last time Everly had witnessed me lose my temper was at that stupid semi-formal after party when I knocked Kyle out. She hadn't been impressed.

Thomas cleared his throat and leaned forward. "I've advised the reporter to drop charges." He stared at me, waiting for me to say something.

"Why?" I narrowed my eyes at him, trying to figure this guy out. He reeked of authority and seemed like an alright guy, but I couldn't understand why he'd advise another person to drop a clearly deserved charge. I'd broken the fucker's nose, and I'd do it again in a heartbeat...but laws were laws.

"His name is Greg Burningham," Thomas replied, waiting for me to recognize the name from somewhere. "Does that name mean anything to you?"

"No. I don't know anybody by that name."

"About a year ago, he tried to break into Ms. Daniels' home," Thomas stated, looking at a paper in front of him. He shoved it over to me so I could read it.

I swallowed hard as I read the police report. It detailed the night that Greg Burningham broke into Everly's house. Photos taken from the security cameras she'd positioned outside her house zeroed in on his face. It was almost hard to recognize him. The man I punched was fit and trim, his hair was dark. The man in the picture had light hair and was overweight. He wore a baseball hat and dark clothes. It was difficult to tell from the grainy photo, but he appeared to have a blotchy face and a fatter nose too.

I clenched my fists so tightly that my knuckles cracked in protest. Luckily, Everly hadn't been seriously injured. According to her statement, he'd told her that he was in love with her and they were destined to be together, then he tried to kiss her.

I shuddered to think of what could have happened had Everly's housekeeper not called the police.

"So." I swallowed again, my Adams apple bobbing up and down while I desperately fought to control my temper. I wanted to flip the table upside down and get the fuck out of here, find that asshole and *really* rearrange his face. "You're telling me that *I'm* sitting in this room, getting interrogated for punching a low-life piece of shit who not only stalked my girlfriend here in Los Angeles, but *also* followed her home to Canada to stalk her some more? And *he's* not in here?"

Thomas sighed, massaging his temple as if he had a migraine. "I've advised Ms. Daniels to press charges again, and she will. He will get into trouble for violating his no contact order. He can still press charges against you because according to the law, the two incidents are completely different."

"That's bullshit," I growled, scowling.

"I know." Thomas smiled without humor. "So, here's what's going to happen. You're going to post bail. You're going to go home. You're going to press charges against him for trespassing on your property. You'll have to return to LA for the hearing and you can either plead guilty or not guilty. If you plead guilty you'll have to pay a fine and probably do community service. It's not a big deal; you'll face no jail time."

"And what's going to happen to this fuckwatt?" I demanded, shoving the police report back on him. "He obviously hasn't gotten the hint that he needs to stay away from Everly."

"I know." Thomas sighed. "Unfortunately, there are a lot of his kind out there. But I think once you guys bring up charges against him, he'll back off."

"You *think*?" I muttered darkly, shaking my head. "That's supposed to ease our minds?"

He chose not to respond, shrugging as if the whole thing couldn't be helped. "I've advised Ms. Daniels to press charges again, and she will. But unfortunately, the two incidents are considered separate from one another. You assaulted him, regardless of the very good reasons, and that is against our laws. So, you'll have to appear in court. Probably in a month."

"Fine," I grumbled, leaning back against the chair. I ran a hand through my hair, tugging at it in aggravation.

Thomas watched me carefully before sliding another document over; my terms for bail. I read it, signed it and handed it back.

"You're free to go, son. But I'd recommend finding a ride. It's a mad house out there right now."

"Why?"

"You're top news right now," Thomas informed me, standing up. He stretched a little, his paunch straining the buttons of his uniform.

He led me out front and told me to wait at the front desk. After collecting my personal items, I was free to go. I peered outside the station doors, seeing the abundance of reporters lining the sidewalk, cameras poised and ready for action.

"What the fuck?" I growled just as my cell phone started to go off. I didn't recognize the number. "What?" I snapped, somewhat aggravated.

"Get your ass out back, dumbass," Kyle's voice came through the line, snapping impatiently before disconnecting. Frowning, I looked behind me. Officer Thomas was still watching me with an almost bemused smile on his face.

"Officer Thomas?" I asked. He raised his eyebrows, urging me to continue. "Is there a back exit?"

"Of course." He chuckled, motioning for me to follow him.

I walked out of the back of the station, seeing Kyle's sleek black Bugatti parked in the back lot amongst the police cars. He was leaning against it, scowling at me.

"Where's Everly?" I demanded, needing to hear that she was okay. Kyle's expression softened for a moment at the mention of her name. I regarded him carefully.

"She's at her place, waiting for you," he answered shortly. He walked around his tiny yet impressive car, opening the driver's side. He gave me a hard look. "Get in."

The last thing I wanted to do was place myself in another situation where my anger could get the better of me, and it was likely that I'd lay into Kyle—especially if he pulled any of his old shit with me. My patience was shot.

Regardless, I didn't exactly have a whole lot of options when it came to a ride and I was desperate to get to Everly, and fast. The Bugatti could get me there fast, even if I'd have to endure Kyle. I stepped up to the car, opening the door warily and squeezing into the tiny vehicle. The interior was all sleek black leather, and very cramped.

I was taller than Kyle, but I still didn't understand how he could sit inside this vehicle comfortably. I was more of a truck guy and always had been. Muscle cars were impressive to look at, and maybe even fun to drive, but impractical for a guy of my height.

Kyle drove down the confusing labyrinth of roads, weaving in and out of traffic wordlessly. His fingers tapped against the steering wheel and his brow was furrowed. I could practically hear the wheels spinning in his head.

I just didn't give a shit enough to ask what was up. I had my own things to worry about; mainly, how badly I had screwed things up for Everly... and with her.

He pulled up to Everly's house in Brentwood and jerked the car to a stop for a moment to roll down his window and look at the video screen.

"Hey, Harris," he said by greeting. The security guard grinned back.

"Hey, Kyle! It's been a while," Harris remarked. I had spent the night at Everly's house and hadn't seen this Harris guy once. I knew that was the point—he was supposed to stay hidden—but still. It bothered me that Kyle seemed to have a close rapport with him.

"I know! Been busy, man. How are the wife and kids?"

"Good." Harris nodded, a wistful smile on his face as the gates swung slowly open, granting us access.

"Awesome! Catch you around." Kyle grinned, tromping on the gas and making the car lurch forward. He drove up to the front of Everly's house. Before I could thank him for the ride, he jerked the car to another sudden stop, causing my head to smack back against the seat. I scowled while he turned to look at me.

"Look, man, I get what you did. I would have done that too had I known," he said. "But next time, think with your head and not your fists. That situation could have been a lot worse. You're lucky."

"I know," I responded, almost grinding my teeth together in annoyance. My hand was on the door handle, but Kyle looked like he had more to say.

"I don't get you two," Kyle admitted, his brow furrowing and his head shaking slightly as he tried to sort it out. "For whatever reason, you work together. You make her happier than I've seen her in a long time...but I've also seen what happens when you break her, and I'm telling you, it ain't fucking pretty and if I have to pick up the pieces again...I swear to God I'll end you."

My eyebrows cocked up and I bristled at the fact that Kyle was telling me off again—and that he was right in doing it. Again. However, it still didn't make the strong desire I had to punch in his perfect white teeth go away.

"I don't intend to break her again, and I didn't intend to break her back then either. And while we're on that subject, asshole...you were no fucking prince charming either."

"I know that." Kyle snorted. "But I didn't have her heart in my hands. I never did and I knew that. That was you, and you crushed it. Don't do it again. Now get the fuck out of my car. I need to get home to my girl."

I shook my head, feeling all sorts of fucked up. For as much as I hated Kyle, his words held *a lot* of truth and I had to admit that it was probably why they pissed me off so much.

I hesitated for another moment, sending him another narrow look. "Thanks...for everything." The aftertaste in my mouth after thanking Kyle wasn't pleasant, but he deserved it. For picking up the pieces, for helping Everly and being there for her when I wasn't, and for putting up with my shit despite the fact that we both clearly hated each other.

"Don't mention it. I didn't do it for you. I did it for Everly and Cadence."

"Well, regardless. Thanks," I said without looking back as I climbed out and closed the door. I heard the tires squeal as Kyle pealed out of the driveway, but I didn't watch him go. My eyes were locked on Everly as she stood waiting in the doorway, watching me.

Her eyes were red rimmed from crying, and she bit her lip while I approached, trying to hold in her agony. I felt like hanging my head in shame from the destroyed way she was looking at me. I shouldn't have been sitting in a jail cell; I should have been holding her, comforting her. Instead, I took it. I didn't let my eyes drift from her face. I deserved to see this; I deserved to see a small portion of pain she felt over what I'd done because I hadn't been there when I *really* broke her.

"I was so worried," she muttered when I took her into my arms. She trembled against me.

"I'm fine," I assured her, kissing the top of her head.

"I'm sorry...I should have known who he was...I should have recognized him." She shivered in my arms. Despite how warm it was in LA compared to Canada, with the sun gone it was a little chilly. I backed her into the house, closing the door behind me.

"You couldn't have known. I saw the photos of what he looked like before. He's obviously done a lot of work to make sure he wasn't recognizable." My hands traveled all over her body, almost on their own accord. I needed to touch her everywhere; I needed to feel her everywhere. I forced them to stop before I asked my next question. "Is Cadence okay?"

"Yeah." She sighed, her face still buried against my chest. "My parents said nobody's shown up for photos or anything. I don't think they'll get swarmed because I'm not there. What did the police say?"

"I'll have to come back for court." I tensed, remembering the facts I'd learned. "I'll plead guilty—I did assault the fucker in front of a bunch of cameras after all. There's no denying it. I'll just have to pay a fine and maybe do some community service or something. No big deal."

Everly sniffled and I let my hands continue their roaming. She shuddered against me when my lips found that sweet spot on the side of her neck, just beneath her earlobe. This time, the shudder was a release.

Her scent was overpowering me and the desire for her was evident, straining against my pants as I pressed it against her. Her breathing increased and I could feel her heartbeat jump beneath my lips. Her head fell back and her eyelids fluttered before she focused on me.

"I need you," I told her, my eyes locked on hers. I swallowed hard. I wasn't just talking about my sexual desire, and she knew it. Hearing Kyle's words had twisted up my heart and mind. I felt this insane need to prove to her just how serious I was, how I wasn't going anywhere. She read that in me, and she smiled, some of the sadness fading from her eyes as she tilted her head.

"Despite this?" she asked, her voice low.

I shook my head, lowering my lips to hers. I kissed her doubts away, leaving the both of us breathless when I finally broke away to look at her again. "There's nothing that could make me change my mind about you. You've always been the best part of me, even when I was too stupid to see it."

"You're not stupid," she whispered, swallowing. She smirked a little. "Maybe a little slow."

I spun her around and pushed her against the entryway so quickly that she scarcely had time to blink. "Am I slow?" I asked her, pressing my hard length against her lower abdomen. I watched the lust explode behind her eyes and I smirked. I'd never get tired of watching the effect I had on her.

"No..." she whispered, her eyelids fluttering against her cheeks. I kissed her senseless, losing myself in the process. My hand moved against her core, rubbing and teasing through her tight, barely there leggings. I could practically feel the heat on my hand. My cock twitched as she whimpered in response.

"And are you mad at me?" I asked, swallowing hard.

"No." She sighed softly. I grinned, pressing against her again as her hands found my chest. I kissed her again, feeding into the carnal urges I felt for her. She shoved against me, breaking the spell of my lips on hers. "Lydia is here," she whispered frantically. "My housekeeper..." Everly clarified at the look of confusion on my face.

"That's alright, Ms. Daniels, I was just leaving." Lydia's voice sounded amused, albeit embarrassed to find her employer in such a compromising position. Everly's cheeks flushed with embarrassment as she tried to tug me away from the door.

"Thank you, Lydia, for everything. I'll see you later." Everly cleared her throat, attempting to sound professional and in control. I could practically see how quickly her heart was beating.

"It was a pleasure working for you, Ms. Daniels," Lydia said, inclining her head slightly.

I kept my back to Lydia, not wanting to turn around when the evidence of my arousal was blatantly obvious. I turned my head to look at her, smiling unapologetically. "It was nice meeting you."

Lydia was standing in the living room, a large bag over her shoulders. Her dark hair was twisted up into a bun and her face was free of makeup. She had a pretty, friendly face and a warm smile that stretched up to her eyes.

"You too, Mr. Dixon, enjoy...your evening," Lydia said before ducking out the front door.

"Are we alone now?" I asked, my voice gravelly. Everly bit her lip and nodded. I smiled dangerously in response. "Good." I said, moving my hips against hers again.

Epilogue

Everly

Six months later...

THINGS WERE FINALLY beginning to calm down after the whole "scandal". Between the breaking news about the secret parentage of my daughter and Grayson's fight with the reporter, Greg Burningham, we were splashed on the covers of several gossip websites and magazines for many months. The incident outside of Heavenly Slices had even ended up on several entertainment shows.

We hired a fantastic lawyer and Grayson counter-charged Greg Burningham with trespassing on his property. I charged him with breaking the no contact order. The slimy jerk was so shook up that he ended up pleading guilty and dropping the assault charges against Grayson in exchange for a lighter sentence.

Eventually, word got out that the man Grayson had punched was someone who had previously stalked me in LA and followed me back to my hometown to continue to harass me from afar, so Grayson wasn't portrayed in a negative light at all, but as a hero. Not that he seemed to care. The only thing Grayson cared about was what I thought of him, what Cadence thought of him.

Luckily, people in our small town didn't even bat a lash about it. I was pretty sure the majority of them had suspected the truth about Cadence, but they'd respected my privacy enough to not be bothered by it. Living in a small town had its perks; the townsfolk were more likely to protect their own...or at least most of them were, the one exception being a certain seething blonde haired nemesis of mine that tried to get her fifteen minutes of fame while attempting to shake the foundation of my relationship with Grayson.

It was quite obvious who the "source close to me" was, especially after she came forward to a major gossip magazine about how she'd hooked up with Grayson. I knew the story was bogus when she mixed up the dates and claimed it was only three months ago when she'd tried to convince Grayson it had been a year ago.

Lindsay didn't have the balls to stay in town after her fifteen minutes, though. She ended up taking the cash she'd made from selling her story and moving out of province. I was a little sad about the whole thing. It was shocking to me that someone I once considered to be a good friend of mine would sell me out like that, but some people are so desperate for attention and fame that they'll do anything to get it.

I had plenty of friends that *wouldn't* sell me out, though. I had Aubrey, Alicia, Kyle, Marcus and Cam. I also had my parents, Cadence and Grayson. I was building relationships with Grayson's dad, step-mom, and sisters. I was able to live a pretty average life. I could drop my daughter off at school without being accosted, and after a while I could even go out for dinner at restaurants several towns over without being completely overwhelmed by screaming fans.

However, I knew I could never really return to a completely quiet life. I was constantly questioned about when I was going to go back to making music, and I was open with my answers—*eventually*. I missed it, but I was happy with being home and focusing on my family. Still, I knew that one day, when Cadence was older, I wanted to return to the stage to focus on a solo career. The idea appealed to me because I could make my own schedule and still make a difference with my music.

I did one interview for the *Morning Margo Show*, discussing my reasons behind keeping Cadence a secret from my fans. The majority of them understood where I was coming from, especially after learning about the creepy encounters I had with the fan-turned-paparazzi-stalker.

Six months after everything in LA went down, I finally agreed to move into Grayson's house with Cadence. I had waited until things felt beyond right. That moment came a month prior when Cadence finally started calling Grayson Daddy.

On the day we brought the last boxes of our things over, I stood in Cadence's new bedroom. Grayson had painted it a soft purple, and he'd bought her a new bedding set. We were arranging her books and little knick knacks on the custom built shelves Grayson had made for her. I placed a photograph of Julia, Cadence and me on one of the shelves just before I felt his large hands wrap around my waist from behind.

"Looks great," he said, nuzzling his lips against my neck.

I smiled, resting my head against his shoulder. "Thank you," I murmured, losing myself to the warm sensation of his arms. Things with Grayson just felt *right*. We'd come a long way from the people we were in high school, and it was for the better. They say everything in life happens for a reason, and it does. I wasn't entirely sure where I would be if life hadn't run its course the way it had, but I was happy with where we were.

I looked at our daughter. She was happily organizing her favorite stuffed animals on her bed, standing beside the Barbie Dream House that Grayson had bought her for Christmas.

"I have something to ask you." Grayson smiled against my skin. Cadence's ears perked up and she turned to face us, watching with those wide ice blue eyes so like her father's.

"Oh?" I arched a brow, turning to face him and slowly wrapping my arms around his neck. "And what is that?"

"Mama," Cadence interrupted. I glanced back at her. "There's something in my Barbie house."

"Better go check it out. Hopefully it's not a mouse infestation." Grayson smirked. "Go on, my question can wait."

I shook my head as I stepped out of Grayson's arms and walked over to where Cadence was. I bent over, peering inside the Barbie Dream House. At first, I didn't notice anything out of place. Cadence had arranged her three Barbies so they were all in the bedroom. The little girl doll stood in the background, while Ken and Barbie faced each other.

"I'm not seeing anything." I shook my head and the motion made the light from the ceiling fan catching on something shiny. I blinked, taking a closer look at Ken. His right plastic arm was extended out to Barbie, and her hands were positioned over her mouth. I picked it up, staring at the shiny white gold diamond ring with a dumbfounded expression on my face.

"Everly." Grayson's voice prompted me to turn my entire body to face him. He was kneeling on one knee, holding out an empty ring box. "Will you marry me?"

The End

About the Author

J.C. Hannigan lives in Ontario, Canada with her husband, their two
sons and their dog.
She writes contemporary new adult romance and suspense. Her
novels focus on relationships, mental health, social issues, and other
life challenges.

Follow her on Facebook and Twitter!
http://facebook.com/jcahannigan
http://twitter.com/jcahannigan

Other books by J.C.Hannigan:

Collide, Collide Book 1
Consumed, Collide Book 2
Collateral, Collide Book 3

Damaged Goods

More Great Reads from Booktrope

Despair **by Ryanne Anthony** (Contemporary Romance) When it came to her love life, Cassidy Wren had a difficult decision to make: her steady boyfriend, who followed her while she chased her dreams or the rock star that set her body aflame.

What the Lady Wants **by Nika Rhone** (Contemporary Romance) The heiress, the bodyguard, and the danger. When Thea finally decides to make a move on Doyle he finds it hard to resist, but his secret could ruin it all. Can he save this new love and Thea's life?

Unconventional **by Danielle Ione** (Contemporary Romance) A hardheaded girl hell-bent on denying her true feelings and a determined rocker with plans of making her see just how right they are for each other, even though they are anything but conventional.

Tripped Up Love **by Julie Farley** (Contemporary Romance) When Heather Meadows loses the only man she's ever loved, her perfect, ordinary life is turned upside down. Little does she know that her world is about to be turned upside down again when one wrong step puts her in the path of a new destiny.

Would you like to read more books like these?
Subscribe to **runawaygoodness.com**, get a free ebook for signing up, and never pay full price for an ebook again.

Discover more books and learn about our
new approach to publishing at **booktrope.com**.

Printed in Great Britain
by Amazon